FOR WANT OF A DRAGON

WENDY DAY

ISBN : Hardcover 978-1-957707-31-0 Paperback 978-1-957707-30-3

First Edition October 2025

10 9 8 7 6 5 4 3 2 1

OPEN SKY
PUBLISHING

DEDICATION

*To the headstrong, obstinate girls
who still believe in true love.*

1

Late afternoon sun filters through the open roof of the dragon keep, casting shadows on the stone walls. I've been grooming this Green Zalia since noon. By the irritated swish of the dragon's tail, I believe we are both eager to be finished.

"Almost done," I say, my head inside his mouth as I work on his rows of razor-sharp teeth. Dragon breath can be horrendous. Fortunately, the minty poultice I use to clean teeth covers the smell of whatever he ate last.

He chuffs in response. I pound the chisel into the calcified plaque on his back left molar and scrape until it comes loose. My elbow holds his long, forked tongue out of the way while I clean. This poor dragon has an unreasonably neglected mouth. His rider should have called me in sooner.

Luckily, we are coming to the end of our time together. I've already polished the crest from his snout to his tail. I've checked his variegated scales, which are softer and more flexible than those of other dragons. He's been patient with me, which isn't always the case. Green Zalia dragons can be temperamental, letting you slip into a false sense of security and then striking out of nowhere. His career patrolling the northern territory's borders had been a long one. He and his rider have earned their retirement in Eshan.

Dragons in service to the Continent stay with their riders from academy to retirement. During their years of active duty, they patrol the borders and fly at the pleasure of the royal families. The academy and territorial courts all have groomers on staff. After military service, the riders take their dragons home, often hiring groomers to care for them.

My client shifts his tail, and I brace myself, waiting for him to settle. I finish scrubbing the molars and double-check my efforts. I move my elbow back again to make sure he is breathing through his nose while I am in his mouth, lest I become a crispy snack. Plenty of groomers who aren't careful are wounded or killed by the dragons they serve. Teeth cleaning is the second most hazardous grooming procedure. The first is expressing the anal glands. They *really* don't like that. A singed hem on my cloak serves as proof.

I did not plan on becoming a dragon groomer. All I ever wanted to do was feel the wind in my hair and the thrill of soaring over the forest canopy as a dragon rider. That is why I braved the journey from Tevyne to Eshan. With every blister and scrape of rough rock against my hands as I trudged through the mountains, my determination to earn a dragon and fulfill my lifelong dream grew.

Two weeks after my arrival, my dream had been shattered. I'd been sitting across from my best friend, Marinn, a half-elf. She'd told me that humans were not allowed to ride dragons without a Fae escort.

"You will need to find a High Fae to fly with you, for those are the only ones allowed to bond with dragons."

Fae is the term for all non-human beings on the continent. High Fae are almost as old as dragons, with magic being passed down through bloodlines. They rule the Fae lands and have little regard for humans.

After seeing my dismay, she schooled her face into a smile and continued, "It's a silly rule. Humans could never be foolish enough to wage war against the Fae. The king's advisors will convince him of that. Don't despair." She grasped my hands and squeezed.

Now, at twenty-six summers, I am no closer to bonding with a dragon. The Royal Council has been unable to change the King's mind about humans riding dragons alone, and the decree stands. At least I get to work with the marvelous creatures. The dragons who call the valley home are not plentiful enough to earn me a significant wage.

I tuck a damp strand of hair behind my ear. Even when dragons breathe through their nose, their mouths are steamy. I reach into my leather tool belt and pull out my shiny plaque hook to chip off the last stubborn spot on the molar. A low growl rumbles through his throat.

I agree. We've both had enough for today. I back out of his mouth, pushing against his teeth until I stand upright atop my ladder. He turns his head and stares at me with a narrowed eye. I pat the side of his jaw. "Thank you. We are finished. You have been most tolerant." Then I slip my hand into a satchel strapped to my ladder and pull out a smoked fish. He sniffs and opens his mouth so I can toss it in.

I ensure my tools are secure in my belt and retreat down the ladder. The bells in the town center begin to ring, and I realize I am late. I fold my ladder and drag it out to my wagon, then wrap myself in my cloak before heading home.

Orthello, a fellow member of the Merchants' Guild and the caretaker of the estate where I'm working, is taking a bundle of tree trunks up to the main house. His secret wish is to become a wedding singer. He has been taking singing lessons and has been invited to sing at one wedding so far, a cousin's. There is only one problem: Orthello is a terrible singer. But no one has the heart to tell him. While his vocal talent is lacking, he has been blessed (or cursed) with confidence.

"Well met, Orthello. That's quite a haul," I say, reaching my hand out to brush it against the bark.

Although I'm tall for a human woman, Orthello towers over me. He must be at least eight feet tall. Resting the trunks on his shoulder, he runs a hand down his bushy, waist-length beard and smiles. "Well met Livvy. Will you be at the revel tonight?"

I brush my hair out of my face. "Perhaps. You?"

He chuckles, his belly shaking with mirth. "Lenora wouldn't let me miss it even if the forest was on fire. She'll be deep in her cups by the time I get there. I must hurry and get this wood chopped before I leave." He looks up towards the keep. "Best get to it."

His wife, Lenora, is known to overindulge on occasion. At Summer Solstice, she ended up on the tavern's roof, naked and declaring she could fly. In my home village, it would have been a scandal of epic proportions. But in Eshan, it was a tale told for a fortnight over the ale-splattered bar and then forgotten. The winter chill should keep her clothes on tonight, but there's no guarantee.

I use a leather strap to secure my ladder to the pushcart and glance over to the slope where my cottage sits, even if I can't see it through the evergreens. My heart still catches when I survey the valley I call home. I didn't know it was possible to adore a place this much. Something in the air fills my lungs with clarity and sets my soul ablaze. Eshan has a wild, untamed spirit that has loosened the knots of social convention my ma had used to try to tie me down.

My feet are light even though my body is weary as I trek down through the valley and up the ridge. How convenient it must be to have the magical ability to port from place to place. Alas, that isn't an option in the valley, even if one did have the magical ability.

Since the Great War, the border between the Fae and mortal kingdoms has been warded to dampen ambient magic. The goal was to dissuade creatures of measurable magic from crossing into the mortal lands and causing harm to defenseless humans. If a magical creature travels too close to the border, it will feel physical discomfort and disorientation.

Dragons, being of ancient primordial magic, are exempt from the wards. Other creatures, like caracals and Field Sprites, have such low levels of magic that they can slip through undetected. Eshan became an ideal location for mortal settlers from Straume and low- or non-magical creatures, such as caracals, from the five Fae kingdoms. Antrais, Ezera, Jura, Lauks, and Ledas all live in harmony.

Still, only a brave soul would attempt the dangerous trek over the Skadaris mountains along the divide between the human kingdom of Straume and the closest Fae Kingdom, Antrais. My home village of Tevyne is five days' travel from the edge of the mountain range, an arduous journey even before you begin to climb. Every year, people perish while attempting the crossing. When I told my parents of my plans three years ago, Ma burst into tears and claimed that, because of me, her nerves would finally end her.

Da had asked me to take a walk in the woods with him. He said he was proud of me for following my dreams. His support was solidified after a lengthy discussion with his trader friend, Craige, who regularly traveled to Eshan, and agreed to serve as a guide and chaperon. He assured Da that I would arrive safely and that he would serve as a carrier for correspondence.

When my courage faltered, it was Da who challenged me

to be brave. He said he wanted to live vicariously through me as I wrote home about my adventures. He had always been a dreamer and would have loved to explore the world. Now it was up to me.

Ma spent the weeks before my departure alternating between chastising me for my wild irresponsibility, tugging at my guilt for leaving when Da was ill, and tearfully pleading for me to stay close to her. Despite the guilt and tears, I could no longer be contained within Ma's conventions.

Now I have joined what started as a community of primarily thieves, outlaws, and adulterers from across Saule, who made the valley their home for generations. Eshan has evolved into a thriving village with established families and a range of amenities. And some, like myself, aren't running from anything. I'm just looking for something—a place where I can choose my destiny, instead of meekly succumbing to my mother's expectations.

2

Tonight is First Fall, the annual celebration of the coming snow. The festival used to be held on the actual night of the first snow, but it was changed some time ago to the first Saturday in November. In anticipation of the celebration, the village is abuzz. Later, I plan to meet Marinn for an evening of cider and dancing.

For now, my deepest desire is to get home, warm myself by the fire, and wash off the day. I avoid the bustling preparations, taking the side road across the valley and up the slope to my cottage. I yearn to bring my family here to visit someday, although I can't imagine my sisters making the journey. And what would Ma think of the gnomes and halflings who live alongside humans? If Da were in better health, he would be here already and find it quite fascinating. Perhaps someday.

Rounding the bend, I see the moss-covered roof of my cottage peeking through the trees. Mr. Bennet, my caracal, is lazing on the porch, drinking in the fading sunlight filtering through the pines. When he sees me, he lets out a throaty growl, and the feathers at the tips of his ears twitch. "Well met, Mr. Bennet. Did you miss me today?" His striped tail slaps against the wooden porch. "I had to kill a rodent for my midday meal. It was most unpleasant."

"Aren't cats supposed to kill mice?" I ask, smiling. He licks his paw, then stares at me. "I am not a cat. I am a caracal."

I park the cart under the moss-covered lean-to on the side of the cottage and start up the steps. "Of course you are," I say. "You are *my* caracal. And you are perfectly capable of hunting for your food."

He hisses when I bend to scratch him behind the ears, and then he lazily climbs to his feet to follow me. "You know, if you insist on leaving me here, you must hire a servant."

I scoff. As if I could afford such a thing. I notice a folded parchment from the crevice of the door, and the familiar wax seal belongs to the man who holds my tenancy. Fantastic. I retrieve the letter but do not bother to open it. I already know its content.

Hanging my satchel on the hook next to the door, I toss the letter on the table and turn to the small pile of logs next to the hearth. Winter has settled into the valley early, and I will need to chop more wood if I don't want to freeze to death before the spring thaw. That is, if I still have a cottage at all by then.

I live on the razor's edge of poverty, without the means to weather unexpected storms, for most of my coin is sent home to my family for Da's medical care. Two months ago, I broke my most expensive chisel on a Cobalt Toris dragon's tooth. The expense was unexpected, but I could not go without it. Now, I owe my landlord a month's payment, with another due in a week.

The parchment taunts me, sitting there watching me tend the fire. Maybe I could use it as a fire starter. I chuckle, and Mr. Bennet rubs his side against my legs as I work, purring. After striking a flint and setting the dried pine needles ablaze, I add logs and stand back to watch the flames take hold. I fill my kettle with water from the wood jug in the corner and hang it on the hook over the fire, taking a moment to warm my hands. Tea will cut the chill and help shake off a day of messy dragon care.

I lift my arm and sniff, making a face. I stink of dragon slobber and fish. Ma would be appalled if I went to the revel in such a state. It could be added to her list of things about me that disappointed her, like being unmarried at six and twenty or working with dragons. I am forever grateful to live in a place that doesn't frown upon independent women.

Still, even independent women should avoid offensive odors if possible. There's no time to boil bathwater, so I'll have to make do with a quick wipe-down and a change of clothes. After removing my tunic, I kick it over into the corner. Dragons don't care about wrinkles, and neither do I. With a cotton cloth, I wipe down my face and torso with water from the kettle. After drying my face, I pull down my hair and finger-comb the long brown tresses. I weave my hair into two braids, dipping my hand in the heating water and smoothing the frizzy strays that have plagued me since I was a girl.

That will have to do. I lift my extra tunic off the hook and slip it over my head, tucking it into my skirts. Crossing to the small cabinet near the front door, I retrieve a pouch of tea from the tin and my mug. The water steams as I fill the mug and let it steep.

Mr. Bennet has curled up on the small rag rug before the fire and hisses at me. I hiss back. "I miss when you were a kitten and sounded like a chirping bird when trying to get my attention. If you had been this disagreeable the day we met, we would not have become friends."

He rolls over in a huff. "And if I had known about the lack of fresh quail and sleeping silks, I would have moved on to another porch." His ears twitch. "I cannot believe you expect me to hunt like a common street urchin."

"It's unfathomable," I say, smiling. It still amazes me that Mr. Bennet can talk. Of course, I knew it was possible. Early in my days in the village, Marinn had sent me home with an armful of texts from their personal collection. I had pored over tomes on magical creatures, the history of Saule, and every edition they had dealing with dragons.

Caracals of this variety can communicate with almost any creature, magically translating their voice at will. Mr. Bennet has taken this skill as a sign that his intelligence surpasses that of those around him. I have given up trying to correct the notion. He has been a constant companion these many years and serves as fodder for my letters home. My family always welcomes tales of my talking cat, and I write about him often. Of course, Ma thinks a talking cat is a foolish waste of magic. I know she secretly enjoys my stories.

My attention catches on the tunic balled in the corner, and I grunt as I move to pick it up and lay it over the back of a chair. The memory of my mother's voice echoes in the room: "A tidy house is a tidy life."

"Is it too much to ask for a simple fur rug to rest upon?" Mr. Bennet turns in a circle and then curls up on the unacceptable rug.

Mr. Bennet is the prissiest animal I've ever met. I'd been here a few weeks when I came home to find him curled up on my porch, his spotted fur and striped tail easily recognizable as a small but potentially dangerous animal. My fear was misplaced. He took one look at me, yawned, and never left. You would think he'd been bred for an easy life in the capital, Kaimas, instead of hunting prey in the mountain climate. In the mortal lands, caracals are predators known to steal off with hens or even baby goats. Twice the size of normal barn cats, they would never be considered a pet.

He eyes me, and as I approach, lazily rolls over and stretches, waiting for me to scratch his belly. I crouch next to him. "I hope you haven't grown accustomed to these glamorous accommodations. We both might end up living in a tree before the year is done."

He growls and paws at me with his claws retracted. "Don't even jest about such a fate. Although we may need to work on your language skills if you define this as glamorous." He lazily scans the room. "Still, I would rather live in a hovel than a tree."

I don't blame him. My gaze wanders to the parchment, and I begrudgingly retrieve it and settle into the chair by the fire. As expected, the letter reminds me that my landlord has a grandson coming in the spring, and my continued tenancy depends on prompt payment.

My vision travels up to the left, where I know his estate stands watch over the valley. I crumple the paper in my hand. I'll have to see if a partial payment will suffice. If not, I only have a month to make some serious coin.

After tossing the letter into the fire and giving Mr. Bennet one more head scratch, I move for the door. If I'm going to meet Marinn, I must make haste.

Most nights, Eshan goes to bed with the sun, but during First Fall, the hamlet is alive with celebration late into the night. Candle lights in glass jars are festively strung across the road, creating a cozy atmosphere. The sound of music drifts out from the central square. On nights like this, I am reminded of why I made the journey to Eshan.

Before I had even arrived, I knew this was where I was supposed to be. My thoughts wander to those early days in Eshan until a banner visible amid the lights stops me in my tracks. An artfully hand-painted sign hangs on posts in the village square announcing the upcoming Drakonas Jousting Tournament. I shake my head in disgust. Our community is about to be overrun with High Fae dragon riders. It is appalling that so few of Saule's citizens are allowed to bond with dragons. Dragons should not be subjected to such limitations, and they certainly should not be used as jousting mounts.

Still, Eshan has buzzed with excitement since we were chosen. The valley's terrain is ideal for competition. I instinctively look up to the shadow of the mountain range, with its natural caverns and rocky outcrops.

While everyone is enthralled with the upcoming tournament, I am dreading it. The presence of dragons is little consolation, as the tournament itself is a poor reflection of the honor dragons deserve. The only ray of sunshine will be the myriad dragon breeds I have yet to see outside of my worn *Field Guide to Dragons*.

3

Thoughts of the tournament flee when I spot Marinn, my dearest friend, standing at a plank and barrel table in front of the apothecary. She is huddled with a tall, bulky Fae man with wings tucked in tight.

Despite their magical reputation and rumors of trickery and glamours, Fae are just as diverse and varied in their appearances as humans. Their magic tends to follow bloodlines, and this affects their appearance. This man is not High Fae, born of royalty, but he does share the pointed ears indicative of both elves and Fae.

He whispers something, and she throws her head back to laugh. Her pointed ears peek out from her silky blond hair that cascades down her blue cloak. If the boys in Tevyne could see her, they would trip over themselves for one word. Perhaps I should take her for a visit to see the hullabaloo that would ensue.

It would be a lie to say it hasn't tested my confidence to have such an exquisite friend. Even for Saule, filled with beautiful, magical creatures, her loveliness is notable. As a half breed, she wasn't blessed with magical abilities, but the way she moves through the world has an ethereal quality just the same. It doesn't hurt that she has excellent taste in clothing. Her father indulges her ongoing need for the latest fashions. Luckily, her unassuming cheerfulness and straightforward manner make it easy to stand by her side, even as a flawed mortal shadow of her many charms.

As soon as she sees me, a smile breaks across her face, and she strolls to meet me on the road, which is beginning to fill with villagers. "Well met, Livvy. How was your day?" She hands me her mug of spiced cider, which I gratefully wrap my chilly hands around.

I return her smile. "I spent the day with my head in the mouth of a Green Zalia dragon."

Her brows furrow. She licks her lips and clenches her jaw as if chewing her worn-out warnings. She is sure I'll die a most horrible death at the hands of a dragon, someday. I watch her wrestle with her words, and then her thoughts change course. "I have some news," she says.

I wait for her to continue, sipping my cider and surveying the scene. Orthello and Lenora are circling the dance floor, both deep in their cups. Lenora's bright orange skirt flows behind her like a sunflower. They dance as if they are the only two people in the world, towering over the rest of the crowd.

"With the Drakonas coming on, my Father is looking to hire a tournament dragon groomer. Obviously, I told him he must hire you."

I choke on the spiced drink and use the back of my hand to cover my cough as I struggle to find my breath. Why she thinks I have any interest in participating is a mystery. It's a barbaric activity. Dragons are regal creatures who should be respected, not flown in a brazen display of brutish competition. It is grotesque.

Marinn smacks my back with so much force that I stumble. "Are you choking?" she asks. I shake my head and force myself to breathe through my nose until my coughing subsides. My eyes water, and I wipe them dry with my sleeve before clearing my throat and meeting her gaze.

Her face is pinched. "Are you well? I thought you might drop dead in the middle of the square."

"I'm fine. Perchance, what makes you think I want anything to do with that horrible tournament? You know my feelings. The riders are pompous, empty-headed fools."

I do not wish to offend her, but *berries*, she should know better. When I meet her gaze, instead of seeing pain, she is smirking. "What are you smiling about?" I ask.

She seems to swallow her smile and set her face in sincerity. "I knew you were going to object, but you see, I've already thought about that. If you are so concerned with the treatment of the dragons, what better way to make a difference than to be in charge of their care?" She raises her eyebrows expectantly.

I scratch my cheek, considering. She isn't wrong. There will be two dozen dragons kept in a series of caves along the mountain ridge. Green Zalias, Red Kurenti, even Black Jouda dragons from the north- dragons I have never seen before. It would be marvelous to work with such a variety. When will I ever have such an opportunity again? Maybe I can teach those pompous riders how dragons are meant to be treated. "What is the pay?"

She claps her hands and bounces on her toes, "Oh, I knew you would be perfect. I'm unsure about the pay, but it will be more than you currently earn." Her voice tips up at the end of the sentence, and she smiles sheepishly.

I grit my teeth. I never should have told her about my money troubles. "Would I still have time for my regular clients?" Even as I ask the question, I mentally scroll through the list and identify dragons whom I would be happy to give up serving. The Orange Zarijos dragon across the valley has singed my hair twice. Then there's the Cobalt Toris dragon, who is nice enough, but her rider seems quite surprised every time he's expected to pay me for my services. No. Even with the challenges, I could not forgo time with a single dragon on my schedule. If they cannot accommodate my current responsibilities, I will not even consider the position.

"I don't see why not. You'll have to ask my father to be certain. The riders will arrive in a fortnight for the opening ceremony and to become acquainted with the mountains. Then they'll return a month later for the actual tournament."

So much for an easy exit from the topic. I flick my chin towards the Fae man, who is looking a bit put-out. "Your admirer is growing impatient."

She turns to him and waves. She beams at me. "He is quite handsome, but he spends too much time at the pub playing dice games to be a suitable partner. I am waiting for the perfect man. I must marry for love."

"Look at us, modern women." I loop my arm through hers. "Let us stay single forever. Men are a diversion from self-determination."

Marinn frowns. "Livvy, someday you'll meet someone dreamy who will make you eat those words."

"Doubtful. If so, I shall add salt and enjoy." I lift my chin.

She laughs. When I first arrived in the village, I was exhausted, almost out of money, and missing home. After securing a room at the inn, I followed the innkeeper's suggestion and headed to the tavern, hoping a good bowl of soup and a solid night's sleep would rejuvenate my spirits.

I had been deep in conversation with the tavern's owner, Jasmine, when Marinn walked in. She was like summer sunshine wrapped up in a person. Ever the optimist, she had shepherded me through village life and introduced me to a family who had a cottage for let. Then Marinn found me a job with the local baker. I had spent six months kneading bread and covered in flour.

One night at the tavern, I saw an advertisement for a course on dragon grooming. I had never heard of such a vocation outside of royal households. But what better way to be near dragons? It was a perfect solution. Most of the course was completed through mail-away booklets and exams. Twice during the course, an instructor would bring an actual dragon into the valley for the practical portion of my studies. It took me six months to complete the course while I continued to work for the baker. The post served me well as I finished my course. The employment with the baker kept my tuition paid and my belly full. Meanwhile, between my studies and rising early to tend the ovens, I began to quietly advertise in all the usual gathering places in Eshan, hoping to spread word far enough to start building a client list.

I had been so excited to meet my first client, an elderly dragon who was as easygoing as they come. However, in my enthusiasm, I'd pressed his tongue too far into his throat, and he gagged. When dragons gag, they spark. By the time I had frantically withdrawn from his mouth, my eyebrows had been singed and my coat was on fire. It wasn't his fault, and I certainly learned my lesson.

Marinn pulls me back to the present and in the direction of the tavern door. "Come along. I require another cider."

4

Two days later, I wake up with Mr. Bennet curled up leisurely on my pillow, his tail smacking me in the face as he stares at me. I crinkle my nose and push him over. "You're tickling me."

He hisses and swishes his tail as he turns in a circle and then settles down just out of arm's reach, burrowing into the quilt. "Don't you dare use your claws on this quilt," I say.

"I am well aware of how fond you are of this," Mr. Bennet says, scanning the bed covering.

When I'd left Tevyne, Ma had handed me the patchwork quilt, each square made of fabric scraps and crafted into scenes from home. She said she wanted me to take part of home with me. It must have taken her months to piece together the soft, worn fabric into flowers and trees. My heart had swelled at the idea that she had been preparing for the moment I left, even if she was outwardly wary.

I groan as I stare at the fireplace embers, willing a log to appear magically. After a few moments, I reluctantly throw off the covers, race across the wide plank wood floor, and stack three logs in the hearth, pushing them around until embers catch and the bark begins to burn. Then I race back to bed and pull the covers up under my chin. It would be nice if someone could invent a way to heat homes that didn't involve such intense upkeep. Perhaps Sam, a friend and amateur inventor, can tackle the problem next.

Curled up under the covers, I watch the flames grow. Outside, enormous snowflakes drift past the window and the wind occasionally whistles through the trees. If I didn't know better, I would believe magic had come to Eshan once again. It would be a perfect day to stay in bed and read. At least the mid-morning bells haven't rung yet. When they do, I will be forced to dress and journey down to the pub.

I reach for the book on the small table next to my bed and run my finger down the edge of the ribbon I used to mark my space. I was supposed to return it to my friend Kessia today, but after spending most of the previous day reading, I still have a few chapters in "Small Business Practices for non-magical people." I'll take any assistance I can get as I navigate a world with all manner of magical creatures with their own customs and communication styles.

I don't get through an entire page before the mid-morning bells sound. I slip the ribbon between the pages and turn over to scratch Mr. Bennet behind his ears. He purrs and leans into my hand, but I reluctantly pull it away. "If I do not ready myself to leave soon, I shall be late," I say, scurrying around the cottage to get dressed. I grab my satchel and head out the door.

When I step into the dimly lit tavern, the smell of roasted boar stew hangs in the air. Jasmine stands by the fire, stirring the enormous kettle before replacing the lid and wiping her hands on her apron. Her gray, unruly hair is pulled into a bun, with a curl escaping to fall forward across her weathered face. She reminds me of Ma. It's such a normal sight from home, and my heart aches. Jasmine spots me, puts her hands on her hips, and smiles, saying, "Well met. Fancy a pint?"

I return her smile. "No, thank you. I'm late. I'll be back for a bowl of that stew, though."

"Off you go, then." She points to the room where the Merchants' Guild meets weekly.

"Thank you, Jasmine."

I unwrap my scarf and pull off my mittens, then pause by the hearth to enjoy the smell of the stew.

"Ah, I almost forgot," Jasmine says. "A trader was in last night and left something for you." She moves over to a stack of envelopes, her dresses swishing as she walks.

I've been hoping for a letter from my family. It has been weeks since I've had word. She rifles through the stack and retrieves a letter, handing it to me. I inspect the handwriting on the front; it's Ma's. And my heart returns to our cottage, watching Ma put quill to parchment by the light of the candles. She works as a laundress during the day, so correspondence has to wait till evening. Ma ensured we knew our letters and numbers by the time we were ten summers old. I hug the envelope to my chest, torn between opening it now and waiting till later, when I can savor each word from home. Trepidation flitters across my heart. Would this be bad news? Another request to come home? Letting out a breath, I slip the treasure into my satchel. "Thank you. It's from my ma."

Jasmine gives me a slight nod, "And so it is." She turns her attention to the bread she's begun kneading, and I proceed to the rear of the tavern.

Through the doorway, members of the Merchants' Guild are seated on benches around a large wooden table. A group of small business owners who meet weekly to help grow their businesses, the group serves as a source of encouragement and a haven.

Today, tension hangs in the air. Everyone seems to be looking at Sam, who is sitting on a stool pulled up to the end of the table. As a gnome, if he were to sit in the regular chair, only his eyes would be visible over the table. Thankfully, Jasmine offers a range of options catering to the diverse needs of the valley's population. Sam's glasses sit cockeyed on his face, and his cloak hangs off his shoulders to reveal the buttons of his vest straining across his midsection. He takes a pull from his mug of ale, seeming unconcerned.

Across from him, Kessia stares. Her tattooed arms are folded across her black sleeveless tunic, and her dark eyes are narrowed in irritation. "It's no wonder your trade is failing. You spend all your time and coin on those silly contraptions."

Sam wipes his mouth with the back of his hand. "If I wanted to be nagged, I could journey home to see my mother."

I smile. Da would like Sam, I am sure of it.

"I'm just saying that if you focused on your carpentry business, you could make a fortune," she says, running a hand through her short black hair.

I watch Sam as I unbutton my cloak. Kessia's not wrong. He talks about taking Colette to his family's estate in Ledus, but a lack of funds keeps them tethered to the valley. He is brilliant, but would forget to eat and wash if it weren't for Colette's reminders. A self-proclaimed inventor, he relies on Colette's glass-blowing trade to pay for his efforts. Luckily, her work is highly regarded, and she is his biggest supporter, happy to let him explore his invention ideas.

Sam taps the side of his head. "My mind swirls with ideas and notions far beyond carpentry. Even now, I am designing a system that will alter the world." He pauses dramatically before announcing, "I'm working on a chamber pot that does not need emptying."

Captain asks, "Where will the shite go? Do you plan to sprinkle fairy dust over it?"

"I, for one, find the idea quite appealing. Please keep me updated on your progress," I encourage. Someday, he will make a true discovery, I am certain.

A smile flashes across Sam's face, and he visibly relaxes. "See, Kessia? Livvy thinks I'm on the right path."

Kessia shakes her head and waits for me to slide onto the bench beside her. She studied tooth mending at a university in Straume, then continued her studies with a specialty in vampires. She was the first human to matriculate from the program. Being close to a vampire's fangs every day is a dangerous choice, but Kessia is fascinated with the creatures. She even dated one for a spell. But she loved the heat of the midday sun more than she loved him, so she ended it saying that she couldn't commit to a life of nocturnal normalcy. However, Kessia's fascination with their ways kept her in the specialty, and she is steadily building a reputation as the region's top dentist.

"What of your new office?" I ask her, pouring myself a cup of ale.

Kessia's face lights up. "Perfection. You come by and I'll clean those stubby canines." She waggles her finger at me.

I bump her shoulder with mine. "And run into a vampire in the waiting room? No, thank you."

Next to Sam, Captain clears his throat. "Shall I step out for my midday constitution while you hen peck?" Captain's eyes sparkle with mischief as he chews his toothpick.

Captain earned his name after spending most of his life on the open sea. As a Dwarf, his mountain clan had been shocked when he told them the sea was calling. Eventually, he returned to the solid footing of rock and soil to find a wife and start a family. But the conch shell rings woven into the braids of his long beard remind everyone that part of him will always yearn for the salt spray and wooden decks of a long ship.

He and his sons had opened a forge on the edge of the village a few summers ago. The last blacksmith was killed after he bragged he could shoe a dragon. When a baby dragon showed up with a limp, he thought it was his chance. He was burned to a crisp after he smacked her on the flank and said, "Easy there, little lady." Apparently, she didn't like being called "little."

Captain has stepped in to fill the need for a smithy. He's gruff and often disagreeable, but I've seen the way he looks at his wife when he thinks no one is watching. He's quite a romantic at heart.

"Where's Orthello?" I ask, noticing he's missing. I had assumed he was in the privy or running late.

"He isn't coming," Kessia says.

Sam nods. "His wife left a candle lit and set the wall of their house aflame."

"Oh, dear!" I say.

Kessia licks her lips. "Oh, it's going to be fine. He is replacing the scorched boards, and they are looking into lanterns to replace the open flames."

As if recalling something, Sam lifts a finger. "I almost forgot to tell you. They are lifting the ban on magic during the tournament."

"They never would," Captain says.

"Well, not during the preliminary phase, but magic will be available for two weeks during the actual tournament. Best protect yourselves." Sam gives Kessia and me a pointed look.

While peace has existed between the mortals and Fae for many centuries, it is precariously balanced on the edge of that ward. It deters Fae from venturing towards the border. Not having access to magic is uncomfortable for the Fae, and it's not something they would enter into lightly. In the mortal lands, there are common elements that dampen the magic, such as gold, which is why it is so valuable as a trading commodity. I glance at Kessia, whose jaw is slack. She clearly is just as surprised as I am.

"Thank you for the warning," she says, "We will indeed need to visit the apothecary for some defense."

Sam gives a satisfied nod.

I slip my thumb under the gold necklace around my neck, a going-away present from Da to help ward against magic. Hanging from the chain is a Huntsman Talisman that is supposed to bring good luck. Kessia wears a similar chain, as it is well known that gold, not iron, suppresses magic.

Captain gives the wooden table two knocks to get our attention. "Please ensure your tournament brackets are filled out if you plan to participate in the village pool." He unfolds a stack of parchment. "I have extra brackets if you would like to make your predictions. Ten coppers to enter."

Sam slides one off the top and squints for a closer look. "This is quite exciting. I'll need some time to run calculations."

Exciting is one way to describe the terrible abuse of dragons. I bite my lip and swallow my criticism.

Kessia notices my discomfort and keeps her voice light when she asks, "Livvy, do you object to jousting or just gambling?"

I suck in my cheeks. "If you must know, I am opposed to jousting of any kind, but especially with dragons."

"Are you not going to be working for the tournament?" Captain asked.

I placed my palms down on the table to steady myself. How did he find out? He's right. If I engage in this endeavor, I will be a hypocrite. "I have not decided. And if I do, it will be in service to the dragons."

Captain rubs his beard and grunts.

Kessia rescues me by discussing how we might utilize the tournament to advance our businesses. I choke back my resentment over the tournament. Either I take the job and violate my values, or turn down the job and give up the chance to help my da. It is a terrible choice, to be sure. I'm relieved when the meeting ends and I can retreat to my cottage with my letter from home.

5

$\mathcal{I}$ sit on my bed with my back pressed against the rough plank wall and unfold the letter. Mr. Bennet is out hunting, so I have the quiet cottage to myself. I lift the paper to smell the faint scent of the lemongrass and rosemary oils Ma loves to use in her house back home.

With one inhale, I'm right back in our little home in the woods. Ma's careful script decorates the page, and I slowly drink in every word. Her letters are bittersweet, pulling me back to the days of daisy chains and dolls, memories that have the softness of distance that seems to blur the rough edges. My sisters are on their way to settling into their own families, happily keeping close to Ma and Da. We couldn't be more different from each other, my sisters and I. Yet I miss Mary Ellen's quiet, contemplative spirit; it always brings a measure of calm whenever she enters a room. And Constance, who wanted nothing more than to be married and have a house full of children. Now she is expecting her second child.

Loneliness nibbles at the corners of my heart. I long for lively family meals surrounded by those who know me best. I yearn to taste the sweet, plump berries warm with the summer sun. These are the moments I curse my wanderlust, wishing I were content with a quiet life. But it is of no use. I am sure that if I were to return, my restlessness would eat me alive if not paid heed.

It is easy to forget the sour looks of disapproval from Ma when I would talk about dragons or leaving Tevyne. While Da loved hearing my plans, she never truly understood my heart. Leaving home had ripped out a root of bitterness that was certainly taking hold and would have grown into a wall between us over time.

At least she is thankful for the coin I've been sending. It's paid for medicine to quiet Da's cough, which has worsened beyond the remedies Ma brews for more minor ailments.

He is now confined to bed much of the time. He is filled with discontent at his loss of vitality. I fear the Da you knew is slipping away.

My heart clenches at the thought of Da lying in bed instead of walking the woods or playing his fiddle on the porch. I should be at his side. But even as the thought crosses my mind, it's no good. The road is perilous. If I did make it home, Ma would either resent me for leaving my employment or be happy to see me, saving her resentment for when I inevitably left again. I could not sacrifice the chance to earn much-needed funds only to satisfy my homesick heart, and that would be a selfish endeavor.

The best thing I can do for him is earn as much coin as possible to pay the Healer. Without my contribution, they shall need to rely on Ma's mending work and jam sales. I must stay here. Otherwise, I might pack a satchel and leave for Tevyne immediately. As I read, I realize Ma has other motivations for asking me when I will return.

William is still without a wife. He always had soft eyes for you.

Perhaps there is a match there? His family is well off and will ensure our security.

Of course, she believes an advantageous marriage is the only hope. William's family's land borders ours, and his mop of unruly brown hair had been a familiar sight in our cottage growing up. One year older than me, we were thick as thieves. He taught me to shoot a bow, and I taught him how to swim. We spent hours with muddy feet, racing through the woods and searching for frogs by the creek.

Of all the boys in the village, he was the least objectionable by a long mark. If I had stayed, he might have been a promising suitor. But I didn't stay, and it is unsurprising but also unfair that she should ask me to trade my freedom for security. Of course, in her mind, it makes logical sense. But she should know by now that my wild spirit is often at odds with her logic. While I will always be fond of William, I don't love him that way.

I let the parchment fall to my lap and turned to stare at the crackling embers of the fire. She worries. She misses me. I ache to see her, as well. But returning to the mortal lands to settle down and marry William or disappointing her by not returning to the traditional path she dreams of are the last things I wish to do.

With an exasperated sigh, I scoot down to lie on my back and stare at the spiderwebs stretched across the window frame. Condensation from the window turns the strands luminescent, and firelight glints off them like stars. My grandma used to say that stars were the loved ones shining down on us from the afterlife. I'm not sure if that's true. Perhaps there are entire worlds, maybe even one where social conventions don't confine women such as me.

I cannot summon the words to quell Ma's worry or desire for my return. Luckily, it will be a few days before Craige returns to the village on his way through to the mortal lands.

It is good to see a face from home, and he happily provides postal service in exchange for items the Fae do not consider treasure, such as enchanted jewelry, scraps of fabric woven with spider silk from the north, and plants native to this region. He is a credit to our family, unlike anyone else who would likely discard the letter, pocket the coin, and disappear.

I tap the quilt until I feel the parchment below my fingers. I fold it carefully and set it on the side table. There must be another option to increase my wages besides participating in the tournament and getting married. I could pick up some work at the tavern. Jasmine has offered in the past. But regularly smelling of ale and having my bottom smacked by drunk travelers is beyond even my loosely drawn bounds of propriety. I chew on my thumbnail. If I can maintain my regular clients and work for the tournament, that should put me ahead. The experience might lead to additional opportunities.

If I am to consider working for the tournament, normal wages won't do. I will have to demand more from those wealthy riders. The tournament attracts visitors from across both lands, and the village is sure to experience a substantial increase in income. Resignation wraps itself around me, and I cannot decide whether it is a comfort or a serpent set on strangling me.

6

The following day, I set out for a nearby hamlet to groom the sweetest Pink Gele dragon. The morning sun glistens off the dusting of snow clinging to the trees. In the valley, the magic is still woven into the soil and roots, even with the ward. The trees are more vibrant. The spices make even the most mundane food explode with taste. If I ever return to Tevyne, I would miss the food the most, second only to the dragons.

On my way through the village, Marinn waves me down. "Well met, Livvy! I'm glad I caught you."

I set down my wagon and let my satchel slip off my shoulder, apprehension taking its place. "Well met," I say tentatively.

"I spoke to my father." She pauses dramatically and then says in a flat voice, "I was misinformed about the coin you would receive."

I rub my brow, a headache threatening to come on. I knew the offer was too good to be true. After spending hours tossing and turning, I couldn't reconcile the need for coin and turning down the opportunity. The light was starting to outline the snow on the pines when I finally resolved to take the job to keep my cottage and send money to my family. Now, what am I going to do? With the toe of my boot, I clear the frost-covered leaves from the space in front of me, preparing to lie on the ground and curl into the fetal position.

Before I can fall into complete despair, Marinn grasps my hands, gives them a light squeeze, and says, "I spoke with my father about the pay…." Her voice trails off. Then she begins to jump up and down, and then continues, "It is more than you make in a year. But half your pay is given at the end of the tournament to ensure you stay. I guess it is standard."

My mouth falls open, the existential crisis forgotten. That much? I could easily pay my rent, send money home, and still have coin left to replace the wheels on my cart. I could even get Captain to make me a custom chisel. He has such a talent for creating beautiful handles.

Marinn settles back on her heels and raises her eyebrows. "Does that mean you'll do it?"

I nod and force my mouth closed. Of course I will do it. I can do anything for a short time. Ignore the riders, care for the dragons. This could work.

She throws her arms around my neck and squeezes. I work my fingers between her arm and my windpipe, threatening to cut off my air and end this endeavor before it starts. It must be her human heritage prompting her enthusiasm. "This is so exciting."

Finally, she releases me and sweeps her hair back from her face. "We will meet all of the riders." She tucks her fists under her chin. "Oh, let's fall in love with best friends, get married, live beside each other, and live happily ever after."

I hate to burst her bubble, but I have no desire to be

tucked away in a house only to wait for my mate to come home, even if it is next to Marinn. If that were my goal, I would settle for William. "The only happily ever afters I'm looking forward to are my da getting healthy and me not being tied down by someone who doesn't understand my need for freedom."

Her smile drops. "He's not getting any better?"

I shake my head. "I'm hoping the coin I send home from this tournament will be enough to pay for advanced Healers, maybe even a Fae Mender."

She nods. We both understand the stark difference between the two lands in terms of healing. The mortal lands typically only have access to non-magical Healers. Finding a Mender to help Da has always been my wish. After I arrived in Eshan, I learned quickly how few Menders existed. My misconception was not unique.

We've seen more than one frantic family member stumble into the village, their most precious possessions laid in offering at the village center. Many had almost lost their own lives making the trip to Eshan on behalf of a child or spouse who was on the brink of death. Most of the time, there is nothing we can do. They need a Mender, and Menders don't live in this village- they are in the Courts and large territorial cities and come at an astronomical cost. The best we can offer in Eshan is herbs and maybe a magical poultice. It breaks my heart when we send them on their way, knowing it likely won't make a bit of difference.

A hawk screeches from a nearby tree, breaking the silence between us. I reach out to touch her arm. "I should be on my way. I have a date with a lovely pink dragon," I say.

Marinn lifts her chin. "I refuse to be envious of your date, even if I shall spend the afternoon staring out the window, pining for a love I haven't met."

I laugh. "You are so dramatic. You realize I am speaking of a dragon, yes? Besides, any man would be lucky to have you."

She shrugs and blows a breath out. "I must get back. My father wants my input on the decorations for the tournament."

"That's a fine job for you," I say. Some might take the assignment as a slight. But her father knows Marinn has a lovely style and will ensure it all comes together nicely.

She wrinkles her nose. "Will you be okay? I know how worried you are about your da. I wish there were something I could do to help."

I shake my head. My heart is heavy with worry, but there is nothing she can do that hasn't already been done. "You helped me secure this post. That's the best thing you could have done. Now I must leave before I start losing my regular clients."

As I'm walking away, pulling my cart, she calls out, "Did I tell you there will be uniforms? Isn't it exciting?"

I crinkle my nose and give her a quick wave before continuing my journey. Uniforms? What kind of uniform might they fashion for me? It's probably something ridiculous. Marinn may be a fashion plate, but I am more comfortable in my simple dresses and tunics.

It doesn't matter. They can dress me like a jester if they want. The more ridiculous the better. Then perhaps the riders will ignore me, letting me focus on my actual clients, the dragons.

By noon, I am deep into the process of cleaning the ridge on the dragon's head. The horns and ridge help filter rainwater away from the dragon's eyes. This dragon has somehow managed to clog its ridge with red clay. "How did you get red clay in your ridge? Did you try to burrow into the northern ridge?" I ask, although it is a more appropriate question for his rider. With the tournament dragons coming from all five of the Fae Kingdoms, I am sure to encounter dragons in a variety of conditions. Who knows what kind of care those riders provide? No matter, while under my charge, the dragons shall be well looked after.

7

Two weeks later, I stand beside Marinn in a crowd of humans, Fae, and other magical creatures from across Saule. Fae are not always the evil beings Ma told us they were. Some are more sinister in their actions, I am sure. But in Eshan, any Fae that I interacted with tended to be, if not good, neutral in their motivations. Most are gifted with magic and have a deep connection to nature. If they are blessed with magic, they can live for hundreds of years.

When I first arrived in the village, it was quite startling to see the great variety of magical beings that populated the area. If the same creatures ventured into my home village, it would be declared that the end of the world was near. But over the years, I've grown accustomed to seeing ogres, elves, gnomes, sprites, and, of course, the Fae, and I relish the fact that our little village provides a peaceful co-existence for all who come with good intentions.

Today is the opening ceremony for the first phase of the Drakonas Tournament. For the next four weeks, the teams will visit the valley and stay for as long as they deem necessary, learning the terrain, training, and planning strategy.

This portion of the competition was added after several unfortunate incidents in which dragons and riders were killed due to a lack of familiarity with the field. Because each range is unique, it makes sense to allow riders to become acquainted with the land.

The real competition isn't until four weeks from now. It will last a fortnight, with a winner emerging through a single-elimination tournament. During that time, the wards' dampening magic shall be lifted. Anticipation skims my skin as I imagine Eshan at full magical capacity. What impact will the change have on the village? I will undoubtedly need additional protection for that time. I have no desire to become enchanted or led into the wilds of the mountains by a nefarious Fae.

I have yet to meet the dragons for whom I'm charged with caring. Many arrived in the last hour and went directly to the ridge to participate in the initial flyover. The Village Square is packed with people sporting hats and flags of their favorite dragon rider, all in anticipation of the first opportunity to view the majestic creatures. The Drakonas Council enters onto a wooden platform, and a cheer erupts. A Fae man with jet black hair and tattoos snaking up his neck from under his shirt uses magic to project his voice across the restless crowd, easily escalating their excitement into a frenzy over the upcoming tournament. He launches into a speech about the event's history. His cloak billows in the wind.

Everyone officially associated with the tournament, including me, was given a uniform of sorts. I run my hands over the thick velvet cloak, adorned with the tournament's insignia, and smile despite my lingering reservations. This cloak is worth a fortune. I bite my lip. Perhaps I could sell it and send the coin home. But it's also the warmest cloak I have ever owned. It may be more practical to keep the cloak and even have the patch removed. I do not want a constant reminder of my compromised morals.

Marinn stands next to me, beaming. She leans in and whispers, "Did you see how handsome some of the riders are? A few are sure to be single."

I breathe out my nose and say, "Oh, Marinn, you are way too good for those men."

"Well, I am sure you will be able to find out if that's true. You'll probably get to know them quite well as you're taking care of their dragons," she says, waggling her eyebrows.

I chuckle, "You are quite immature sometimes, you know that?"

"Sometimes I swear that you're made of stone. Some of us happen to appreciate romance. This ceremony is taking forever!" Her voice takes on a whiny edge.

She is right. Last week, I bought Captain a pint, and he filled me in on what to expect. He has attended a couple of tournaments during his many travels, and regaled me with the drama and pageantry. However, he failed to mention the number of speeches that open the ceremonies.

The Duke of Antrais starts by welcoming every dignitary in attendance, even the human dignitaries from Straume. I shift on my feet. I had no idea dignitaries were so plentiful. I stifle a laugh and tug on Marinn's sleeve, pointing her attention to one of the village council members sitting on the stage. His red nose dips with his chin, and then jerks up.

Marinn purses her lips. "He is not representing the council well at all. Father will be appalled."

I'm not sure what her father is going to do. I cannot fault the drowsy council member. If I had access to a stool, I might nod off as well. In front of me, a woman holds a little boy who, when we first arrived, was jumping up and down with great excitement. Now he's drooling on her shoulder, sound asleep. My attention snaps back to the speaker when he says, "And now for the moment you have been waiting for."

He raises his eyes to the sky behind us, and everyone turns to follow his gaze. Gasps of surprise, excitement, and delight erupt as the sun is blocked out by a line of dragons crossing over the valley, low and majestic. If it weren't for the cheering and screaming, I imagine we could hear the beating of their wings.

I shield my view from the sun and watch. Despite every doubt I've had about the tournament, my eyes fill with tears, and a smile gets caught in my throat. How is it that I have the honor of caring for these dragons? My heart aches as I picture my da handing me the *Field Guide to Dragons*. He was so proud of that gift. Oh, if he could be here with me. He would be so happy. This is what dragons were meant to look like, gliding across the open sky. My heart swells at the memory of the first time I saw a dragon.

In my sixth summer, I had been tasked with picking the blueberries that grew along the side of our cottage. I had just popped a berry into my mouth when I felt a deep rumble under my feet. The forest fell silent, and a shadow swept the ground, swallowing our homestead. I looked up, wondering where the sun had gone, and my breath caught in my throat.

Dragons were rarely seen in the mortal lands. It was likely to be the only time I would see one in my lifetime. It was hard to tell the color while it was in shadow, but I could clearly see its tail swishing as it soared across the sky. When it roared, my hands rushed to shield my ears from the sound, fear joining my fascination. Still, I couldn't look away. The sun shimmered off the burnt orange scales as it cleared the cottage; it was the most beautiful thing I had ever seen. Even after it had melted into the horizon, I watched for a few minutes more, hoping for its return.

Finally, Ma had called from the house, "Livvy, what's

happening out there? I felt a rumble. And what is that racket? Are you finished? I have a pie to make." Her attention was quickly diverted to my crying baby sister.

"Almost finished," I replied absently, my gaze still turned to the sky.

Ma had clucked her tongue and said, "Hurry up, girl. You're picking berries, not planting a garden."

I was about to ask her if she had seen the dragon, but she had retreated into the cottage. Dropping my eyes to the basket of berries, I stared at the shades of blue that now seemed flat and dull. How could I be expected to return to my tedious chores after seeing such a glorious sight?

Later that night, we crowded around the table, and my da and I shared our stories of seeing the dragon. Da had been in the Tevyne when it flew over, on an errand for the man who ran the mine where he worked. "It was great luck that I wasn't stuck underground today." His voice stuttered as a cough forced its way into the middle of his story.

Sometimes, he coughed hard enough to turn his face red and leave him struggling for breath. Ma blamed it on the dust in the mine. When the hacking had quieted, he described how the whole village was in an uproar over the sighting. Ma had focused on feeding my younger siblings, her lips pursed as she looked furtively at Da. She had no time for dragons. But Da would have loved this.

I hold my breath as the dragons disappear over the hillside on the other side of the valley. As much as I hate this tournament, I have to admit the flyover was impressive. I know I have a stupid smile on my face, but I can't help it. When I turn to look at Marinn, she grins back at me. I say, "Have I thanked you for getting me this job?"

She schools her face into a serious expression and taps her chin with her finger. "Let's see. You have been annoyed, begrudgingly willing to think about it, and resigned to the truth that you have no better option. But, I'm not sure any of that constitutes a thank you."

I put my hand over my heart. "Well, thank you."

She dips her head in a slight nod. "You're welcome." She spins around, absorbing the energy and excitement of the crowd. "Isn't this just the best?"

I nod. Marinn is loving the crowded square and the excitement buzzing through the air. I could be just as happy with the view if I were alone in a clearing. But either way, my heart is full. Once the last dragon is out of sight, the crowd starts to disperse, heading home for supper or making a long trip back to the neighboring hamlets.

"All of the riders are meeting at the pub tonight. We should go, and you can help me get acquainted with them," Marinn says.

"Your father will permit you to go to the pub?" Her father hardly lets her out of his sight. A rowdy pub full of strangers seems like it would be off-limits.

She tips her head. "He doesn't know." She brushes off the front of her cloak and continues. "My father has spent weeks preparing for the tournament. He's meeting with the judges. They will labor over the rules as they drink all of the good wine from our cellar. I'll simply tell him we're going for a walk or something." She waves me off.

I would prefer to curl up in my bed in front of the fire and finish the chapter on Red Kurenti dragon care. But Marinn has been such a good friend to me, the least I can do is accompany her on her quest to meet the riders. Likely, they will be as insufferable as I assume, so the evening promises to be short.

The dragons will spend tomorrow getting acclimated to their keep, and I'm not expected to begin my work until the day after. I should have plenty of time to finish my reading and triple-check my supplies. I ordered some specialty formulas from the apothecary and a new set of chisels. Hopefully, I will not be expected to express anal glands since this is a temporary assignment, and they should have taken care of that at home.

Marinn is staring at me, eyes wide and expectant. "Alright. I will go," I say.

She throws her arms around me. "Thank you, friend." A small child with pointed ears and bright red hair pushes between us, causing Marinn to let out a little shriek and pull back. He tugs on her skirt. "Miss Marinn, where's my mother?"

She tousles his hair and says to me, "This is Osso. His Father is one of the judges."

I smile and squat down to his eye level. Then I hold out my hand. "Well met, Osso. I'm Livvy."

He looks up to Marinn, who gives him a slight nod. Then he shakes my hand. "Well met."

"And how old are you?" I ask.

"Six summers."

I raise my eyebrows as if impressed. "You are quite tall for six."

He straightens and lifts his chin. "I'm the tallest in my class, right Miss Marinn?"

She pats his head. "Of course.

He beams.

"Osso, your mother is just over there," Marinn says, pointing to a woman with a haggard face and a baby on her hip. "She must be worried. Go to her and we'll see you later."

I stand and watch Osso race to his mother, who lets out a relieved sigh and pulls him to her side.

Marinn turns her attention to me. "You must join me for dinner. Our cook is making enough food to feed the entire village."

I stifle a sigh. I am not interested in a formal dinner after such a long day. Marinn must notice my reaction because she quickly follows up with, "We can take our plates and eat in the library. Then we'll slip out later."

My mouth waters. Their cook is the best in the valley, although I'd never say that to Jasmine. The cakes that come from Marinn's kitchen are enough to cause me to abandon almost any plan. If she's cooking for all those fussy judges, the food will be fantastic.

8

Although an increasing number of people choose to live in Eshan as a long-term plan, many buildings reflect the transient nature of past residents. The village has a cozy but dingy, sharp-edged feel to it, except for Marinn's house. The light blue timber-framed house with gingerbread trim painted in yellow stands in stark contrast to the thatched-roof cottages and clapboard wood buildings. The love story behind the unusual architecture is novel-worthy.

Marinn's father is a wealthy merchant who inherited several businesses. He was born in the human lands, ordinary in every way. He isn't particularly tall. He has always been a bit thick around the middle and wears spectacles. But while he was visiting the elves in Lauks to discuss a trade agreement, he had met Vittoria. He was captivated by the young elf, and despite family expectations, Vitorria found the young man witty, charming, and kind.

After they were married, they decided Eshan was the perfect place for them to settle. Elves are tight-knit communities, and Vittoria was desperate to stay as close as possible to her family. Additionally, her pointed ears and ethereal beauty would stand out in the mortal land. On the other hand, Marinn's father made his fortune in Straume and needed to be accessible to his enterprise.

The manor was a gift from Marinn's father. If Vittoria must leave the lush landscape of her Realm, she should have the finest house in Eshan. It took three years to complete, as Marinn's father had specialty wood, glass, and paint brought from the other side of the mountains. Marinn told me stories of a home filled with music, laughter, and love. Marinn's mother had died in childbirth along with Marinn's younger brother when Marinn was three. They stayed in the house where memories of Vittoria lived beside them.

Marinn meets me on the porch and takes my hand, leading me through the side door into the butler's pantry. Steaming platters and bowls crowd the counter top, waiting to be carried to the group of men and women huddled around the dining table. Once our plates are loaded with boiled potatoes, chicken, and green beans, we proceed into the library. The smell of rosemary and lemon trails behind us. In front of the fire, we balance the plates on our laps while we eat and talk.

"Just think, you could meet a handsome rider, become the caretaker for his dragon, and travel the world with him. Would that not be amazing?" Marinn asks.

I chew a bite of potato, marveling at the perfect seasoning and buttery flavor. Thankfully, she continues to talk without waiting for an answer.

"Of course, my father seems to believe I will grow old in this house and never leave. But my feet long for the sands of distant shores and the unsteady deck of a ship on the open sea. This is my chance to fall in love with someone who can take me away from here."

"Well, unless he ties you to a chair, your father cannot force you to stay here if you want to go."

"True. Once I am married, he no longer has a say over my choices."

Marinn's father had done his best to raise her after her mother died. Unfortunately, his efforts were a bit exuberant and left Marinn feeling smothered most of her life.

We eat in comfortable silence for a while and then sneak into the kitchen for mini cakes made with jam and fruit. When we are sure Drakonas Council and the dining room are engrossed in their rule discussions, we slip out the back door and make our way to the pub. I might have attempted to stay and eavesdrop on the proceedings, but Marinn was determined to meet the riders.

The excitement of the day lingers in the air, despite most of the village being tucked in for the night. A warm glow can be seen through the steamed-over windows of the pub. As we approach, I grab Marinn's arm and pull her to a stop. "Are you sure it's appropriate for us to be here? It might not be safe for us." There's something about the fact that the building's occupants are almost all likely strangers that makes me cautious.

She shakes off my grasp. "These are not traders or vagabonds; they are respected dragon riders." Her eyes flash with frustration.

"Very well, then. But if anything dangerous or untoward occurs, we are leaving immediately." I'm not a prude, especially after living in Eshan for a few years, but I keep my guard up around strangers, especially when they are Fae. There are simply too many unknown elements.

Marinn holds up her little finger. "Pinky promise."

I link fingers with her, and she smiles. I can't help but appreciate her sanguine personality. I may have braved the trek here from my village, but small talk with a room full of strangers makes me sweat. The thought of having to awkwardly walk through the door and have everyone turn to look at us makes me want to crawl into the watering trough and drown myself.

My only consolation is that they'll be looking at Marinn, not me. She has a way of drawing the light to herself and then basking in it. I don't mind being in her shadow. The last thing I want is the wrong sort of attention from dragon riders. No, I need to be taken seriously as a dragon groomer. Luckily, Marinn is sure to excel in this environment, leaving me to enjoy the show.

As we approach, the door to the tavern bursts open, and two men stumble out, singing a bawdy tune. One of the men wraps an arm around the other and rubs his knuckles on the man's head. "You owe me coin. I knew that woman wasn't interested in you. Your round ears and pudgy middle are off-putting."

We pass the men as one of them insists on heading to the treeline to relieve himself. Marinn giggles and yanks me forward. "Let's hope the men we meet tonight are more enchanting than those two."

A wave of ale-soaked heat hits us as we enter. Luckily, everyone is deep in their cups and conversation. I scan the room, finding only a smattering of faces I recognize. "Is there anybody in particular you desire to meet tonight?" I ask her.

Marinn bites her lip and nods, a moment of uncharacteristic shyness. I study her. She is nervous. I might think they're all repugnant, but she loves following the tournaments with her father and clearly has her favorites. "I can't wait to meet Thaddeus Cedar."

I wrinkle my nose. "Isn't he known as Thaddeus the Great?"

She claps her hands in front of her and says in a dreamy voice, "Yes, because he *is* great. He is here all the way from Lauks and will give the last victor a real challenge. Besides that, he's painfully handsome."

Oh, *berries*, it's going to be a long night. She has romanticized these men in her mind. Perhaps once she gets to know them, she'll see I am right about their excessive pride. I will find no joy in it. I like being proven right, but not when it's at the expense of my best friend.

Marinn, who has seen Thaddeus a few times at other tournaments and in the capital, has spent hours telling me all about his curly auburn hair, which he wears pulled high on his head in a leather strap so it flies out behind him while he rides, and his sparkling green eyes. He's been connected with a few princesses from the realm and even a fellow dragon rider over the years. It was rumored that he was a sorcerer, ensnaring women with his charms. That is probably why she likes him. She's always been drawn to rakes.

9

____

A barmaid squeezes around the tables with ale sloshing over the tops of mugs she's working to deliver. My nose twitches from the musky smell of working men. The boisterous laughter and chatter drown out my thoughts. Behind the bar, Jasmine pulls drafts as fast as she can, her brows furrowed in concentration.

Fae men and women stand a foot taller than their average mortal counterparts, and it's hard to see through the crowd. I rise onto the tips of my toes and strain to find a place to sit. Two barstools are open on the far side of the tavern. I grab Marinn's hand and make my way across the room. We slide onto the stools, and I'm grateful for the cocoon of space we've carved out. Jasmine flashes me a tired grin. "Well met, Livvy. Mug of ale?"

I nod. Then she notices Marinn by my side, and her smile slips for a moment. "I didn't expect to see you. Your father knows you're here?" One eyebrow creeps up her forehead.

I watch Marinn's throat bob, and she lifts her chin. "He knows I'm out with Livvy. And I will have a pint of ale, please."

Jasmine nods. "As you wish." She turns and grabs two pints from the counter and sets them before us.

Marinn leans in and says over the din, "Have you seen Thaddeus Cedar?"

Jasmine's eyes flit to the side, and I follow her glance. Sure enough, in the corner holding court is a tall, red-headed man who has to be Thaddeus. A brown-haired Fae woman with iridescent black wings tucked in tight has her hand on his arm and is staring at him adoringly. His attention is focused on a tall and muscular man with black hair tied back at his nape. The woman is a fool if she thinks Thaddeus to be interested. Perhaps he likes fair-haired women, which puts Marinn in a favorable position. I chuckle and swig my ale.

Marinn squeals and tugs at my sleeve. "I knew he would be here."

I lean my elbows on the bar and watch her smooth her hair, then twirl a strand around her finger. Her eager optimism fades, and she starts to look uncomfortable, even shy. "You should go introduce yourself," I say.

"I couldn't. It isn't polite." She bites her lip. "Perhaps if you come, too. His friend is nice-looking. You could help ease the introduction."

I shake my head. "No, thank you." I need at least two more pints before she drags me into talking to the brainless idiots who would not know a healthy dragon molar if it bit them in the arse.

She sticks her lower lip out. "Don't be such a sourpuss. It's not as if I'm asking you to propose to the man. Just come with me so I can meet Thaddeus."

I suck on my teeth. We'll never get these seats back. Then again, once Marinn sees how ridiculous they are, we can leave. I roll my eyes and drain my ale in one go. Marinn grasps her mug and waits for me as I push my mug toward

Jasmine and wipe my mouth with my sleeve. The barkeep chuckles and slides a fresh brew over to me.

I lift the mug in thanks and then turn to Marinn. "Onward."

I motion for her to lead the way, and she eagerly begins to weave a path across the room. As we venture into the sea of patrons, I realize we should have planned our strategy. Ma would be scandalized. According to her, respectable women do not approach strange men without an introduction.

Marinn's bravado starts to give out halfway over to the men. Perhaps she realizes our impending lack of propriety. When her steps falter, I crash into her with a grunt. She stops and turns around with her eyes wide. I rest my hand on her shoulder and say, "You are beautiful. You are available. It will be fine."

She takes a deep breath and sets her jaw. "Alright, I have a plan."

I chuckle. I'm not sure exactly what she is scheming to do, but it will be fun to watch.

She strides towards Thaddeus. As soon as she gets close to him, she rotates her body and then steps backward as if bumping into him. When she pivots, she's all fluttering eyelashes with her palm over her heart. "Oh, I'm so sorry I didn't see you there."

I stifle a laugh.

He gives her a rueful smile, then feigns concern, looking her over. "Are you all right? Have you been hurt?"

Marinn's face flushes, and she folds her arms in front of her. "I am quite well. I believe I have stepped on your toes."

He lifts his boot and flexes his ankle. "No harm done."

I stand awkwardly as Thaddeus and Marinn quickly fall deep into conversation. She cannot stop smiling, and he seems just as enchanted. I glance longingly at Jasmine. I may need another ale as mine shall soon be drained to the dregs to endure this interaction.

My attention shifts to Thaddeus' friend. His guarded gaze briefly meets mine before he looks away, becoming deeply interested in a set of stag horns on the wall. I clear my throat and say, "This promises to be a spirited tournament. Are you a rider?"

He looks at me, his lips pressed into a thin line as if he's annoyed that I dare interrupt his stag horn gazing. I shift uncomfortably. Did he not hear me? Perhaps he doesn't speak the common tongue?

Finally, he says, "What other reason would I have for coming to Eshan? It is not exactly a bustling center of commerce and art."

This man is quite full of himself. He is proving me right about dragon riders on every count.

Marinn gives me the side eye and lifts her chin towards this man, encouraging me to keep talking to him so she can keep talking to Thaddeus.

I suck in my cheeks. If not for her generous friendship, I would saunter out of this tavern right now without a look back. Instead, I smooth my hair and try to rescue the conversation. "Right. I'm sorry, I don't know your name."

The muscles in his jaw twitch and he does not respond. Am I annoying him? Did he not hear me? Finally, his view drops to his mug and then up to me. "My name is Asher. Asher Covington."

I force a smile. "Well met, Mr. Covington."

Before he can respond, Jasmine calls over to me, "Oy! Love! Got a fresh pint for you!"

"Please excuse me, I'll be back presently." I weave my way back to the bar, gladly accepting the fresh drink. Perhaps it will make this conversation feel less awkward. "You rescued me, Jasmine. Many thanks."

"Rescued? Do you know who that is, Livvy?" She starts to laugh, and I can't help but feel like it's at my expense.

"You know I don't follow the tournament. I don't know who any of the riders are," I say stiffly. "I care more about the dragons."

"Asher Covington is famous. He won the last tournament and is favored to win again. He's even known throughout the mortal lands, and has been linked to royalty, human women of great status, and even wealthy widows- not that he needs the coin." Her voice is growing slightly breathless as she gushes. "He is royal, and rich."

I glance back through the throngs of drinkers and survey the cut of his perfectly fitting tunic and the supple leather of his black riding boots. It all makes sense. Despite his many rumored attachments, Asher Covington seems like a snob. Unfortunately for me, Marinn is giggling behind her hand as Thaddeus whispers in her ear. I swallow, thanking Jasmine as she winks. Returning to my friend's side and my own unpleasant conversation, my mouth instantly fills with sand. I'm grateful for the fresh mug of ale.

After a few moments of awkward silence, Asher says, "Are you here for the tournament, or do you live in this village?

He says the word "village" as if he's just sucked on a lemon, and I tip my head, cheeks flushing with ire. "You may be surprised to find that I adore Eshan. The tournament offi-cials seem to agree with me."

He blinks rapidly. "You are quite sure of yourself. Perhaps they should make you an official ambassador." A smile plays at the corners of his mouth.

"I don't appreciate strangers coming in and insulting where I live."

"I did not mean to insult you or your village. It is simply not what I'm used to in terms of accommodations and company." He lets his gaze scan the room. Is that a sneer? His half-hearted apology does nothing to soothe my indignation.

Before I can respond, he leans over and says something to Thaddeus that I can't hear. Thaddeus looks at Marinn and then at him, fervently whispering something back. Asher glances at me and gives a stern shake of his head. Finally, Thaddeus blows out a breath and smiles at Marinn, brushing his lips against the back of her hand and bidding her good night. Her face falls as she realizes Thaddeus is leaving, and she can do nothing about it.

This is Asher's fault. I wasn't enjoying our conversation by any means, but I'm every bit as worthy of his time as Eshan is. It's not as if I have a horn growing out of my forehead.

Before Thaddeus goes, he reaches into his pocket and pulls out a pin connected to a ribbon imprinted with an image of a dragon. He presents it to Marinn, who eagerly accepts it. She smiles brightly as she takes the pin and examines it closely. He gives her another nod and follows Asher out of the tavern.

Marinn's face has gone from ecstatic to heartbroken and back to ecstatic in about 15 seconds, and she seems to be holding onto that feeling as she turns to me. "Isn't he the best? He is sweet, and such a gentleman."

I swallow my cynicism and smile. "He seems nice. And I think he enjoys your company."

I finish the last of my ale and set the mug on the table, hoping she's ready to go since Thaddeus is leaving. Sure enough, she slips her arm through mine and pulls me towards the door. Once we're outside and the cool air hits my sweat-drenched neck, she says, "Can you believe that we met famous dragon riders? It's just too much."

"At least some of them are amiable," I say with very little

enthusiasm. "As happy as I am for you, my interaction did not yield anything close to your results."

She crinkles her eyebrows. "Was Asher not cordial? Was it not a pleasant conversation?

I chuckle. "Pleasant? No. Asher is a snobby, unpleasant man."

"Well, if he cannot see how amazing you are, then it is his loss. Count your blessings; if he had liked you, you'd have to spend more time with him."

As we walk towards Marinn's house, she prattles on, replaying her entire conversation with Thaddeus. Then a deep, menacing growl rumbles from inside the treeline, followed by a sound I can only describe as bone-grinding. We freeze.

arinn and I both stop breathing at the sound. A growl in the dark is never a good thing. At best, it's a stray dog or bobcat, which I am reasonably confident I could fend off with my dagger. But here, it could be a bear, timber boar, or any number of magical creatures that roam Saule. Animals that venture too close to the border find their magic silenced, which can frighten them and cause aggressive behavior.

I slowly scan the area for anyone who might help defend against the mystery creature. The road is empty. Behind us, distantly, a bawdy round of singing breaks out in the tavern. It taunts us as it echoes across the quiet. Would anyone hear us, even if we scream? We likely wouldn't make it the fifty yards back to the tavern, and I cannot bring myself to turn my back on the woods. Our best chance at shelter is the inn. If we can make it there, we'll be safe.

As I lean in and whisper, "We need to get to the inn," I unclasp the sheath and slide my blade out. We turn to watch the woods and begin to walk slowly backward towards the inn, which sits towards the edge of town. A stick breaks, and

I can make out a large shadow. That is no dog. Marinn's breaths are coming in short gasps. She is going to faint if she does not calm down. I squeeze her arm, and she lets out a whimper.

It is unusual to have such a predator this close to the village. Perhaps the tournament is attracting more than just dragon enthusiasts. The animal lets out another growl. Before I can stop her, Marinn shrieks, then turns to run.

I have no desire to remain behind to discover what is lurking in the shadows. We race towards the lantern-lit porch of the inn. Marinn strides up the stairs, attempting to take two at a time. I am right behind her, fear coursing through me. It isn't often that I am afraid out here. But my heart is pounding in my ears as I push her up the stairs. "Hurry!"

Marinn stumbles and we collapse in a heap on the porch, both of us letting out another shout. The door flies open. I look up to see black leather boots. "What is going on out here?" a stern voice asks.

Marinn and I scramble to our feet, catching our breath. It's only when we are sure-footed that I dare turn to the woods, expecting to see a maw dripping in anticipation of making Marinn and me its next meal. But there is nothing there. I shift to see who it was that likely rescued us from sure death, and am met with a set of gray eyes. It's Asher. *Berries.*

Marinn smooths her hair and speaks through choking tears. "There was an animal or something, growling." She points to the treeline. "It was just over there."

I nod in agreement. Asher moves to step off the porch, but Marinn grabs his arm. "No, you mustn't".

"I am quite capable of navigating these woods." Asher jogs down the stairs and surveys the treeline. After a moment, he scratches behind his ear and puts his hands on his hips, an ear tipped towards the woods. "I hear nothing. If something was there, it must have fled when you screamed."

I straighten my spine. *If?* I exercise healthy caution in the woods, but it takes something formidable to make me feel threatened enough to turn tail. There was something there, and it was formidable and huge. I'm sure of it.

Before I can respond, the door to the inn opens again. Thaddeus steps into the threshold and surveys the scene. "Has something happened?" He looks at Marinn and me, then descends the stairs, where Asher tells him about our encounter. From their expressions, it appears as if they are taking our concerns seriously, which is a credit to them.

Marinn is pressed against the wall next to the door, her arms wrapped around herself. She sniffles. I blink back tears. The last thing I want is for them to see me cry. There is a wide belief among the Fae that mortals should not live in their lands. Most Fae see themselves as superior to humans, even if they are not born with magic. They believe humans to be a fleeting annoyance barely worth consideration. I must work twice as hard to prove I can handle myself.

Thaddeus strides to the edge of the road, right in front of the trees, as if daring the creature to attack. After a few moments, he seems assured that there is no longer a threat waiting to attack and returns to the porch, looking up to where Marinn and I take refuge. "You've had a fright. Come into the drawing room, and I will fetch us some warm cider. Once you have gathered yourself, we will escort you home."

The idea of warming by a safe fire with a mug of cider is appealing, so I turn to enter the inn. Marinn touches my shoulder. "I have twisted my ankle on those blasted stairs. I can't walk."

Her eyes shine with tears, and I notice she is leaning against the wall not just for safety, but also to avoid putting weight on her foot. I bite my lip. "If you lean on me, can you make it inside?"

I look at Thaddeus and Asher, standing at the bottom of the stairs, still glancing between us and the woods. "I can try."

I lean down so she can wrap her arm around my shoulder and then push the door open. She hobbles a step over the threshold and cries out in pain. In a few strides, Thaddeus is there, scooping her into his arms and carrying her to a chair by the hearth. He gingerly lowers her into the wooden high-backed seat and pulls another chair over in front of her. "Which ankle have you injured? I will ask my Healer to examine you. For now, you must elevate your foot."

She motions to her left boot. He carefully lifts her foot and sets it on the chair. She brushes her skirts down, her cheeks flushed. "Please don't go to any trouble. I'm sure I'll be fine if I rest here briefly."

Thaddeus stands. "Nonsense, I shall return in a moment." He strides off towards the stairs to the second floor.

I move to sit across from Marinn, placing her foot in my lap. I unlace her boot and gently remove the shoe. She winces and sucks in a breath. "Sorry," I say. "Can you move your toes?"

Marinn wiggles her toes. "Thank goodness," she says.

"Shouldn't we wait for the Healer?" Asher asks. I forgot he was even here. He's leaning against the wall, looking put out, as if it's our fault we were almost dragged into the woods by some gigantic carnivore and now poor Marinn can't walk.

I bite back a retort as Thaddeus returns with a balding man in tow. The Healer is pulling off his glasses to wipe sleep from his eyes. He's in his dressing robe and has a small leather satchel with him. He clears his throat and kneels to examine Marinn. I stand and the Healer slips into the seat I had vacated.

When Marinn flinches at the Healer's touch, Thaddeus rushes to her side and takes her hand. The Healer continues to examine her foot. After asking her questions and looking at her ankle, he wipes his brow with a blue hankie. "Well, it is not broken. But it is quite sprained. I will give you a potion to speed up the healing process. And this ointment will relieve the pain. You must stay off of it for the next few days." He unscrews the top from a small jar and scoops out white cream that he smooths across her ankle.

Marinn groans. "But there's so much happening and I don't want to miss it."

She's right. There are a dozen events she plans to attend. Her face is crestfallen. The only possible consolation is the fact that Thaddeus is still holding her hand.

The Healer turns to Thaddeus. "She must take care for the next few hours. You will need to ensure no weight is placed on her ankle, even if the pain is diminished. Can you ensure she gets home?"

Thaddeus nods dutifully.

"I can get her home," I say, standing abruptly.

Marinn throws me a look of dismay, her jaw set. I blink rapidly. Of course, she would rather have Thaddeus accompany her home. But I am not leaving her alone with any man. I scuff my foot. "It might be beneficial for you to escort us home, given everything that's happened tonight." My mind flashes back to the growl, and I shiver.

"I shall come as well," Asher says, "in case I am needed." He pulls at the hem of his jacket.

The Healer closes his bag. "Very well. Remember, two drops of the potion every morning and night for three days. Keep the ankle elevated, and you should be much improved soon enough."

We all thank the Healer, and Thaddeus shakes his hand.

I help Marinn put her sock back on, but when I try to slip her boot on, she shrieks, and I decide to carry it instead.

Thaddeus scoops her into his arms as if she weighs nothing. Marinn wraps her arms around his neck and looks at me over his shoulder, her face lit with excitement despite the pain. I shake my head and follow them out the door. Only Marinn could care more about a romantic gesture than her very real injury.

Asher and I follow along in silence. Once Marinn is safely delivered home, I bid the men a quick goodbye and retreat to my cottage, refusing their offers of escort. Once I cross into the wooded path from the village, I bite back my regret as fear threatens to overtake me. I was a fool. Ma would say that it serves me right if I am eaten by a beast in the night while walking alone. Thankfully, the walk is quiet and peaceful, and as I reach the porch of my cottage, snow begins to fall.

11

Two days later the snow gently blankets the ground, crunching under my feet as I walk. I avoid the sunken wheel treads, now frozen mud, on the road. The sounds of the village are muted into an idyllic scene. After dropping my cart at the cottage, I set out to visit Marinn. She has been confined to her bed as her ankle heals.

Her elf blood means she will heal more quickly than humans, so she should be back on her feet in no time. If I suffered the same injury, I would be out of work for a few weeks, which would be a disaster. "Well met," I call out, pushing her partially open door wider and entering her room.

"Well met," Marinn says, smiling brightly and looking like an elven princess propped up against her headboard with feather pillows stacked under her ankle. Across from her bed, Asher and Thaddeus quickly rise from two wooden chairs I recognize from the dining room. What are they doing here? My heart warms at the evidence of their gallantry. It's a rare gentleman who takes the time to check in on an injured damsel- or a smitten one.

I go to Marinn's side and kiss her cheek. Only then do I turn and nod a greeting towards the men. They return the gesture and sit. "Thank you for keeping her company." I slip off my velvet cloak and cross the room to hang it on the hook next to the door.

When I turn around, Asher is staring at me. As if struck by an afterthought, his chair scuffs against the floor and he rushes to stand again, motioning for me to take a seat. I shake my head slightly and turn towards the bed. But when I step forward to pass him, I stumble, tripping over the edge of the thick woven rug. Asher reaches out and takes my hand to keep me from falling. I look down at our entwined palms, and he immediately lets go, as if burned.

I mumble my thanks but don't meet his eyes. I cannot. My fingers tingle from his touch and my heart races. How peculiar; maybe it is merely the result of him squeezing my fingers too tightly. Perhaps I imagined it. I swallow, push the thoughts out of my mind, and move to sit next to her.

From the corner of my eye, I see Asher and Thaddeus share a look.

I smile and say, "Thank you for caring for her so diligently. I am officially relieving you of your bedside duties."

Thaddeus slaps his thighs. "We should take our leave and give you some time to catch up."

Marinn sits up on her elbows, "Oh, must you go?" She sticks out her lower lip in a pout and drops back onto her pillow.

Thaddeus stands and comes to her bedside, grasping her hand, "We are going to the tavern for a meal, and then we shall return. You rest. I want you to meet my dragon once you are on your feet."

Marinn squeezes his hand and smiles. "Alright."

I watch Marinn, her face aglow with infatuation. I am

filled with trepidation at the pace of this possible relationship.

Asher follows him out of the room, pulling the door shut behind them. When the latch clicks, I weave my arm through Marinn's and turn to her. "How are you feeling, friend?"

She is glowing. "Oh, Livvy, can you believe it? He is just as a young man ought to be. He was here for two hours. We talked about all sorts of things. Of course, Asher was here as well, but he did not have much to add to the conversation. He is most reserved." She wiggles in her bed, giggling. "If only you could be this happy. I think I love him."

"So soon? My, that is quick," I say without thinking.

Marinn's smile melts away at my unintentionally icy response. Trying to salvage her good spirits, I continue, "If his behavior is any indication, I believe he is well on his way to falling in love with you."

That makes Marinn kick her feet in happiness, at least until she moves her ankle and then lets out a yelp. "I wish he had a friend other than Asher. It would be magical if both of us fell in love."

I chuckle. "Maybe I should write to William back home and invite him to come here. Ma has us married off already."

Worry clouds Marinn's eyes. "Oh, Livvy, you cannot settle for some boring man. You deserve to find someone brave and noble, like you."

I pat her hand. She is sweet, but I'm not sure I would use those words to describe me—more like stubborn and reckless. But I do not correct her. It's nice having someone who sees the best in me, even if she's wrong.

The family cook brings up a tray of soup and, upon seeing me, retreats to the kitchen for a second serving. We sit with our backs against her wooden headboard and enjoy our meal. Once we have eaten, Marinn recounts every word of her conversation with Thaddeus. Her voice begins to trail off, and her eyes are heavy. I smile and give her a big hug. "You might want to sneak in a nap before your prince charming returns from the tavern," I tell her.

She groans, "Did I fall asleep again? I am mortified." She smooths her hair.

I stand and reassure her, "I imagine you have had a hard time sleeping through the night. There's no shame in that."

"Must you go?"

"I need to talk with your father. Tomorrow is my first official day working for the tournament, and I need to solidify my schedule."

Despite her halfhearted protests, I pull her bedroom door shut and set off to find her father. As I reach for the banister, I stifle a yawn. I've been so excited since my post was finalized that I've scarcely been able to sleep. Maybe Marinn and I could both use a nap. It will be a busy fortnight. I am eager to apply all the lessons I have learned.

In her last letter, Ma told me that my new position is all Da has been talking about, telling anyone who comes within earshot. I cannot be sure she meant it as a compliment, but I take it as such. I will need to write home and update them on my progress once I officially begin my responsibilities. My heart swells with the thought that Da is proud of me.

Twenty minutes later, I am walking out the front door of Marinn's house when Asher and Thaddeus ascend the stairs. Thaddeus has his hand on his stomach, his head thrown back, laughing at something Asher has said. Asher smirks. Catching them in this unguarded moment casts them in a different light. They seem almost boyish, authentic. Asher sees me and immediately pulls the curtain down on his mirth.

We exchange nods and pleasantries, and then they are through the door, and I am on the road. Should I put them off to let Marinn sleep? She would be furious if I cost her the chance to see Thaddeus. I pause to turn to look up at Marinn's bedroom window. What must they think of us? I cannot figure them out. Thaddeus is more accessible, to be sure. His obliging and cheery disposition makes him easy to be around. But is Asher the prideful snob, or is there someone more underneath his hard exterior?

12

"You are as jittery as a cat in a room full of rocking chairs," says Mr. Bennet, watching me check my pack for the tenth time.

I count my brushes. "I want to ensure I don't forget anything."

He absently licks his paw. "It is not as if an item could simply jump out of your bag and run away."

I pause. "Perhaps not, but you have been known to steal my tools from time to time. One can never be too careful."

"Your accusations wound me." Something catches his attention in the corner of the room. He jumps to his feet and springs towards this invisible foe with a snarl. He leaps and claws the air, a one-sided war. After a few moments, he settles. Seeming satisfied with his efforts, he strolls across the cottage like a victor who has defeated a mighty enemy.

I chuckle and slip a water skin into my bag. Finally, I close my satchel and slip on my cloak. Taking a deep breath to calm the trembling in my hands, I am ready. "I should return before dark."

My first meeting is with Thaddeus Cedar. The dragons

have each been assigned an area in which to make camp with their riders. Most of the dragons are residing in the naturally occurring caves along the ridge. A few have been given space in the woods, by the lake, or in ruins scattered throughout the valley from the Great War. As I hike up to the cave assigned to his dragon, competitors sweep across the canyon. When I was young, I was thrilled to see even one dragon. Now, with so many in the air simultaneously, it is awe-inspiring.

I cannot imagine the terror of being hunted by dragons. After the Great War, treaties were enacted between the Fae, humans, and dragons to protect humans from being hunted. In some regions, there are still reports of humans being snatched into the air by the talons of dragons and carried off to their deaths. Thankfully, those instances are few and far between, as dragons tend to stay away from the human lands altogether, and the punishment for such a crime committed by dragons is swift and brutal. The world is dangerous enough without dragons choosing me as their next meal.

I have added an extra blade to my arsenal when I travel, and the Drakonas Council purchased a mule, now named Ranger, to pull my cart—another perk of my position. While I walk, my nerves still sizzle, and I cannot determine if it is from the danger in the woods or the danger in the rider. Asher threatens to invade my thoughts at every turn.

Perhaps it's just that I have been on edge since the incident with Marinn and the growling. Either way, the quiet of the woods is no longer a comfort, but the silence before the storm. The only consolation is that the village population has temporarily swelled to three times its size, with encampments erected throughout the valley. The occasional voices filtering through the woods keep the edge off my fear as I weave my way up the mountain.

A deep laugh greets me as I approach Thaddeus and his

crew gathered around a fire outside the entrance to a cave. They are passing a leather of liquor, and Thaddeus has his head back laughing. When he sees me, he says, "Well Met, Livvy. Are you ready to meet my mount?"

As if on command, the ground rumbles, and a blue-scaled head peeks out of the opening, sniffing. Thaddeus strides over, running his hand over the cerulean blue scales behind her frilled ear. He steps backward as the dragon lumbers forward into the sunlight. She looks like a shimmering lake with scales of every shade of blue. "This is Starlight."

He turns to the dragon, who chuffs in acknowledgment. "This is Livinia. She is here to serve you."

I step forward and bow. Cobalt Toris dragons don't like to be thought of as subservient to humans. All dragons demand a certain level of deference, but Cobalt Toris dragons are especially sensitive to disrespect. "Well met."

She steps forward and lowers her snout. I tentatively reach out and stroke her scales. The first interaction with a dragon sets the tone for the entire relationship. Being humble when around dragons has always served me well. Besides, she could electrocute me if she wanted to, so being humble is prudent. She allows me to do a quick examination of her from snout to tail. When I am finished, I thank her for allowing me to assist her.

I step back, and after a minute, she lifts her maw and turns toward the cliff's edge. Thaddeus pulls me against the rocks while she leaps off the edge, her wings extending to glide before she pumps the membranous appendages. Rocks crumble into the ravine below. The wind blows my hair, and I watch as she soars towards a clearing that has been stocked with cattle and sheep. I admire her gliding past the ridge and out of sight. When she disappears, I let out a breath.

"Where are you off to?" Thaddeus says to three men who

have abandoned the fire and are gathering their things to leave.

"We ran out of ale. Going to the village to find more," says a stout, bearded man in a gruff voice.

Thaddeus chuckles. "Good. Do not get lost in your cups at the tavern. There is much to do."

The men nod and disappear down the trail.

"Can you tell me more about your dragon?" I ask, gratefully following him to the fire to ward off the mountain chill.

"She needs the scales on the inside of her hind legs checked regularly. She habitually flies too close to the trees and tends to return with branches stuck in them."

I nod and reach into my satchel for my scroll, ink, and quill. Usually, I can easily remember the needs of my dragons. But with thirty-two to look after, writing things down is unavoidable.

"Will you be staying here during the tournament or down in the village?" I ask. Many of the riders set up elaborate camps near their assigned den. Others leave their dragons at night and stay down in the village.

"When the tournament begins, I will stay here. My family will join me for the duration. I am thankful for the impending presence of my kin."

I nod. It is good to know he is close with his family. That says a great deal about a person. "Is the magic ward causing you discomfort?"

He shakes his head. "Not really. My ability is transfiguration. My alternate form is a lionaire. I am quite comfortable in this skin." He pats his chest.

"A lionaire? That is fascinating. I have never seen anyone shift before."

"It is quite a thing to see. Just be sure to shield your eyes. The light we emit is blinding."

I smile. "I will." For the next few minutes, I frantically scribble notes about his dragon.

Thaddeus watches, asking me questions about my work. Then he clears his throat. I turn my attention to him, shifting on his feet, looking unsure of himself. He tugs at the hem of his long jacket. "Do you think Marinn would be open to an offer of marriage?"

The question catches me entirely off guard. I am not sure how to respond. The courting process is a bit more straightforward than in the mortal lands, but there are still plenty of social conventions to mind. And he has only known her for a brief time. I settle for, "In general, yes. Beyond that, I believe she should be the one to answer."

"Of course. I didn't mean to be impertinent."

He looks so uncomfortable as he bites his lip that I am compelled to give him a reprieve. "She is having a reception at her home tomorrow evening. Are you planning to attend?"

A smile breaks across his face. "Yes, I am looking forward to seeing her again." His smile falters, and he wrings his hands. "Can I ask for your discretion about my inquiry?"

"Your secret is safe with me."

He gives me a nod and smiles. Then he claps his hands together. "Have you met with Asher?"

I school my face into neutrality. Why does the mere mention of his name taste like a salty pickle? "Not yet. There are quite a few dragons I have yet to see."

"Ah, well," he stammers, "I'll leave you to it. I'm off to the village to rescue the tavern owner from the bawdy stories my men love to tell."

He turns and starts down the path towards the village. I roll up my scroll and tuck it into my satchel along with my ink and quill. Then I move on to the next cave opening. If I had a dragon, I might want it to be a blue one. However, color is no guarantee of temperament.

Docile and pleasant, Starlight is perfect for Thaddeus and proof that dragons and their riders seem to blend their personalities. That doesn't bode well for meeting Asher's dragon. If he's anything like his rider, it will be an unpleasant experience, to be sure.

13

___

The next afternoon, I meet with two Red Kurenti dragons who are mated and share a covered rocky outcrop on the village's east side. Their riders are twin brothers, a rarity among the Fae, who share deep sea-blue eyes, platinum hair, and a curious disposition.

As I work, the brothers ask me endless questions about my life in the mortal lands. They are fascinated by how we survive without magic. They come from a long line of magic wielders and are having a difficult time being unable to use their magic due to the wards on the valley. I chuckle as they complain about simple tasks that require work when magic is not available.

"Explain again how you made your way to Saule without a steed, dragon rider escort, or portal," one of the twins says. He leans casually against the cave wall, his eyes twinkling.

I smile as I check the scales of the female dragon who had a boulder when she was rescuing her fallen rider during practice.

"There is a trader, Craige, who frequents our village at home. He gave me a map to Eshan, and that became my guidepost. I made my plan, and the next time he came through, I asked if I could accompany him. He agreed to serve as a chaperone. It's unsafe and improper for women to travel alone in the mortal lands."

They nod in agreement because the same is true here, at least among the High Fae. "But wasn't it an arduous journey?" the other brother asks.

"To be sure. Worth it all the same."

The brothers excuse themselves to enjoy the meal currently being cooked by their servant over an open fire outside the cave.

My mind wanders to the lonely nights sleeping on the ground and the moments when my feet were covered in blisters. I considered turning around more times than I'm proud to admit. The little things kept me going, like a hearty bowl of stew from a fellow traveler to break up my diet of hard tack and stale biscuits. Once we saw a cluster of moon moths, their enchanted wings glistening in the moonlight as they danced above our heads while we readied for bed. I had never heard of them, but Craige had impressive knowledge of magical creatures and was able to teach me. "The moon moth is a sign that magic is close by. They are a good omen, to be certain."

The final part of the trip was the most challenging. A well-worn but somewhat hidden trail wove through the hills on the edge of the mountain range. "This trail is only known to a small group of traders." Craige had said with a wink. "Less chance we encounter desperate travelers or double-crossing sorts."

I knew the moment we crossed the border. One step to the next, everything shifted. The leaves on the trees shimmered. My skin tingled as it met magic for the first time. Everything was a little brighter, larger. Craige looked to see me grinning and said, "It is a delight to see your first encounter with magic. But be wary, girl. This land is full of dangers you cannot comprehend. manticores, sprites, pooka, and a host of other creatures that would kill you just for sport."

He must have seen my distress because his stern face softened. "Ah, not to worry. The magic along the border and into Eshan is warded to dampen its power. Most magical creatures choose to avoid the area as the spell is uncomfortable for them. I will keep you safe until Eshan. Besides, the worst of the creatures are found much further into Saule, where the magic is at full power."

He was right, because I had only encountered magical animals on a handful of occasions. And I still can't be sure the growl Marinn and I heard wasn't merely some large cat or wolf. But that second noise from the animal had sounded hell-sent. I have no idea what kind of creature could make that noise. Marinn is sure it was a werewolf, but she was always a bit dramatic.

Even so, I never leave my cottage unarmed. My confidence grows as I engage the riders. Instead of viewing me as a silly mortal girl, they treat me with respect. It makes me wonder what the tournament officials told them about me. Not only are they respectful of my position, but the riders are surprisingly affectionate towards their dragons, treating them with kindness and reverence.

I'm also learning more about the tournament itself. My da was always interested in the tournament, drawing me into conversations about the riders and match outcomes. My righteous heart had decided early on that the tournament was a repugnant display of Fae male pride, lording over the dragons. What gave them the right to use dragons so casually as entertainment? And why were there no women riders? He couldn't answer these questions, so I refused to engage with him about the tournament. Now, of course, I wish I had learned everything he knew. Thus, my education is coming late, but first-hand. So that is something.

Each match has three rounds. Making contact with the opposing rider using the gold-tipped lance earns points, but knocking the rider off his dragon is an automatic victory. If a rider is knocked off his dragon, the dragon must fly down to retrieve the rider before they hit the ground. Watching the riders practice with their lances has proven that jousting is more dangerous for the riders than the dragon.

Yesterday, I watched a rider on a Green Zalia dragon lose his grip on a sharp turn and plummet to the earth. I held my breath, sure I was watching someone die. It was horrifying. Then, miraculously, his dragon dove down and swept underneath him, catching him as if they had practiced the maneuver a million times. The entire village erupted with joy at the successful catch.

When I'm finished with the Red Kurenti dragons, I bid their riders goodbye, grateful to have met them. I am certain I would find their mischievous and inquisitive tendencies potentially dangerous under different circumstances. But with the wards in place, they are somewhat harmless. It's always best to keep a level head about just how different they are than mortals. Still, my heart is full as I ruminate on my day. I wish my da were here to share it with me. Perhaps he can come to visit if his health allows.

14

————————

Two days later, my limbs are heavy with exhaustion as I pull on my boots. I have been rising with the sun and not coming home until long after the lanterns are lit. It is some consolation to be able to send money and herbs from the apothecary home to my da. I wish I could do more. In her last letter, my ma asked me if I knew any Fae Menders who could come to our village and heal him. Of course, there are Menders in the village for the tournament, but unless Da travels here, there is nothing to be done. The amount of money it would cost to convince a Mender to travel to Tevyne is more than I will earn in a decade. And even if Da traveled here, there is no guarantee a Mender would see him.

I sigh as I hook the cart to Ranger. I push Da into the corner of my mind and focus on the task at hand. I am missing the Merchants' Guild today, a sacrifice necessary to meet my tournament obligations. As the riders begin to depart the village and the atmosphere quiets down, there are fewer options for escorts to and from the dens. That means that any trips I make will have to be solitary. I have my two blades and a hatchet. If I run into anything in the woods, I'll have a fighting chance.

I travel to the west end of the village, past Sam's cottage and blacksmithy. I wonder what new invention the gnome is working on? The road narrows into a trail, weaving between the trees in a gentle slope up the mountain. Despite all of the walking I've been doing, I still get winded sometimes. And I am huffing. I blow a strand of hair out of my face and sigh in relief when the trees thin to reveal a break in the hillside with a row of cave openings.

A man appears at the entrance of the cave. He doesn't see me, instead looking towards the sunrise, stretching his arms over his head, his tunic lifting to the edge of his britches. His blond hair gently waves to brush his shoulders. My throat closes up. I've seen some handsome men this week, but he ranks towards the top for certain. I unroll my scroll with the list of riders and dragons. Julian Kilric from Ezera. Asher is from Ezera. Perhaps they know each other?

I slip my fingers under the harness of Ranger and proceed. Julian hears me and turns, smiling. I smile and give an awkward wave. He puts his hands on his hips, "Well met. You must be Livinia."

I bring my rig to a stop. "Well met. You can call me Livvy. And you must be Julian?"

He nods, looking at me sheepishly from under his eyelashes. "I'm afraid my dragon is in a terrible mood this morning."

I am unsure of how to respond. I've dealt with disagreeable dragons before, but I don't know this dragon yet, and it gives me pause. "Perhaps I should return at a later time?"

He chuckles. "Not necessarily. Just give her a minute, and she will approach."

"All right." I scan the area and bite my lip, searching for a topic of conversation. "Are you enjoying the village?"

"Of course. It is a charming location for the tournament." He looks at Ranger. "Would your animal like some water?"

I follow his line of sight to Ranger. He's the first rider to ask that question. How considerate. "Thank you, we stopped at the stream down the path. He is satisfied."

Julian smiles and fishes something out of his cloak pocket. It's an apple. He holds it up and flicks his eyes to Ranger.

I nod and laugh. "I cannot stand between Ranger and an apple. He will never forgive me."

Julian holds out his flattened hand with the apple sitting in his palm. Ranger sniffs and then pushes his lips down onto Julian's palm. The sound of his teeth crunching into the apple makes me smile. "You have made a friend for life," I say, slipping my satchel off my shoulder and setting it on the ground.

Julian is open and amiable, unlike another rider I know. Asher's face and distant gray eyes flash in my mind. The two men are a study in contrasts.

Julian pats the side of Ranger's flank and says, "I'll go check on Zelena." He disappears into the cave.

I nod and wait, scratching Ranger between the ears.

A few minutes later, Julian scowls as he appears at the cave entrance, and the pounding feet of an agitated dragon follow behind him. I swallow a smile. "Everything all right?"

He gives a quick nod and seems to remember himself, blowing out a breath and pulling his face into a smirk. "You know how dragons can be. Zelena knows she is to be tolerant of your efforts."

I clear my throat, drawing forward everything I know about Green Zalia dragons. I haven't come across many outside of my regular client. They have bad tempers and a penchant for deceit and turpitude. Still, the variegated green scales take my breath away. Softer than other dragons, the scales make them more flexible in flight and battle. Her wings begin as a deep shade of emerald and lighten as they extend to the tips, where the color resembles the color of eucalyptus leaves.

I peer at the back of her head. Most green dragons have a fin that runs from the snout to the tail, which I think would interfere with the ability to ride them. Zelena's fin stops at the base of her long neck, flattening into a rumble of bumps down her back. I step forward and introduce myself. A growl comes from low in her throat. I stop, put my hands out to show I am no threat, and wait. Julian steps forward, "Zelena, don't be rude. Let Livinia complete her work, and you can hunt. I heard some new steers have been added to the fields."

Zelena's pupils dilate, and she swings her maw toward Julian. She huffs and lowers her head to the ground. I look to Julian, who waves me forward. While I work, Julian stays close. I cannot decide if his proximity is reassuring or proof that I should be wary of his dragon. Perhaps both are true. Either way, I make it through my exam unscathed.

As soon as I step backward, Julian pats Zelena's crest, and she immediately raises her long neck and moves toward the cliff. I wipe my brow with the back of my hand and watch Zelena lift into the air, flapping her mighty ombre wings. When she disappears behind the mountain, I turn to Julian. "Her scales will require extra attention. Be sure to inform me if she has any issues so we can address them quickly. Has she injured them before?"

He wipes his chin. "A few times. Because she is more flexible, she has the propensity to impale herself on sticks and such by flying through restrictive terrain. Nothing serious, but I shall keep an eye on her."

I listen intently. Those are precisely the kinds of things I am preparing for. I will add the previous injuries to my notes. "Thank you. That is good information to note."

"I cannot afford a regular dragon groomer, so I am forced to maintain her the best I can," Julian says with a frown.

This doesn't make any sense. Dragon riders are wealthy. "Surely dragon groomers are plentiful in your kingdom?"

"Aye, but I am just a lowly rider, too poor to afford such a service."

"I was under the assumption that those with dragons did not have to worry about coin," I say.

"True, unless life deals you a losing hand," he says. "No matter. I am grateful for your presence." He bows dramatically.

This must be a sore subject. I clear my throat and smile. "I'll return in a few days, unless you send for me sooner." I find myself gazing at him from under my lashes, hoping he does indeed send for me sooner.

The corner of his mouth turns up slightly. "I'll be here."

15

The sun has long set when I join a group gathered around Marinn's dining table for another formal dinner. Marinn and I are seated across from each other. Her ankle is healed, and as we'd found our seats, she had joyfully showed me her new shoes. I long to speak with her about Julian, but she is happily chatting with Thaddeus. Her lilac dress perfectly complements her flushed face as she shyly looks down at her plate. He seems equally enamored with her as he offers to refill her goblet. They make a handsome couple, but it takes more than a lovely appearance to forge a successful partnership.

I sip my wine and glance around the room. I usually enjoy these events, primarily because of the food. I am seated beside a tournament official, a robust man who smells like onions and talks while he chews. Even so, he is the better option for conversing, because my other dinner companion is Asher. Marinn had warned me she was going to seat us together, even over my objections. She had explained that there were tensions among a few of the guests that meant they could not be seated together, and if she were to sit next to Thaddeus, I would need to suffer with Asher. As expected, he has been taciturn and sullen all evening. Perhaps he ate a bug on the way over from the inn.

I stifle a laugh and dip my head. I feel his gaze on me. Someone kicks my foot, and I look up to find Marinn staring at me with her jaw set. Fine. Message received.

I glance over to where Asher is deeply engaged in corralling peas onto a spoon. He glances sideways at me, opens his mouth to say something, and then seems to think better of it. Across from me, Marinn and Thaddeus smile shyly, stealing glances at each other.

With a sigh, I lean forward and pluck the wine bottle from the middle of the table to refill my goblet. More wine should ease the awkwardness, at least on my end. There is no reason we can't at least be civil to each other, and civil people converse when seated together. Maybe he needs some encouragement. "Are you finding your training satisfactory?" I ask.

"Yes."

I wait for him to continue, but he doesn't. Am I such an unappealing dinner partner? Does he not understand how to interact in such a setting? It's not as if this is his first time in a social situation. Unless I want to face onion breath all evening, I will need to increase my efforts. I search for something that might spark a conversation. "Is it difficult returning to defend your title?"

He sips his wine and says, "Not particularly."

Does he even want to be here? Just like him to take for granted the opportunity to fly in the tournament. I would give anything to ride a dragon. "Is your family looking forward to seeing you defend your title?" I try again.

He grunts. "My aunt will be attending."

"Not your parents?" I ask.

He shakes his head. "No. They are otherwise occupied." He slices into his roast beef and continues to eat.

I reach for something to say without being intrusive. Why would his parents not attend? "They must be pleased by your accomplishments."

"I believe they consider me adequate. Any exceptionalism is directly tied to Honora." There was no malice in his voice, just admiration for his dragon.

I pause. What am I to do with this rare show of humility? I would have thought he would take credit for the victory. He talks of his dragon as a companion, not an animal to be used. "What happens if you lose?" I ask.

He sits back and puts his hands on his lap. He leans down towards me, but keeps his eyes averted. "If I fail, my family loses its status, my aunt will be disappointed, and my father has vowed to disown me."

"Disown you?" He can't be serious. It is a contest, a sport. It's not as if lives or a civilization depend on the outcome.

"Indeed." He glances at me and then lowers his gaze. "Winning the Drakonas has been my assignment since I bonded with Honora. Becoming a dragon rider was an opportunity to make my father proud and bring glory to my family. I must win. With your station, you would not understand the pressures of a high-profile family."

I stare at him. Why must he appear to have a heart and then prove it is made of stone? "You are confused, sir. The nature of the predicament you face is not uncommon. Even we peasants have parents with expectations for what we should do and become."

He gives his head a slight shake as if clearing his thoughts. "You misunderstand me."

It's too late. I have no desire to help remove him from the hole in which he sits. "Perhaps you are right."

With that, I turn my attention to my plate, my potatoes

taking on fascinating intrigue. Even as I begin to chat with the other dinner guests, I remain keenly aware of Asher's presence. I have yet to meet anyone else who can raise my heart rate so quickly for all the wrong reasons.

Thaddeus meets my gaze from across the table beside a smiling Marinn. "Marinn told me your father is the reason for your love of dragons."

I look to Marinn, who raises her eyebrows and shrugs. My heart warms as I think back to my childhood. "Oh, yes. When I was a little girl, my da spent more money than we could afford to buy me a *Field Guide to Dragons*. It is my most treasured possession."

The wife of one of the judges, dressed in yellow brocade that clashes with her orange hair, says, "I didn't know the humans could read."

A ripple of laughter hits me like needles, and my face flushes with embarrassment, or perhaps it's indignation.

Thaddeus, ever the gentleman, ignores them and asks, "And did you send it out for binding?"

I shake my head. "No. That is not something we could afford. But Ma was skilled in all manner of homemaking and bound it for me, although she complained the entire time."

Marinn leans forward. "Livvy may not be skilled in sewing, but she has other talents."

She leaves the comment hanging in the air, full of innuendo. I grind my teeth. Someone at the end of the table chuckles.

Marinn scans the group with feigned admonishment and continues, "What I meant to say was that she has been an asset to the village in many ways and is a credit to her profession."

I am more than ready for the attention to shift to someone else. I clear my throat and turn to Marinn's father.

"Tell us how you made it possible for the tournament to be held in Eshan."

He wipes his mouth with his napkin and proudly launches into a detailed report of the selection process. The group is captivated by his boisterous tale, and I am left to eat my meal in peace.

16

When I reach home, Mr. Bennet weaves between my feet as I angrily kick off my boots. "Stop trying to kill me," I say, stumbling over him and thrusting out a hand to brace myself on a chair so I don't fall. Guilt twists my mouth as he looks at me indignantly. I'm not vexed with Mr. Bennet. No, the menace in my life is the high-born man who believes himself better than everyone.

Reaching down, I scratch Mr. Bennet behind the ear. "I'm sorry." I rub my hands together, wishing the hearth was already ablaze. All those tales of everyday magic have left me wishing for a bit of that convenience. It must undoubtedly make life easier.

"I have been waiting all day to tell you the news," Mr. Bennet says, watching me.

"What sort of news?" I ask. Moonlight streams through the window. I can see my breath, so I quickly light a fire and then the candle next to my bed.

"That man you and Marinn speak of, Asher," he begins.

I whip my head around to face him. "What about Asher?"

If a caracal could smirk, I'd swear Mr. Bennet was doing so now. "Yes, that is the one. He stopped by this morning."

I unbutton my dress, slip it off my shoulders, and replace it with a woolen tunic. "You must be mistaken." I peel off my fur-lined tights, a gift from the tournament committee to keep me warm, and replace them with woolen pants and thick fur-lined socks.

Mr. Bennet jumps onto the bed and continues, "I was sitting by the window, as I often do, and that man sauntered up onto the porch as if he held the deed."

I hang my dress next to the fire to dry the snow-soaked hem. "I just dined with him, and he made no mention of it. How odd. Then again, getting conversation out of him was like pulling dragon teeth. You are quite certain? Asher was here?"

"Of course, he knocked on the door. I hissed in an effort to dismiss his company, but he did not notice me. I fear he was here for nefarious reasons, the way he paced and mumbled. I was prepared to defend our homestead if necessary." He puffs out his chest.

"And was it necessary?" I ask, pulling back the covers.

"Luckily for him, it was not. I would scratch his eyes out if he meant to harm you."

I lean over and kiss his forehead. "You are the best companion a girl could ask for." Why was Asher on my porch? Perhaps his dragon needs assistance? Surely he would have mentioned it at dinner if it was important, unless he didn't want gossip circulating about his dragon.

Abandoning my bed, I head to the door and yank it open, searching the porch and crevices for any sign of parchment. Nothing. Frustration creeps up my spine. Is he trying to vex me? Why make such an effort to come here and not so much as leave a note? I huff and retreat to the warmth of the cottage, slamming the door behind me. My frustration blooms into irritation, although I cannot pinpoint why.

"What on earth are you doing? You let in the chill." Mr. Bennet complains.

I toss another log on the fire. "It is not important. Although I must say, Asher Covington is the most exasperating man I have ever met."

"If he returns, I shall scratch him till he bleeds."

I sigh. "Don't do that. We have given him too much of our attention already." Crawling under the covers, I grab my book to settle in for some reading. My legs twitch with restlessness. When I realize I have read the same paragraph three times and retained none of it, I slam my book shut. What gives him the right to tromp around my porch and then fail to disclose his visit? Asher Covington is a rude, boorish, snob. The entire dinner was infuriating. How dare they think so little of us as to be illiterate?

As if in protest, I have the sudden urge to write home. I cannot pour out the poisonous account of the dinner, lest I confirm Ma's opinions. Perhaps I can fashion the tale of dinner into something sweeter, mentioning the eligible men and connections I am making. Who doesn't love a little creative embellishment? Actually, Ma detests fanciful hyperbole. But she will be none the wiser if I choose my words carefully.

I leave my cozy cocoon to retrieve writing supplies and move to the table with my candle. I tap the quill on my jaw, contemplating what to tell her. I craft my letters to be read out loud to my entire family, affirming my decision to travel to Eshan and, at the same time, that I have not forgotten our sweet cottage in the woods. Obviously, their curiosity will be centered around the tournament and the riders that have overtaken the valley.

Dipping my pen into the ink, I give a short recounting of

dinner, focusing on the positives and only mentioning Thaddeus and Marinn by name. I quickly move on to Julian. My heart warms thinking of his good-natured smile. I share his humble and diligent care of his dragon and his kindness towards Ranger. Next, I write about the blue-eyed twins and share snippets of their curiosity for the mortal realm. When I've exhausted that story, I move on to other candidates.

In the line of riders running through my brain, my mind keeps landing on Asher. What to say about him? Ma once told me that the Saule royalty was too high for their inseam. Not that she's ever met any Fae royalty. I think the comment was meant to dampen my interest in Saule. It didn't work. The pull of magic and dragons was too strong.

I learned to leave her words floating in the air, never to take root in my mind. She was right about one thing, though. I have never met anyone with more disdain for those he deems beneath him. He seems perfectly at ease with Thaddeus. Then again, Thaddeus is so affable that I find it difficult for anyone to be at odds with him. He hardly deserves praise for befriending someone so easy to like.

After crafting several tales, I finish the letter by asking after everyone in the village. Ma relishes sharing gossip, although she would never admit it is anything besides relevant village news. She has a propensity to know everyone's business. That knowledge is a weapon she uses to maintain her status in the village as a woman of virtue and a model of motherhood.

The candle is burned down a peg when I sign my name, fold up the note, and melt my wax press over the flame to seal up the correspondence. When it's finished, I slip it into the pocket of my cloak so as not to forget it tomorrow when I go to the Merchants' Guild.

Back in bed, I stare at the ceiling beams and try to forget what it looked like when Asher wiped a bit of frozen cream from his lip during dessert. He lifted his finger to his mouth, and as he brushed his finger across the cream, his lips slightly parted. Then I realized I had been staring at his uncommonly handsome face, and I am sure my cheeks flamed red hot as I looked away.

I pull my pillow over my face to smother the memory. Why did he have such an effect on me? No matter. It will take more than a pretty face and a bit of cream to raise Asher's standing in my book.

17

At Merchants' Guild, we gather around the usual table, bowls of stew before us. With so many strangers in the village, the familiar chatter is a comfort. Sam gives us an update on tournament gambling odds. The group, especially Orthello, is tuned in to his every word; there is some serious coin on the line. While he answers questions, Jasmine delivers a tray of food. Conversation takes a break as we enjoy the mid-day meal.

"Are you finding the dragons in the tournament to be cooperative?" Kessia asks me as she picks at a turkey leg.

"They can be unpredictable," Captain says, throwing me a knowing look. He once told me about a tournament he attended where a dragon turned on its owner, throwing the man off and attacking him with fire as he fell. According to Captain, the crowd was surprised and delighted, even when the rider was burned to a crisp by his mount.

The Fae grow bored easily and revel in unpredictability and excitement. They also have an innate sense of fairness that extends to their handling of dragons. If a rider violates his partnership with disrespect or betrayal, they might well believe that he deserves a brutal fate. Of course, put in those terms, I'm not sure I disagree. Not everyone can, or should, bond with a dragon.

Kessia snaps her fingers before my face, pulling me into the conversation. "Sorry," I say, "Yes, I am having a wonderful time with the dragons, despite my distaste for the tournament. Getting to work with this many dragons - it's more than I could have dreamed possible."

"And the riders?" Kessia asks, raising an eyebrow and smirking.

I pour a cup of cider from the pitcher in the center of the table. "We shall see. I meet with Asher Covington this afternoon."

Captain sucks in a breath. "He is favored to win the tournament again this year. I've seen his dragon; she's a sight."

I run my finger around the edge of the cup. "Yes, well, let's hope Honora is more agreeable than her rider."

"So you've already met Asher?" Sam asks, looking up from a paper he is sketching on.

I nod. "His talent for jousting must far outshine his propensity for conversation."

"Who needs conversation when you have wealth and accomplishment?" Kessia asks, leaning back on the bench and surveying the table for agreement. Then she leans in. "I heard his family demands he make a good match this year."

My attention snaps in her direction. A match? I did not know the Fae cared about such things. They live long lives and usually do not rush into binding ceremonies unless they find true love. There are only a few reasons for a proactive search for a mate: money, power, or posterity. Which is he hoping to secure by such a match? I cannot fathom Asher making a grand gesture of love. "I pity the woman forced to spend her life with him."

Kessia raises a brow. "You've imagined it?"

I scoff. "Of course not. I believe love is possible, but I have never met a man worthy of the effort."

Sam pushes his spectacles up his nose. "You would be wise to keep your heart from hardening. I cannot imagine my days without my sweet wife."

I smile at him. He has such a tender heart. "You two are a rare partnership indeed. If I could find such a match, I might be willing to entertain the idea."

Kessia turns to Sam. "Perhaps you have a cousin?" She bites back a smile.

I smack her arm playfully. Sam chuckles.

Kessia clears her throat. "I require some advice."

Captain leans in. "Bring it forward, then."

"I am struggling with the issue of personal protection." She folds her hands on the table and lowers her eyes. "When meeting with new clients, I understand there's a danger. Well, truth be told, the danger remains even with my most loyal of clients, but rapport goes a long way. They know better than anyone that a skilled dentist is hard to find."

We nod in agreement. All of us have expressed concern and reservations about the unique dangers of Kessia's profession in the past. She's usually been the first to dismiss them as unnecessary, but if she's coming to us, she must really be in over her head.

"Based on our collective knowledge and experience, I wonder if you have any advice on how I might protect myself in case things do not go as planned," she stammers.

I put my hand over hers. "I can't imagine the courage it takes to walk into the lair of someone who could so easily kill you. While dragon grooming has its share of danger, I could never willingly groom a dragon with a taste for human blood."

"Did something happen?" Captain asks.

Kessia swallows. "Yes. I was meeting with a new client.

She was complaining of pain in her left canine. I was examining her, as I usually do, and she bit down on my finger.
Luckily, I was wearing my dragon hide gloves and was able
to yank my hand away, but it was close."

I look to Captain and Sam, who may have some ideas on
how to help.

Captain scoffs, "I'm surprised you're only facing this now.
A dangerous occupation, to be sure."

Kessia's face twists into a frustrated frown. She puts her
hands flat on the table. "Obviously, I am aware there are
inherent dangers. When in school, we learned to resist mind
control. We studied vampire history and traditions. I have
taken some precautions already, including gold-threaded
clothing and gloves made of spider silk to prevent punctures.
I want to ensure there are no other things I should consider."

"You have indeed taken great caution," Sam says. He holds
his finger in the air. "I have an idea. What if you had a
machine that made a special kind of light? One that passes
through your body but not your bones or teeth." He opens
his mouth and points at a molar. "And if there is rot, it would
pass through that enough to show a different color. Then
you would know where and if a patient needed treatment,
reducing the need for up close examinations."

I usually indulge his hare-brained ideas, but my nerves
are frayed today. Still, I pity the misunderstood genius. "Your
idea may work, but perhaps Kessia needs something more
immediate," I offer, forcing Kessia to meet my gaze and
raising my brows a silent message reminding her to be kind.

"Right, of course," Kessia says, patting his hand with hers.
"Perhaps that is a future solution."

He smiles at her. "I'll work on it for you."

"Wonderful." She gives him a weak smile.

When he's done with his machine, maybe Sam can invent
something to make Asher stop being such a prat.

Orthello has been inhaling a plate of turkey and potatoes. He finally speaks. "You should head to Kaimas and have a gold-infused tattoo inked on your body. Gold-infused blood tastes rancid for Vampires and will help ensure you don't become dinner for your client."

"Excellent idea," Sam says.

Kessia looks to me. "We should go together. I am sure you could also use extra protection against magic."

I haven't traveled far beyond the surrounding hamlets. If I travel outside the valley, I will no longer be protected by the ward-binding magic. I might be enchanted to believe anything the Fae wanted. Humans have been known to be made to dance at a revel until their feet bleed. The Fae can glamour leaves and mud to look and taste like the finest meal; they could laugh at me as I ate, and I would still have no choice but to thank them for their hospitality.

Not all Fae have natural magic, but they have access to runes, spells, and other concoctions they can use to cause mischief. Some Fae believe they are entitled to enslave or even torture humans for their entertainment. Every few years, we hear of someone from around Tevyne who disregarded the warnings and found themselves in a desperate situation. Luckily, it is a rare occurrence.

"I would love to visit the capital," I say, "But I am not sure the danger of traveling beyond the wards is worth the trip." Perhaps if we had an escort…

As if reading my mind, Orthello continues, "It's a dangerous journey and even going with an escort isn't a guarantee of safety. I'm happy to accompany a traveling party, but it might take a few weeks to arrange."

Sam and Captain nod. My heart swells. Although I miss my family, Eshan has become the home of my heart. And these people are the family I never could have imagined I would need.

18

After Merchants' Guild, I depart for my next appointment, which I am dreading. The weather has warmed enough to turn the road into a muddy mess and cause sweat to break out on my brow as I hike up the mountain. I am fond of walking, but with every step, Ranger and my cart threaten to abandon our journey and sink into the thick mud. My skirts are a mess, and my boots are coated when I finally reach the break in the trees.

Asher is standing outside his assigned cave, arms at his side, hands clenched. His face is stoic, as usual. No matter. I am a professional and will behave accordingly. "Well met, Asher."

"Well met, Miss Livinia." He offers me a surprisingly warm smile. "Have you had a pleasant day?"

My heart skips a beat. So he can smile. "Very pleasant," I say, tying Ranger to the hitching post and retrieving my tool belt, scroll, and writing utensils. When I turn towards him, he's watching me. Suddenly, I feel quite shy. His gaze burns into me, and I force myself to meet his eyes as I approach. I clear my throat. "What brought you to my cottage yesterday?"

He shifts on his feet. "I stopped by hoping to confirm our appointment."

How do I respond to this? Does he believe me fickle? Is he being considerate or condescending? I tilt my head pensively. He clasps his hands behind his back and softens his scrutiny. This man is strange. I lick my lips and decide to move on. "Can you introduce me to your dragon?"

"She is out hunting, but should return shortly."

I narrow my eyes. "She is not present? Did you not know I was coming?"

He clears his throat. "Yes, of course. We had a particularly long training session this morning, and she was, well, hungry." He looks sheepish, running a hand through his hair.

I chuckle. "Not much to be done about that."

He nods and shifts his gaze to the east, which is where Honora must have gone. I watch him watch the horizon, considering. What had Honora deemed worthy in Asher? Gold Vesti dragons are renowned for their nobility and reputation as defenders of good.

"Honora must love the view from here," I say, admiring the sprawling vista and the lake in the distance.

"Indeed. She has led an interesting life." He turns to look at me. "Did you know that Vesti dragons can shapeshift?"

I nod. I did know. They can even become humanoid. What I never fully understood was the bonding process. Perhaps Asher could shed some light on the subject. "How did you come to bond with her?" It is unusual for a Gold Vesti to bond. They tend to be solitary creatures.

He stares out at the view. "When I was a boy, I used to ride into the countryside on my horse. It was my only escape from the chaos of palace life. Although I am not directly in line for the throne, my family often stayed at court." He bends down and picks up a rock, then tosses it off the side of the cliff. "One day, I was out on a ride and my horse got spooked. He threw me, and I landed hard, twisting my knee. I was miles from town and had no idea how I would get home."

"That sounds awful," I say.

"Yes. I hobbled towards home the best I could, but night began to fall, and I knew I would soon no longer have the sun to guide me. And it is not wise to be caught in the forest after nightfall."

I nod. There are dangerous and evil creatures who traverse the woods. It certainly isn't the place for a child, Fae or human."What happened?" I can picture Asher as a boy, hurt, alone, and afraid.

"I stopped at a small stream for water. While I was bent down to drink, I heard a branch crack behind me. When I turned around, I was faced with a redcap. He was staring at me, a sickle in his hand."

I hang on to every word. Redcaps are goblins and among the most dangerous of magical creatures with a thirst for violence. They are known for soaking their hats in the blood of their enemies. Asher was lucky he escaped with his life. I will him to continue, eager to hear the rest.

"As you can imagine, I was terrified. I believe my short life flashed before me."

I shift on my feet, impatient for the rescue.

"The redcap started for me, raising his sickle in the air. I hid my face and waited for the darkness to claim me. Instead, the ground rumbled. I dared to look and saw expansive wings filling the sky. It was Honora. She swept down, grabbing the redcap in her talons. The redcap was too surprised by the attack to react. I watched his face, full of terror, as Honora flew out of sight. Then all I heard was screaming."

"How horrendous."

He peers at the horizon. I wish he would look at me when he's talking. It is awkward standing next to him, having this conversation with little eye contact. Is he uncomfortable speaking to me when I'm facing him? I cannot comprehend why. I believe I am easy to talk to, even if he seems to be the exception.

Finally, he begins again. "I tried to be brave, but I knew other creatures in the woods would be just as dangerous as the redcap. When the sound of flapping wings returned, I scrambled over to hide as best I could under a thicket. I was sure the dragon was returning to eat me. She flew into the clearing and landed. As I hid my face in fear, a bright flash of light leaked through my fingers. When I looked up, it was no longer a dragon, but a woman standing there. She appeared as if dipped in gold, but otherwise could have been a Fae courtier."

"Did she transform right there in front of you?"

"Yes. She told me she was there to protect me. And she carried me home through the woods. When we arrived at the forest's edge near the castle gate, she set me down and told me she would return in dragon form when I was old enough to bond. And when I turned fifteen, she returned."

"And she's been with you ever since?"

Asher nods. He brings his hand to his brow to shield the sun. "Ah, here she comes."

I follow his gaze to a small dot in the distance, rapidly growing larger as it gets closer. Her gold scales are blinding in the sunlight. She is the most beautiful dragon I've ever seen. As she approaches, I can see the many horns on her head and her long tail trailing behind her.

Honora lands between the cliff and the cave. Her touchdown shakes the mountain under my feet. Asher reaches out and takes my arm to steady me.

"Thank you," I say, my voice catching in my throat—heat

courses through my fingers up my arm. I look down at where his fingers wrap around my forearm, skin to skin, fire passing between us.

He nods, lets go of my arm, and wipes his hand on his trousers. Without another word, he strides toward his dragon and explains who I am and why I am there, speaking aloud for my benefit. Bonded dragons and riders can communicate nonverbally.

What's with this man? He wipes his hand off as if I were covered in dirt. Am I that disgusting to him? I wait until he motions for me to approach. As I get closer, I notice the distinct smell of saffron, common for Gold Vesti dragons.

Honora is enormous. She is larger than any other I have seen in the tournament so far. As I bow, she chuffs and lifts her muzzle in recognition. Asher moves to lean against the side of the cave. I tell Honora that I'm going to do a basic examination to ensure she is clean and healthy. She lets out a soft growl, almost a purr, and I get to work.

Thirty minutes later, I am done, looking her over from snout to tail. I pat her crest and say, "Thank you for letting me examine you. You are ready for this competition."

Asher has been a silent observer, but I have been keenly aware of his presence. I feel his attention on me as I load my tools into my cart.

"You are very thorough," he says, breaking the silence.

"Yes, well, it is my responsibility to ensure the dragons are safe while in the village. It is a pleasure to work with them." I fumble with the buttons on my coat. Looking to change the topic of conversation, I ask, "Will you be at the tavern this evening?"

"No. I do not enjoy crowded spaces with cheap ale. My last visit was under duress."

I clench my jaw. How can he be congenial one moment and a pompous snob the next? It's enough to give me whiplash. I do not have time for small talk with anyone who thinks they are above me, which he obviously does.

"Good day," I say abruptly. I turn and untie Ranger, leading him away from Asher and Honora. I resist the temptation to glance back and see if Asher is watching me. As I walk, I review our interaction, trying to make sense of this man.

What is wrong with me? He told me one story about his childhood, and now my heart is conflicted. Is that enough to overcome his blatant snobbery? Then there's the way his dragon bonded to him. Gold Vesti's are excellent judges of character. That means something. I absently look at my forearm where he touched me. It's hard to deny the spark that coursed through me.

Berries. The end of the tournament cannot come soon enough. I shake off the confusing interaction and focus on the bowl of stew waiting for me at the tavern. I am pleased Asher won't be there. I can eat in peace and go straight home to crawl into bed, reading until I fall asleep.

19

———

As I walk back to the village, my mind keeps returning to the hillside with Asher. I can still picture him as a little boy, terrified in the woods. I run my fingers along the velvet needles of the evergreen common to the valley. They are not so different than the mortal land evergreens. I've heard tales of woods to the West that are ancient groves with tangled, gnarled branches and leaves as big as serving platters. There are fairy fruit trees that bloom in spring, with carnivorous flowers eager to snatch passing insects. I long to see them in person, but any significant travel I do should be to the east.

As the image of home brushes against my thoughts, I sigh. Ma wants nothing more than for me to return, marry William, and find contentment as a wife. I'm not opposed to marriage, but not to William. I think it will be challenging to find a man who is not distracted by silly pursuits and yet gives me the freedom to work. Does such a man exist?

As I round the bend on the path, I am halted by the same growl and bone-crushing sound that caused Marinn and me such a fright. Ranger's ears perk up as well, and he begins to stomp his feet, pulling at the bridle. "Shhh," I urge, stroking his snout.

A branch snaps to my left. I slip my dagger from my waistband. My heart pounds as I scan the woods for any sign of movement. I run through the list of weapons on me. I'm not sure if I am quick enough to do any damage with my dagger, especially if the creature is a bear or wolf.

The woods are silent, as if the entirety of the valley is holding its breath. The only thing I can hear is the sound of my heart beating. I chew my lip. Do I proceed and pray the creature's attention turns elsewhere? I cannot stand here as an offering for lunch. I take Ranger by the bridle and move to the opposite side of the path from where I heard the noise. "Sorry, old boy," I say, "But if it's you or me, I want to live."

Ranger chuffs in response, his baleful eyes condemning me.

I blow out a breath. "Fine, I'll save both of us."

I move forward tentatively, rolling my feet to keep noise to a minimum. Another crack of a branch makes me jump, and the rumble of a growl follows. My hand grips the dagger so tightly that my knuckles turn white. I cannot outrun anything on this rocky path. Climbing a tree is an option, unless it is a large cat or a bear; they are likely better climbers than I could hope to be.

Ranger shakes his muzzle, spittle hitting my cheek. My attention is focused on the woods to my right when a branch cracks on the left. I whip my head around. Is there more than one? I cannot fight two predators at once. I will surely lose.

What am I going to do? My regular clients live much closer to the village than where the riders are positioned. When I took the assignment, I had not considered the potential danger of the trek. I tuck myself next to Ranger and continue down the path. The world begins to spin when I realize I've been holding my breath. I force myself to inhale

through my nose. The last thing I need to do is become unre-
sponsive. Sweat breaks out on my forehead, despite the chill
in the air. If I get eaten on this trail, my mother will forever
use me as an example of what happens when you don't listen
to her.

Another crack on the left. I lift my dagger, prepared to
fight. Then my breath whooshes out in relief. A man in a red
velvet cloak and blond hair hanging loose over his shoulders
steps onto the path before me. He gives me a lazy smile and
says, "Well met." He puts a hand on his heart and gives a
slight bow.

It takes a moment to steady myself. My emotions
endeavor to catch up with this reprieve from likely death. It
is Julian. "Well, met," I pant.

"Are you out here alone? I was tracking a timber boar that
was seen in the area."

My shoulders relax. I am so relieved to see another
person I could kiss him. A timber boar makes sense. With
those caves being used by the dragons, there are bound to be
some displaced animals who usually dwell within them. "Did
you hear the growling, then?"

He looks past me into the woods. "I did indeed. Did you
happen to see anything?"

I shake my head. "I did not."

"Well, I shall accompany you back to ensure your safety."

Normally, I would bristle at such an offer, but today I am
very grateful. And besides, he has a pleasant disposition and
perfectly green eyes with lashes that are worthy of the envy
of any woman. I fight a blush and say, "Thank you, sir."

As we walk in companionable silence, I sneak sidelong
glances at him. His cloak has a dragon crest embroidered on
the front.

"Are you from Antrais?" I ask, making an educated guess

based on his self-reported lack of fortune and what I assume are limited finances for traveling great distances.

"No, I am from Ezera originally. But I grew up in Lauks."

My curiosity is piqued. It isn't often that I have the opportunity to converse with someone who has seen multiple kingdoms. "What are those kingdoms like?" I ask, then look at my feet, embarrassed by my limited knowledge of the world. "I have not had the chance to travel beyond the valley since settling here."

Ignoring my self-recrimination, he launches into a description of Lauks. As we walk, he shares entertaining tales of hunting and dragon riding. It is a luxury to be at the receiving end of such tales. Most men are not so forthcoming with information.

When we reach the main road, he pauses. "I have enjoyed our time together, Livvy. My plans include supper at the tavern. Perhaps you might be interested in joining me?"

My heart flutters. This is the kind of man I would enjoy spending time with. "Of course. I shall buy you a pint in thanks for my rescue."

He chuckles and gives me another slight bow. "Till then." He smiles broadly and then turns to walk into the village.

Julian. His name tastes sweet on my lips, and my fingers seal my mouth closed lest I giggle like a silly schoolgirl. I watch him for another moment until Ranger turns towards home. I pat his side. "I agree. You have earned grain and a rest after almost sacrificing yourself for my life."

He pulls his lips back as if offended and snorts.

"You know I adore you," I soothe.

He rubs his head against my shoulder, and we start for home.

20

After ensuring Ranger has his well-deserved reward of grain and fresh water, I make my way to the door of my cottage. Mr. Bennet, who has been sitting on the porch, follows me inside, saying, "I abhor your commitment to these outsiders."

"The dragons?" I ask, closing the door and immediately stripping off my tunic. Slipping on a day dress, I begin the tasks of working my fingers through my knotted hair.

"Indeed. You know I am loath to be left alone. It's as if you have forgotten your commitment to me."

My brows furrow. I abandon my tresses and crouch down to take Mr. Bennet's face in my hands. "You are my dearest companion. No man or dragon could ever mean more." I smile and kiss his nose.

He purrs. "I suppose it is only a temporary distraction."

"Exactly, " I say, standing and separating my hair into thirds, then weaving it into a braid across the back of my head and down over my shoulder. "I shall ask Jasmine for any gristle left in the kitchens and bring it home to you."

He saunters over and rubs against my leg, and I wipe my

face with a cold cloth and survey my reflection in the looking glass. I'll never be a great beauty like Marinn, but my appearance isn't entirely unfortunate. "Please stay close to the cottage. I would hate for you to end up as a dragon snack."

Mr. Bennet leaps onto my bed. "I shall stay safely inside and await your return."

A half hour later, I enter the dimly lit pub and find Julian sitting at the bar. The tavern is buzzing with men who, I assume, are connected with the tournament. It seems each rider has an entourage with them, swelling the population of the valley considerably.

"Well met, Livvy. Let me buy you a pint of ale," Julian says from his bar stool.

"I believe I owe you. But I shall let you buy the first round." Jasmine is washing mugs and lifts her eyebrows as I respond. I stick my tongue out at her and slide onto the stool next to Julian.

Jasmine sets fresh pints in front of us. Julian slides coins across the bar in return. I consider stopping him and offering to pay, but think better of it. It would be impertinent despite his financial situation.

He lifts his mug. "A toast, to a lovely woman in a lovely village."

My cheeks heat. Is my flush from pleasure or embarrassment at his attention? Probably both. Nevertheless, I raise my mug and they clink it with his. "Thank you," I say. We have so much in common, including an understanding of what it is like to live without the excess enjoyed by some.

We spend the next few minutes talking about the tournament. Julian is nothing like Asher. He is charming, friendly, and easy to speak to. I'm on my third pint of ale when Jasmine asks him, "Do you think Asher will be able to defend his title? He seems to be the favored rider."

A cloud passes over Julian's face, and he sets his mug

down and leans in conspiratorially. "If I were a betting man, I wouldn't trust his odds."

Jasmine tilts her head. "What do you know that we don't?"

Julian leans back and waves her off. "Nothing. I'm just not one of Asher's admirers."

The door to the tavern bangs open, and a group of men I recognize as locals comes through. They take a table in the middle of the room. Jasmine moves from behind the bar to get their order. I turn my attention to Julian. "Do you know Asher well?"

"Very well," he replies. "We grew up together."

Grew up together? How did I not know this? It seems like Asher would have mentioned something. But then again, he's not exactly forthcoming with information.

I wait for him to take a swig from his ale, and then he continues. "My mother died when I was born. My father was high-ranking in the guard until he was killed in a training accident. Asher's family took me in, letting me work with the dragons and attend classes, all with the hope of raising my station in honor of my father's service."

"How awful to lose your parents." I cannot imagine growing up without my family. It is impressive that he has accomplished so much.

He nods. "It was. Asher was to become a rider. When I showed interest in jousting as well, Asher decided he didn't want competition. So he poisoned his father's opinion of me, and I was tossed out of the keep, left to fend for myself."

My blood heats. How could Asher be so cruel?

"I had to join the military and chase my own dream of becoming a dragon rider. I was penniless, but Asher couldn't have cared less."

"Is it uncomfortable being so near him during the tournament?" Without thinking, I reach out and place my hand on his forearm. It seems so natural for us to be talking like this, and I know how hard it can be trying to prove your worth.

Julian smiles sadly. Then he raises his chin. "No. If he doesn't want to see me, he must be the one to go. I will not give up my dream of winning this tournament for anyone."

I agree. My heart hurts imagining him as a young boy and losing his father. "I can't imagine losing my da. He's sick, and I worry about him so."

"I'm sorry to hear that. Is there anything that can be done?"

I shake my head. "Not unless you can find me a Fae Mender willing to travel to Tevyne. Otherwise, we are doing what we can, but..." My voice trails off, and I stare at a chipped spot on the bar. My vision blurs, and I blink back tears.

Julian smacks his hand on the counter. "All hope is not lost."

I lift my head to meet his eyes, questioning.

"When I win this tournament, I will bring a Mender to your father. Together we shall defeat death." He punches the air with enthusiasm.

I giggle, then swallow it down. When did I become the kind of woman who giggles? I stare at the mug of ale. Was this my third? Fourth? It's too early for me to be this deep into my cups.

He gently lifts my chin with his fingers and meets my gaze. "I'm serious. I will help your da, and perhaps we could set up house in the mortal lands. It sounds like an adventure."

Is this a proposal? I hardly know him. "We will see." It is the only reply I can conceive. I have always wanted to hold to my freedom and have never fantasized about love or marriage for its own sake. Security alone isn't enough to bind me to anyone, or I would go home and marry William like my mother wishes. All things considered, though, I believe I would put all of my own wishes aside if a suitor had the power to bring a Fae Mender to Da.

"When can I see you again?" he asks.

I turn on my stool so that our knees touch. "If you want to see me again, you must come to the street revel. There will be dancing, and I will perhaps save a space for you on my dance card."

Julian finishes the last of his ale and sets the mug on the counter. He lifts my hand and kisses the back of it. "Save a dance for me, Livvy."

Warmth spreads through my core. "I'll try," I say, as if I have a line of suitors out the door waiting to fill my dance card.

He slides off his stool and gives me a quick wave before walking out the door. Jasmine moves to take his empty mug. "That one is sweet on you."

"What? No, he's not." I bite my lip. I hope he is.

She stares at the door as if Julian will walk in any second. "He seems pleasant." She turns her eyes to me. "You could do worse." She smiles slyly.

"Yes. Indeed." I finish off my mug and hop off the stool. "I must go. I have dragons to groom!" I drop into a deep bow and then laugh at myself. Jasmine shakes her head, chuckling. It's a good thing I'm done drinking, at least for now. Upon leaving, I am met with sleet assaulting the village. I don't actually have another dragon to groom today. If I did, there is no way I would have had so many cups of ale. Dragon grooming is dangerous enough without going into the endeavor less than stone-cold sober. However, I will stop by and make sure Marinn is cleared to dance with me at the revel.

arinn is sitting on her front porch, wrapped in a blanket, a book open on her lap. A smile breaks across her face when she sees me. "Well met, Livvy!"

I dash up the sunlit stairs and kiss her on her cheek. "How are you today?"

"Quite well. I have something for you." She slips her hand under her blanket and retrieves a stack of envelopes. "Father was at the tavern and brought these back for me to give you. With everyone in the village, Jasmine is overwhelmed with the post, so Father has been helping where he can."

"Thank you." I scan the return address of the first letter. Ma's careful script graces the envelope. She faithfully writes, and her message is likely to contain general news from home. The following missive is addressed in blocky print to "Livvy Lou." Only Da addresses me so informally. He doesn't often write, and my heart flutters in anxiety. Hopefully, he's not writing with bad news. I bite my lip and slip it to the bottom of the pile. Bad news does not age well, but a few hours make no difference.

The third letter is from William Collins, my dear childhood friend. What could he have to say? Perhaps it's just a friendly communication. Maybe he has settled down with a nice girl from the village. It is thoughtful that he made the effort to write. Curiosity has long been a vice, so I run my finger along the seam, unfolding the paper.

"Isn't William the gentleman to whom your family has promised you?"

I nod. "If my mother has her way." I smile at the familiar, messy handwriting. *"My dearest Livinia,"* it starts. I moan at the intimate greeting and look to Marinn, as if she can rescue me from the text.

"What's the matter?" She closes her book and hugs it to her chest like a shield against bad news.

I take a deep breath. If I read it aloud, she can share the misery, if there is indeed misery to be endured. I begin again, and at the greeting, Marinn says, "Oh, my. That sounds serious."

I continue. "I write to you to ask for your hand in marriage. I have spoken with your ma and she has assured me that you are in want of a husband. As you are my oldest friend, it seems only right that we should build a life here. We shall be comfortable on my family's land, and you can focus your energy on home and hearth. Surely it is time that you let go of the silly obsession with dragons and focus on more important things. Know that if you agree, your family will also be provided for. Please reply at your earliest convenience."

I drop the parchment onto my lap and stare at the mountainside. My heart pounds and my cheeks are on fire. My jaw is set. I feel Marinn's eyes on me as she waits for my reaction. It takes me a moment to identify the feeling taking root in my center and growing like a berry bush in full bloom.

Betrayal, anger, and frustration all cast a shadow over the bright sunny day. How dare he? Did Ma put him up to this? I rip open the letter from Ma and scan the words.

"Oh, Livvy." Marinn pats my knee. "What does your ma say?"

I speak slowly, every word fighting to get past my gritted teeth. "She says I should be grateful for the offer of marriage and that I am unlikely to get any other. She says I should get my head out of the clouds and come home straight away." I scoff, crumpling the paper in my fist.

"She cannot make you wed him," Marinn says, her voice full of conviction.

"No. She cannot. How could she do this to me?"

"Does your da agree with her?"

I glance down at the final envelope. "I do not know." I stare at the edge of the envelope. Do I dare find out? Dread dances along the edges of my heart. If my da does agree, what am I to do? My heart pounds as anger swells inside my chest.

I slowly unfold the third note. Is it truly to be my death sentence? Awareness flickers in the periphery of my mind that I am being hypocritical on this issue. Why was I not filled with rage when Julian suggested it? Perhaps I am being unfair.

"Go on, it can't get any worse."

Oh yes, it can. Although I know this letter could contain information I don't want to know, I still smile at seeing Da's greeting. *"My dearest Livvy Lou."* Oh, I used to loathe his pet name for me. Now I chuckle, appreciating the familiar greeting. Perhaps he remembers all that pet name evokes.

"Want to read it aloud?" Marinn asks.

"My dearest Livvy Lou, Your ma is most concerned with getting you settled. To that end, she has conspired to renew

William's affections toward you. If it is your desire to be wed to William, I can have no objection. However, if you do not wish to marry him, hear me clearly. From this day forward, you will be a disappointment to one of your parents. Your ma will be disappointed if you don't marry him, and I will be disappointed with you if you do."

I cover my mouth in shock and lift my gaze to Marinn's, who is staring at me quizzically. "I don't understand," she says.

I close my eyes for a moment, the pressure that has been building inside me fleeing as quickly as it has come. I can't keep the smile off my face. "My da is on my side. That's all that matters. I will not move to Tevyne. I will not wed William."

"If you are not to marry this William, is there anyone else in whom you've taken interest?" She runs her palm along the arm of her chair and waits for me to answer.

It is a loaded question. Maybe it's the menagerie of emotions that have plagued me the past few minutes or the lingering effects of the ale, but I stare at a bird perched on a low-hanging branch and say, "I find Julian to be an appealing man."

Marinn nudges me with her elbow. "I knew it. Please tell me everything, spare no detail."

I pick a piece of lint off my skirt. "He is charming, intelligent, and has shown an interest in not only me, but helping my da." My cheeks heat as I remember our conversation, my hand on his arm, the details of his life that he shared with me. It was all so intimate. The tips of my fingers absently touch my lips. His lips are soft and full. I imagine he is a good kisser.

"Is this a serious proposal?" Marinn asks, snapping me out of my daydream.

I shake my head. "Of course not. Although if it were to

become a great love, it should certainly be more pleasant than spending time with that terrible Asher."

"Oh, he is a horrible man," Marinn agrees, nodding.

I let out a snort. "Indeed. I would not marry Asher for all the coin in Saule."

22

The next day, I am up before the sun and race through my dragon duties. I promised Marinn I would be over mid-afternoon so we can ready ourselves for the revel.

When I'm finally seated in front of her vanity, she buzzes behind me, debating how to style my hair. She insists on using an iron heated in the fireplace to curl my hair and pin it into an elaborate creation that is entirely impractical. I'm not sure how I'll ever remove all of the pins. I watch her reflection in the looking glass as she claps and jumps up and down. "You are a vision, a princess."

She has managed to tame my hair into the best style it's ever seen. I bite back my conflicting emotions. I do look lovely. Perhaps a bit of effort in my appearance will be worth it. Impulsively, I reach up and pinch my cheeks to add some color.

She smacks my hand away. "I have rouge and coal. Let me apply it for you."

I sit patiently and pray she doesn't paint me too dramatically. Even coal use is frowned upon by Ma. Marinn gently swipes the heated coal stick across the bottom and top of my lids. Her eyes narrow in concentration as she gingerly taps rouge against my cheeks and lips, smacking her lips together for me to mimic. She frowns when I laugh at her intense pursuit of beauty. Finally, she steps back. "You are perfect."

I smile in the mirror. I do look quite lovely. "Are you certain you don't have magic?" I ask, for that is the most obvious explanation for my transformation.

She flits across her room, picking up dresses strewn across her bed and considering each one. "Oh, don't be daft. You have all the raw materials to be a beauty." She turns to me, holding up a dark green gown. "What do you think of this frock?"

I nod. "It's beautiful. I think it's a wonderful choice for you."

She shakes her head. "Not for me, for you."

My hand caresses the material. It must have cost a fortune. "Are you positive?" I ask. The last thing I want to do is borrow a dress and damage it.

She smiles. "Yes. I ordered it for you as an early solstice gift."

"You did not," I say, incredulous. This is an extravagant present, to be sure. How could I ever respond in kind?

She waves me off. "I cannot wear this shade of green. It makes me look sallow. I got it for you. Try it on. I bet it fits you like a glove."

I peel off my tunic, and she helps me into the frock. She laces up the back and then spins towards the mirror. "I knew it. Have a look," she says.

She's right. It's a perfect fit. She puts her hands on my shoulders and leans in. "And with the fires, it should be warm enough so there is no need to cover it with a cloak. The whole world deserves to see this dress, especially Julian."

I pivot and throw my arms around her. "You are such a dream. Thank you."

She pulls back. "I think Julian will be fond of the color as well. It matches his dragon, yes?"

I nod. She's right about the dragon. I've never had a garment so fine. "What about you?" I ask.

She holds up two dresses, royal blue and burgundy. "Which do you prefer?"

I consider. "The blue. It matches your eyes." With her long platinum hair and beautiful smile, she could wear a potato sack and still be lovely.

An hour later, we are both dressed and seated at the dining table with Marinn's father. The cook prepared a roasted duck. I have no idea what seasonings she uses, but it is better than anything we dine on in the mortal lands.

"Father, will you be attending the revel tonight?" Marinn asks as she slices her duck breast.

He chews a bite of potatoes and then says, "Yes, but only for a little while. I shall leave the evening to the young." Then he points at her with his fork. "Be mindful of your surroundings. The valley is rife with beings of every kind. Stay in the village and stick together."

"We will, Father." She nods, her eyes wide with innocence. Once he returns to his food, she meets my gaze and stifles a laugh.

When dinner is finished, we leave for the revel. Lanterns are strung between buildings, and small fires sit within stone circles every few paces down the center of the road. Villagers and throngs of visitors mill about the village. The entire scene is quite magical. Arm in arm, we weave through the crowd. I know Marinn is watching for Thaddeus. I have an eye out for Julian.

I'm happy to see Captain, Kessia, and Sam all seated together at the tavern. I wave at them and continue towards a haggard-looking Jasmine, who is doing her best to keep up with the demand of the swollen crowd. She manages a smile for me and hands me two pints of ale before I can even ask.

"Well met, Livvy. I adore your dress," she says. Then, surveying both Marinn and me, she says, "You two are trouble walking." She winks.

Marinn chuckles and weaves her arm through mine. "Thank you, Jasmine." Jasmine smiles and turns to speak to another patron. Marinn sees someone across the room and waves, releasing her hold on me and flitting over to them. She disappears into the throng of people.

I watch the festivities while enjoying my ale, but it's taxing to be "trouble walking" without my accomplice in crime. I'm beginning to grow anxious. I'm unaccustomed to the attention being drawn to the green dress flattering my figure, and after a few minutes, I begin to search for Marinn. Where has she gone?

Finally, I spot her talking to Kessia. I can make out snippets of them conversing about the music starting soon. Kessia plays the lute and will be joining a group of locals outside. She looks fiercely beautiful and dangerous. Although she is as human as I am, she has an otherworldly quality that is hard to ignore. I sigh and collect my thoughts. Secretly resigned to the futility of my efforts to look pretty, I glance around the tavern.

This is the most varied collection of creatures I have yet seen in Eshan. I imagine the Capitol will be even more diverse. Hopefully, Orthello will have an update on our trip soon. I am eager to explore the city.

In the glow of the firelight, the Fae are easy to spot as they tower over everyone else. A banshee holds court at a corner table, surrounded by those seeking predictions about the tournament's outcome. A female hob stands on the edge of the bar and regales a group of fauns with a tale. Humans and hobs share a pitcher of ale. A troll is hunched over a plate of meat, his beard brushing the table as he shovels shredded chicken into his mouth. Ma would be shocked at these fairy stories come to life.

I smile. In moments like this, I am still in awe of the fact that I am here. When I left home, all I had was a dream and a map. I have much to be thankful for. It's a shame that it doesn't include Julian dancing with me, because it seems he's not coming, after all. So what if one man decided not to make an appearance?

Besides, since when did I need a man to make me happy? Although Julian won't be at the revel, we can still have a wonderful evening. With a renewed sense of scrappy independence, I grasp the mugs and turn to Marinn, handing her one.

"It's time for me to play," says Kessia, finishing her ale and slapping Captain on the shoulder. "I had better see all of you outside dancing."

He scowls playfully. "You'd just as soon see a pig flying as me dancing."

Kessia laughs and grabs her lute, heading outside. As she passes through the door, my breath catches in my throat. It's Asher and Thaddeus. I step to the left to shield myself from view.

Asher looks well. His black coat is buttoned up to his chin. His jaw sets as he scans the room. He hates crowds, that much I've deduced from our brief interactions—time to find the dancing that's about to start. Just as I am determined to make my escape, I notice him studying me. Even from across the room, his gaze burns into me. The corners of his mouth tip up just a bit before he gives a slight nod.

I immediately avert my gaze. If anyone were going to skip tonight's festivities, I would rather it be Asher. With him here, I'm destined to be dragged into his presence by a lovesick Marinn.

Sure enough, Marinn grabs my arm and points to Thaddeus. "He came!"

"Let him come to you," I say, more out of self-interest than anything else.

She dips her chin, considering. "You're right. In fact, let's go outside. If he wants to see me, he should make a bit of an effort."

"Indeed. I'm confident he shall come find you once dancing begins," I say.

We secure a jug of spiced ale to take outside and move towards the door. Thank goodness. I could use some fresh air.

23

Outside, the band is in full swing. Couples step and twirl, effortlessly weaving and moving around the area carved out as a dance floor. We squeeze between the spectators and find space next to a table. Marinn is almost immediately asked to dance by a visiting Fae.

I spot Kessia, perched on a barrel and playing along with her lute. Her eyes sparkle as she taps her foot along with the music. She is quite talented.

When I was young, Ma wanted me to pursue the pianoforte. She said that music was a perfectly polished pursuit and would help raise my marriage prospects. She arranged lessons for me in the servants' quarters of a local manor. My teacher had perched next to me on the bench as I plunked out scales. She looked down her pointed nose with displeasure. I don't believe anyone else could do a better job making the pianoforte both difficult and tedious. I went to two lessons and then quit.

Ma was furious; she was sure I could have been a great musician. Fortunately, she was able to pass on her love of music to my younger sister, Constance, who has excelled in her playing. Constance plays for gatherings in the drawing room of that same manor where my musical talents died.

I stand on the edge of the dancers, leaning against a high table and drinking spiced ale. Marinn spins and laughs as several gentlemen from the village fill her dance card. When Thaddeus appears, her entire demeanor changes. As he approaches, kisses her hand, and speaks, she is captivated. Her face flushes with color, and her smile is shy. She may flirt and twirl with many men, but she is only prepared to love this one. They take to the floor and are soon lost in the magic of the music.

I continue to scan the crowd for Julian's blond hair and green cloak. As the song ends, I sigh and turn to refill my cup from the jug. Standing on the other side of the table is Asher, staring at me. He's wearing a starched, white-collared shirt and a black coat. His hands are balled into fists by his side. I'm surprised to see him here, since he does not favor crowds. I awkwardly stammer, "Oh, well met."

His throat bobs. "Are you searching for someone?"

I loathe to admit I'm looking for Julian, although I can't pinpoint why. Julian isn't at fault- Asher is the problem. "No. I was admiring the general splendor of the evening."

"I see," he says.

I grasp for something to say. "I thought the merriment of drinking and dancing wasn't for you." I fill my cup with spiced ale and take a drink.

"It isn't, but Thaddeus insisted."

I smile. "Thaddeus and Marinn seem to enjoy each other's company."

"Yes. I believe he is asking Marinn to dance again." He lifts his chin, and I turn to see that, indeed, Thaddeus is taking a smiling Marinn by the hand and leading her to the middle of the floor. Two dances in a row; she must be thrilled.

I use the chance to scan the area for Julian. Where can he be? I do not wish him to see me talking to Asher. We stand awkwardly, and then, to my relief, Asher excuses himself to retrieve a pint.

I watch as the song winds down and Marinn eventually makes her way to me, her brows knit together. "What's the matter?" I ask.

She takes both my hands. "I have terrible news. I'm afraid Julian isn't coming."

"Where is he?" My heart drops, and I realize how happy I was at the prospect of spending time with him.

"I am not sure. Thaddeus told me that Julian had to leave town for a few days."

I frown. Disappointment sinks my mood like a stone thrown into a pond. It sinks further when I realize I'm disappointed in my disappointment. Julian was just a rider who bought me a mug of ale. I shouldn't have let my heart run away with my imagination.

Marinn's father calls out her name. He is seated at a table with a few of the riders and a pitcher of ale between them. "Marinn, come, let me introduce you to these fine fellows."

Marinn gives me a sheepish grin. "Duty calls."

She prances away, leaving me standing alone. I sip my spiced ale and watch the dancers. I hate to admit how disappointed I am that Julian is not here. It would have been nice to dance with him. Now the evening feels spoiled. Would anyone notice if I slipped out and headed home? If Julian is not coming, there is no reason for me to stay.

Before I can make my getaway, Asher appears at my side and says, "Miss Livinia, may I have the next dance?"

It takes a moment for my brain to catch up with his request. Before I can come up with an excuse, I find myself saying, "You may."

He gives me a slight bow and turns to walk away. I am left

in shock. When I find Marinn to share this astonishment, she is seated next to her father, who is introducing her to the table. I bite my lip and wait for her to return. Kessia catches my eye and mouths, "What was that?"

I shrug. I cannot explain to her how I agreed to dance with Asher. I don't understand it myself. I down my spiced ale and consider a refill. But it would be just my luck that I would need the privy right when I am supposed to dance.

I chew on my lip and wait for the song to end. I have no one to blame but myself for this dreadful predicament. I will have to bear it with dignity. As the music comes to a crescendo and then fades out, I straighten my sleeves and wait for my torture to commence.

"Miss Livinia." Asher's voice comes from behind me. I spin around to find tentative gray eyes and an outstretched hand.

I stare at his fingers for a moment. I would have guessed him to have the smooth hands of the wealthy. But the calluses prove his have seen some work. I slide my own callused hand into his and try to ignore the heat that passes between us. I meet his gaze, but his face betrays nothing. He tips his head to the side. "Shall we dance?"

I nod and let him lead me onto the floor. We form lines for a well-known longways dance. As the music starts, I find myself swept up in the loveliness of the movement. Asher is quite good. That is to be expected given his station. I'm just glad Marinn forced me to learn the popular dances and practice with her. Between counting steps and trying to spin without getting dizzy, I spot Marinn. Thaddeus has found her again. The lantern flame flickers across her face as she laughs with abandon at something he is saying. I wish I had a softer, carefree heart. I am like sandpaper next to her silk.

"Did you have a pleasant day?" Asher asks.

"Very pleasant." I spin and then continue, "I met an old friend of yours. Julian."

He purses his lips and then says, "Julian has his charms. He makes friends easily."

"But he has managed to lose your friendship."

"Indeed."

"And is it an irreversible breaking?" I tip my head to judge his response.

"Why do you ask such a question?" Asher asks, holding my gaze as our shoulders brush and we spin.

"I am trying to discern the truth of your character." I search his face for any tell.

"Have you made any conclusions?"

I grind my teeth as we change directions and move together, his hand changing positions to the center of my lower back. All my attention is centered on that spot, warm under his touch, even through my dress. "Very little."

He leans in till I can feel his hot breath on my cheek. "I shall endeavor to provide you with more clarity in the future."

My breath catches in my throat. His eyes are so close I can see they are tinted with blue. A few heartbeats later, the song ends, and cold air replaces his warm breath as he steps back, bows, and turns to retreat. I sniff and blink rapidly, trying to orient myself. A storm of emotions clouds my vision.

Thankfully, a tug at my arm returns me to the moment. "Did you just dance with Asher Covington?" Marinn asks, eyes wide with confusion.

"I dare say I did."

She chuckles. "And what of it?"

I shake my head and stammer, "I do not know."

She giggles and tips her forehead to lean against mine, grabbing my hands and whispering, "Oh, Livvy. Since Thaddeus likes me, are there matching wedding dresses in our future?" She giggles and pulls me over to where Kessia stands on break from playing.

Kessia watches us approach and smiles. "There you are. I was waiting for you," she says.

"You are a most talented musician," Marinn tells her.

Kessia smiles, "Thank you." Then she shifts her attention to me. "Dancing with the enemy then?" She raises an eyebrow.

Marinn nods, "She is deep in enemy territory, to be sure."

I laugh. "At least Marinn has found her knight in shining armor."

Marinn gives us a sly smile. "We shall see. And Asher?"

I open my mouth to respond and then snap my jaw shut. What do I say? I hate the way my heart thuds at the sound of his name. I detest that I can still feel his fingers on the small of my back. At the same time, I fight a smile at the prospect of seeing him again.

24

The next morning, I roll over in bed and groan as Mr. Bennet hisses at me to let him out. My head pounds, and I'm loath to get out from under my blankets. Alas, Mr. Bennet moves to stand on my shoulder, letting his claws peek out to prick my skin. "Stop it," I say, batting him away. "You're lucky you're not an outdoor cat."

Mr. Bennet huffs. "I waited until I had no choice but to take action." He bounds off the bed and struts for the door, turning back to ensure I am following orders.

I'm thankful for my wool socks as I wrap the quilt around my shoulders before skittering to the door and cracking it open for him to exit. Once he's slithered outside, I turn my attention to the hearth. The smell of the pine needles I use to light the fire fills the cabin. I take the water jug outside to fill it with fresh snow to melt.

Marinn's voice breaks the early morning peace. "Oh, Livvy! I am so glad you are home."

I turn to see her running up the path. She's waving a letter in the air.

"What on earth is the matter?" I ask.

She stops short of the porch steps and bends over, her hands on her knees, struggling to catch her breath. I can't help but smile. She should start accompanying me on my rounds and build up her stamina. Panting, she says between breaths, "I received a letter from Thaddeus."

My eyebrows rise. Why is he writing her when he could cross the village and speak in person? "Come in out of the cold and tell me about it."

She follows me and takes a chair near the fire. I let the blanket drop from my shoulders onto the bed and slip into a knitted sweater. Then I set out to make tea over the fire with the water collected from melting snow. Marinn patiently watches me, her fingers running along the edge of the folded parchment.

"What has Thaddeus to say?" I ask.

She covers her eyes with a hand, using the other to hold out the parchment. "I just know it is bad news. I cannot bear to read it. You open it."

She pinches her fingers when I reach out to take the parchment, causing a tug of war. I smile as she grimaces. "I can't read it if you won't give it to me," I say.

Finally, she groans and lets go.

I settle into the other chair. "I do not understand why you would be so afraid to take in his words. He likes you, you know he does."

She folds her hands in her lap and looks at the fire. "It was delivered early this morning. When father gave it to me at breakfast, I couldn't bear to open it."

This was so unlike her. She was ever the optimist, sure that everything would work out happily ever after. Yet here she is, wound up like a ball of twine. Hopefully, I can put her out of her misery. I slip my finger under the seal and open the letter. "Shall I study it and summarize, or read it aloud in its entirety?"

She sniffs. "Read it and summarize. Then I can pore over it if I want."

I nod and begin to examine the text. I glance up halfway through, and she's watching me intently, probably looking for any expressions that give away the content.

It's not good news. Thaddeus and Asher have left the village. Thaddeus has a family obligation he must attend to. He does not know for certain when, or if, they shall return before the start of the tournament. My heart sinks not only for Marinn, but for my flicker of hope that Asher may turn out to be something more than a prideful dragon rider.

When I finish reading, I let the letter fall into my lap. I chew my lip as I contemplate how to share this turn of events with Marinn. I hate to be the bearer of bad news.

"I can wait no more. What does it say?" She is sitting on the edge of the chair, her foot tapping the floor in anticipation.

I swallow and say, "He had to depart for home. He's gone."

"What do you mean?" Her voice holds a rough edge of panic.

I hold out the note, and she snatches it from my palm. She begins to read, her face hiding nothing as she processes what he has written. Her face pinches, and she frowns. "Why would he leave?"

I stand to retrieve the boiling water and add pouches of tea to two cups. "It sounds like he has a family obligation of some kind."

"What kind of obligation?" she asks.

"I don't know. I'm sure he has a good reason." I keep my voice even and face schooled in neutrality. Marinn is on the verge of an emotional breakdown, and I cannot be the one to push her over the edge.

She shakes her head. "No, it's obvious that he does not love me."

I present her with a cup of tea and take my seat. "I'm sure he'll be back for the tournament, then you will find he is more in love with you than ever."

Marinn's blue eyes fill with tears as she rereads the letter. "There is nothing to be done. I am destined to die an old maid."

I pat her knee. "You must keep your faith. All shall be resolved."

She sniffs and wipes her eyes with the back of her hand. "I should go. My father will be looking for me. I am to get a new dress today."

I force a smile. "That sounds pleasant."

"It would be if I had a reason to wear it." She meets my gaze, looking forlorn. "I am having it made in purple, his favorite color." Her lip trembles.

I set my tea on the table and lean over to wrap my arms around her. "I have a dragon to see today, but after, I will stop by, and you can try on your dress for me. I promise to be properly appreciative of your beauty."

She sniffs. "Alright, but I shall look hideous and puffy from crying."

I wipe a tear from her cheek. "Then you mustn't cry."

She lifts her chin. "I shall try."

25

Although I try to maintain a cheerful outlook for Marinn's sake, inside I seethe. How dare Thaddeus raise her hopes and then disappear without a good reason? I knew the riders were rakes. I had hoped Thaddeus was different. If he does not return with love in his heart and a ring in his hand, I may have to push him off a cliff, along with Asher, for good measure.

At least I shall not worry about running into Asher after our dance. That is a point of sunshine, at least.

And what of Julian? Why had he not been at the revel? Did he decide I was not worth his efforts? Not even a note of explanation? I hate that disappointment sits alongside my other emotions regarding men. My universal conclusion is that men are generally odious and unworthy of my attention.

At least I get to groom a new breed of dragon today. I have never seen a Copper Varis dragon before and have been looking forward to it. I've read that their copper scales take on a green patina as they age, just like the metal cupola on Marinn's house.

I work my way up to the crumbling stone fortress. It was

built before the village existed as an outpost during the war. The one remaining turret can be seen from the village, but I've never ventured up the hill to explore. The fortress fills me with trepidation as I imagine what it must have been like: war between King Nassar and those united to defend the freedom of dragons and mortals alike. If it weren't for the Fae who fought with the mortals and shared the secrets of gold and other magic-dampening elements, we would have been destroyed.

I blow out a breath and set my mind to the task at hand. Copper Varis dragons tend to be lean and sinuous. They have a pair of backward-angled, scale-covered horns. Unlike other dragons, they have cheek ridges and jaw frills. I had to order a special brush with extra soft bristles to clean those areas without harming them.

As I approach, the skeleton of the fortress rises; the shadow it casts is sure to swallow the path as the day wears on. I scan the ruins for any sign of the rider or glint of scales. "Ah, there you are," a man calls out in a lilting voice.

I use my hand to shield my view from the sun. A man in a ruffled pink shirt under a dark brown coat and breeches waves at me with a long-handled paintbrush. A canvas is perched on a stand, and I can make out broad strokes of color, but no detail.

"Well met," I say, leading Ranger to where he stands.

"Oh, yes, that is the appropriate salute." He gives a deep bow and says dramatically, "Well met. I am Leonardo Penton."

Most of the riders are serious, athletic brutes. While Leonardo looks like he is perfectly capable of riding a dragon, I cannot fathom that he would want to. Paint a dragon? Sure. But not ride in a tournament. His carefree demeanor is refreshing. I can tell I'm going to like him. "What are you painting?" I ask.

He turns to his canvas and then waves me off. "It's a doodle, a lark."

I step forward to better view his progress. "You have a lovely gift for color." He has captured the gray-blue sky contrasting with the green of the trees, vibrant under the filtered light.

When I turn my head, he has the paintbrush between his teeth, his arms wrapped tight around himself, and he leans back, studying his painting. Plucking the brush from his teeth, he shoves it into a pocket on his coat. I open my mouth to warn him about the paint on the end of the brush, but then stop. He likely knows the brush is wet, and I bet his pocket is an art piece with wild colors.

"Right. You must be here for Metsaloo?" Without waiting for me to answer, he begins to scan the horizon. "Where is that dragon?"

As if on cue, a dragon appears on the edge of my vision, rounding the mountain with his entire wingspan perpendicular to the ground. It's spectacular. He straightens and comes straight for us, flying so low that the trees bend to his will. I tie Ranger to a tree while keeping my eye on the dragon.

He hovers above us for a few moments before gracefully descending to land. He puffs out his chest, a statue adorned with large, glossy bands of scales that are smooth, metallic copper with a subtle patina. I am astounded by the beauty of his turquoise eyes, reminiscent of the ocean I've read about in books. Before we can interact, Metsaloo's attention is caught by the painting Leonardo has been diligently working on. The ground trembles beneath my feet as he approaches to get a closer look. A chuckle escapes my lips, as I remember that Copper Varis dragons are fond of fine art. Perhaps that's how Metsaloo and Leonardo crossed paths- over their shared passion for art. It makes perfect sense.

Leonardo takes a step forward. "Ignore my silly scribbles,

Metsaloo. I want to introduce you to Lavinia, or would you prefer Livvy?"

"Livvy is perfect." I nod and smile. I turn to the dragon and meet his eyes, bowing respectfully. "I am delighted to meet you. I am here to serve at your will." I place my hand over my heart to convey my sincerity, and he dips his head slightly in acknowledgment.

As I begin my initial examination, I ask, "How did you meet?" After hearing Asher's story, I have asked for the story of every rider. These tales reveal a great deal about the nature of the dragon, the rider, and their relationship.

Leonardo smiles, lounging on the remnants of a rock wall stretching across the field. "Ah, that is a tale. I was painting beside a river, and suddenly, this dragon appeared. I was so lost in my art that I did not hear him approach. Can you imagine? Now, he was much smaller as he was still relatively young. I was a very young man, more of an adolescent myself if you will. Ahh, such good times." His voice trails off.

I finish examining the dragon's claws, and he chuffs.

"Oh, right. Where was I?" Leonardo says.

"You were on the riverbank painting," I say.

"Yes, of course. There I was, standing beside this beautiful dragon, who was focused on my painting with such intensity. As you know, his kind loves to hoard art. Even though I thought it was rubbish, he seemed to appreciate it. After offering him the piece, he showed me the lair he had at the time, full of beautiful paintings. I've no idea where he got them from, and I did not ask. But it was clear we shared a love of art, and we've been together ever since. He shows me beautiful things he'd like me to paint and add to his hoard. And he lets me ride him and bring him out to these silly tournaments to joust, mostly because I promise him lots of good food while he's here."

"Food is an excellent motivator," I say, nodding. Then I

reach into the cart for my tools and tuck them into my belt. I am glad to have only one dragon to see today. Leonardo's love of storytelling is sure to extend this appointment.

I examine the large, smooth, glossy bands of scales. There is such a beautiful variety in dragon breeds. Not only the scales, but horns, wings, talons, and of course, color. It's no wonder Metsaloo appreciates art. He is a living work of art himself. Leonardo stays close by as I unfold my ladder and climb up to give Metsaloo's teeth a polish.

"Is that safe?"

I look down at Leonardo, whose face is pinched. He pulls a flask from his jacket pocket and twists off the cap.

I smile. "It's perfectly safe. Don't worry. In fact, if you would like to get back to your beautiful painting, I will come to you when I'm finished."

Leonardo seems to consider for a beat, then nods. "Alright." He turns his attention to Metsaloo, "Be a good old fellow. I'll have a finished painting for you before long."

When I complete my work with Metsaloo, my heart is lighter than when I started. But as I guide Ranger down the hill, my thoughts return to Marinn. She must be so forlorn. I cannot fathom sitting in my cottage just to ruminate on my dance with Asher and the sudden absence of the three men who have disrupted our lives. Yes, a visit is certainly in order.

26

The moon is peeking through the trees as I cross the porch, and a board creaks under my feet. As I lift my hand to knock, Marinn's father opens the door, relief flooding his face when he sees me. "Ah, Livvy. So glad you're here. Perhaps you can bring some relief."

I offer a sympathetic smile. "I shall try. Where is she?"

He lifts his chin towards the top of the stairs. "In her room."

"Thank you," I say, unwinding the scarf from my neck.

"If you like, you are welcome to stay tonight. Marinn could use the company." He looks at me hopefully.

I shove the scarf into my satchel and study him. I imagine it must be difficult being the single father to a daughter so full of excitement and vigor. Her emotions are like the tides, pulling the world to her mood. He is a boat tossed upon the waves. He runs a hand over his hair and sighs.

"Of course."

His shoulders relax and he flashes a weak smile. "Thank you."

I slide my hand along the polished banister and climb the

stairs to Marinn's room. The door is shut and when I try the knob, it is locked. She only locks her door when she is distraught. I rap my knuckles gently against the wood. "Marinn, please, may I come in?"

The latch clicks, and through the gap in the doorway, Marinn appears with red-rimmed eyes. She takes one look at me and bursts into tears, which I suspect has been her condition more often than not today. I push through the door and fold her into a hug.

"Oh, Livvy, it's hopeless."

She sobs on my shoulder, and I pat her back. "It cannot be all that bad."

She sniffs and pulls out of my embrace. "Unless you have brought news to the contrary, how can you say the world has not ended?" She pulls a handkerchief from the pocket of her dressing gown and retreats into her bedroom, curling up on the chair by her window.

I slip my satchel off and unbutton my cloak, hanging it on the hook next to the door. There are two choices when she descends this far into despair: solve the problem or distract her. I decide on the latter. "At least gowns do not fly off into the night without warning. Did you receive your new one?"

She waves a hand to her wardrobe. I cross the room and pull open the cabinet. The dress is stunning. I have never seen fabric such as this. There is an iridescent quality to the weave that reminds me of dragon scales. "Oh, Marinn, this is exquisite." I lift the hanger off the rack and hold it in front of me, then spin around. The candlelight flooding the room reflects off the silk, changing color with every shift in movement.

"It is lovely, isn't it?" she asks.

It is uniquely enticing. This may be just the thing to get Marinn to focus on something besides Thaddeus, which may lessen the weight of her melancholy. I flash her a bright smile. "I am sure there will be many occasions for you to show the village this dress. You are going to look like a dream."

Marinn turns her gaze to the window. "I shall never wear it if I cannot wear it for Thaddeus."

In moments like this, I'm struck by the unfairness and complexity of being a woman in this world. I came to Eshan to find a safe harbor, yet Marinn is drowning in a man's rejection, and I cannot seem to rescue her from the swells.

I begrudgingly return the dress to the wardrobe and take the seat across from her. I tap my foot on the wood floor, chewing on my nails. I consider descending into despair alongside Marinn. "I wish there was anything at all I could say, dear friend."

"There is no cure for my aching heart," she bemoans.

I survey the room. She feels everything so deeply. But she can't hide in here forever. No, she needs an adventure that doesn't revolve around men. I lean forward and take her hands, "I am not sure about a cure, but maybe a change of scenery would take the edge off the pain. Don't you have an aunt in Jura? This might be the perfect time for you to visit."

For the first time since I arrived, a glimmer of light shows in her blue eyes. "Oh, a trip is a wonderful idea."

I smile in satisfaction. "Yes, you could return in time for the tournament and have a thousand tales to tell."

She rises abruptly and begins pacing. I watch her as she gestures randomly, working something out in her mind. Finally, she pauses and faces me. "I will travel, but not to Jura."

My brows furrow. "Where else would you go?"

She smiles confidently. "I should go to Lauks. I have a cousin there, and it is where Thaddeus resides. If he truly went home to his family, he would be there."

I sigh. This trip was supposed to get her away from Thaddeus. "Could you travel there and back in a timely manner?"

"You forget, all I must do is move beyond the valley to access portals. And I will have access to magic through my cousins. They are elves."

That makes sense. I imagine Marinn would love to have magic, but I am grateful she does not. If she did, living in the valley would be most difficult.

Her face brightens, and I can tell she's working out a plan in her mind. "I shall write to them tomorrow."

She crosses to a cupboard in the knee wall of her room and opens the small cubby, revealing a trunk. It scrapes across the wood floor and snags on the rug. With a grunt, Marinn lifts the end of the trunk to drag it closer to her wardrobe. Throwing open the latch and lid, she stands and places her hands on her hips.

"Shouldn't you make your inquiries before you pack?" I ask with a smirk.

She begins to select items to pack. "I shall send a letter tomorrow. Surely they will come straightaway if Father assists in the persuasion." She looks at the half-filled bag. "This is just my first round of packing. You know that when I travel, it takes me several attempts to compile the perfect travel collection."

She's right. This should keep her occupied until the hour she leaves.

But her enthusiasm wanes as she looks at the purple dress, hanging as a reminder of the boy she may not have. Flopping onto the side of her bed, she hangs her head. Just like that, tears are filling her eyes again. She abandons the trunk and curls up on her bed. "I am a fool. This will never work."

"Oh, Marinn. Perhaps we should sleep. Everything will seem brighter in the morning."

She scoots over to the edge of the bed and slips under the covers. I excuse myself to use the privy and then change into one of her nightgowns. When I return, she blows out the candles. We lie in the dark, the moon's light shining through the window. I listen to her sniff as tears continue to fall.

There is no balm I can offer for her heart. Soon, the exhaustion of the day catches up to me, pulling me into a dreamless sleep.

When I wake, Marinn is still asleep. I consider rousing her, but decide it's better to let her be. Her blond hair is spread out on her tear-stained pillow. She snores softly. My limbs are heavy with disappointment at all that has transpired. It takes everything I've got to drag myself out into the pre-dawn chill and back to my cottage to let Mr. Bennet out for the day. As I stand in front of my unlit hearth, my breath clouds in front of me. I check my supplies and run through my list of remaining dragons I need to see—three more days. Then I get a break.

$\mathcal{A}$ few days later, Marinn and I stand on her porch watching her father grunt as he heaves her trunk onto the wagon. Her cousins arrived late last night to transport her to their estate for a fortnight. Her father readily agreed to the idea of getting her out of the house and away from thoughts of Thaddeus. Marinn failed to disclose the additional reason for her departure —that her cousins live near the Cedar family estate. She believes there is a reasonable chance she will meet him while she's in the city.

"Are you sure this is a good idea? When I suggested travel, it was to get away from all of this, not run towards it," I say.

Marinn wipes her palms off on her skirts. "I am sure."

"What if you do not see him? Won't it make your broken heart worse?" I ask. I can't imagine her sinking further into despair.

She takes my hand. "I shall leave it all up to fate. I will enjoy a nice trip with my cousins, and if I happen to see Thaddeus, then all the better."

I bite my cheek. She is putting on a brave front but her confidence in this is fragile.

Picking a piece of lint off her cloak, she says, "Surely I could not have imagined his affection. If so, I will be most embarrassed about it."

"I cannot pretend to know the reasons for his behavior change, but I'm sure things will come around right." I squeeze her hand.

"I hope you are right, Livvy. "

I give her a nod that I hope conveys confidence. A smile plays at the corners of her mouth, but doesn't reach her eyes. Instead, she kisses me on the cheek and descends the steps to climb into the wagon with her cousins. With one last wave, she's gone, and I am left alone.

After stopping at the apothecary for more mint poultice, I head to the cottage. The view from where I walk is rather gray. The dragons have mostly gone, and with them the excitement of the past few weeks. Although they could have stayed in the village until the tournament began, the magic wards deter riders from lingering.

Marinn has been gone for a mere hour, and I already find myself restless and lonely without her. I should have volunteered to go with her. It might have been an excellent opportunity to travel under the protection of her family, who are of high social standing. A fortnight is too long for me to be away from my clients. Hopefully, Orthello will soon be ready to go to the Capitol. It will be nice to have a solid plan to look forward to, especially if Julian will not return until the tournament starts.

When I reach the edge of the village, Sam strides out from between two buildings, dragging a bundle of what looks like discarded rubbish precariously tied with a rope. "Sam, what are you doing?"

He pauses and works on the knots of his haul, which is threatening to burst out of the bindings. "I have an idea for the most amazing invention."

I watch him struggle and grunt with effort. "Do you need help with that? Would you like me to accompany you home?" I ask.

He straddles the load and pulls the rope tight. "Oh no, I've got it."

"What are you building? Is it the machine for Kessia?" I can't imagine what concoction requires this collection of items. There are jagged boards, pieces of metal plating from a discarded suit of armor, and several glass bottles tucked between scraps of fabric.

Sam says, "Oh yes, I am working on that. My plans are taking a bit longer than I had predicted. But don't you worry."

I chuckle. "All right then." I turn to continue on my way.

"Oh, Livvy," he calls out after me. "I have forgotten myself. Colette charged me with inviting you to our dinner party."

I turn, so many questions filling my thoughts. Do he and Colette host parties? If so, I've never heard of one. I've imagined their home as a hovel full of rickety, failed inventions. But perhaps I'm wrong.

"It is the day after tomorrow at seven o'clock. I believe that is what my wife told me," he says, knitting his brow together. "Lenora will be there along with Orthello, and some other folks. It is sure to be a lively discussion all the way around."

I cannot help but smile. If Lenora and Orthello are there, it should be quite pleasant. The invitation comes at the perfect time, as I am missing Marinn. "It sounds lovely."

Sam rises on his tiptoes and rocks onto his heels, grinning. "Perfect. Colette will be so pleased." He starts to walk away and then turns to me. "Livvy, you are always welcome to help me with my inventions."

I smile. "Thank you for that. I may take you up on it."

I watch him dragging his bundle down the road towards his home, and out of nowhere, the back of my eyes prick with tears. Why am I filled with emotion at a simple dinner invitation? I do admire the life he has built with Colette. I run my fingers under my lashes and shake off the moment.

As I walk, I reflect on the past few weeks. There is much to entertain. When I think of my meetings with Asher, melancholy is soon joined by a seething frustration. I do not have the introspection to pinpoint the reasons for my frustration, except that my heart beats faster whenever he is around, and I don't know if it's because I want to push him off a cliff or crush my lips against his. Perhaps both. No matter. He is gone until the tournament begins, and I shall busy myself with preparations for the coming chaotic fortnight. At least I have a proper dinner invitation to look forward to, and the Merchants' Guild is tomorrow. Perhaps Jasmine will even have some mail for me.

When I enter the tavern, Jasmine reaches below the bar and retrieves a letter. "This arrived last night."

I stride over and take the letter. I do not recognize the script. How odd. I break the seal and unfold the parchment.

Dearest Livvy,

I must apologize for my sudden departure. It could not be avoided. I shall return in time for the tournament and look forward to your company.

. . .

ours truly,
    Julian

houghts of Asher vanish. Julian is a man of good character, strong constitution, and no fear of sharing his affection for me. I clutch the letter to my chest. This fortnight cannot pass fast enough.

28

The tavern is blissfully quiet now that most of the riders and their traveling parties have vacated the village until the tournament begins. It's not surprising that they left. The magical wards are uncomfortable for anyone who has magic, which many of them do. When they return, the wards will be down.

Meanwhile, this break allows me to care for my regular clients and catch up on my reading. Best of all, I was able to send my landlord a complete payment and send funds home. If Marinn comes home happy, my world will be set right again.

The smell of the roasted chicken and winter squash Jasmine prepared for the mid-day meal has my mouth watering. I tear open a soft roll, still warm from the fire-baked oven, and inhale the yeasty goodness. I could eat this same meal every day for the rest of my life.

"I hear that Asher Covington has returned to the village," Captain says.

My ears perk up, and the bread is suddenly stuck in my throat. Is Thaddeus with him? It would be terrible if Marinn were on her way to Lauks and he were in Eshan. Before I can ask, Sam speaks.

"This is one time his lack of magic may serve as an advantage against his competitors if he can conduct additional training," Sam explains.

Kessia leans forward. "If I see him, I shall invite him to join us at the tavern tonight."

"Oh, please don't," I blurt out, then clamp my jaw shut. Everyone at the table looks at me.

Kessia tips her head to the side. "Why ever not?"

I cross my arms, wishing I had kept my mouth closed. Silence hovers as they wait for my answer. How can I explain my frustration? Finally, I throw my hands in the air. "It's just, he's so rich."

Captain strokes his beard, "Rich? He can't help it if his family has money."

I shake my head. "He has no real sense of humility. He acts as if we are beneath him, when nothing could be farther from the truth. It's exasperating." I am met with blank stares, as if I am speaking another language.

Sam leans forward. "He's always been pleasant to me."

Orthello grunts, chewing on a toothpick, "I agree. You might be mistaken here, Livvy."

I suck in a breath. Am I required to bow down to the whims of these riders? Of course not. My opinion may be jaded due to my close interactions with him. If my fellow guild members spoke to Asher for more than five minutes, they would appreciate my perspective.

"Does she perceive him to be a snob, or is she fond of him and cannot admit the truth?" Kessia asks, biting back a smile.

My mouth drops open. "Cursed be the day you are accused of such madness," I say.

Kessia laughs and pounds her fist on the table. "I knew I was speaking the truth. You do like him."

I lift my chin. "I shall not dignify your comments with an answer. He may come to the tavern or not. Either way, it is of no consequence to me. "

Kessia continues to grin like a madwoman.

Orthello clears his throat, "Perhaps we should move on to the business at hand."

"Yes, yes," Sam agrees, "There is a trip to plan."

My shoulders drop as the subject changes. I am grateful for the diversion.

"Livvy, can you get away for a quick trip to Kaimas?" Kessia asks.

I bite my lip. I've always wanted to visit the capital, but can I spare the time? There is a great deal to prepare before the riders return. Yet, if I do not go now, when will I ever have the opportunity? "Yes. I believe it's possible, depending on the timing. But won't the journey take many days?"

"Magic works outside the ward, remember?" Orthello says.

My interest is piqued. "What kind of magic?" I ask.

"Portal doors are scattered throughout the Kingdom. They do not work for traveling between Kingdoms, but once you are inside the border and away from the wards, they are available. We shall ride out and catch a portal door located about an hour away," Orthello explains.

"See, Livvy, we will only be gone for a day. Surely you can spare a day for your good friend." Kessia bats her eyelashes at me, and I laugh. Her piercings, tattoos, and short hair do not naturally lend themselves to feminine antics. But her effort pays off.

"Alright, I will go."

Orthello smacks the table, "It's settled. I will prepare a list of items needed for the village. The markets in Kaimas are plentiful."

Excitement lifts the hairs on my arms. This was sure to be

an adventure. I would need to borrow a horse, ensure Mr. Bennett was cared for, and delay my clients for a day.

"Is three days' time too soon to depart?" Orthello asks.

I catch Kessia's gaze, and she smiles, raising her eyebrows in question.

"That would be fine," I say. Then I turn to the men and say, "Can you escape your responsibilities for the day?"

Captain smiles, "It would be my pleasure. I'll secure horses for our ride."

My heart swells as I consider the people around this table. Each of them has profoundly impacted my life. This sojourn to Kaimas could not come at a better time.

As the meeting ends, Sam jumps on the table and crosses to me. "I'm looking forward to showing you my workshop this evening."

I gather my dishes to return them to Jasmine at the bar. His glasses slip down his face as he waits for me to respond. I smile and say, "I would not miss it for all the gold in Straume."

Captain lets out a slow whistle, "I am not certain you are making a good deal with that one."

I chuckle. "Either way, I shall be there with bells on."

29

Standing before the rounded wooden door of Sam's cottage, I stomp the snow from my boots and pull the brass gargoyle door knocker. The thud of metal against wood is muted, but effective. Almost immediately, the shoulder height door swings open, and I'm met with the smell of rosemary and roasted garlic.

Colette stands below me, smiling. An apron looped over her neck, cockeyed and tied under her ample bosom. "Livvy, well met." She retreats a step to make space for me to duck under the doorway and enter. After I am safely inside, she excuses herself and disappears into what I assume is the kitchen.

I take a minute to survey the surroundings. The inside of the house is not what I had pictured. This room is a library of sorts. It is cozy and uncluttered, with shelves lining the wall filled with books of every kind. My fingers itch to run across the spines and inspect the treasures within.

A small set of chairs sits before a fireplace half the size of the one in my cottage. Will we be expected to sit in the gnome-sized furniture? I grin to myself, imagining us huddled around a pint-sized table. Then the grin fades as I realize it could be a possibility.

Sam bustles over, offering to take my cloak. "Livvy, I'm so glad you're here. I cannot wait to show you my latest invention."

Before I can respond, Colette's voice calls out from the kitchen, "Oh no, you may not take her into that horrible workshop tonight." She peeks her head into the doorway. "No inventions- you agreed."

Sam's shoulders heave, and he says, "Yes, darling."

Then, to me, he whispers, "After dinner, we can sneak out to my workshop."

I lean in conspiratorially and say, "I would like that very much."

Perhaps it's because he reminds me of my da, my heart is soft towards this peculiar portly gnome.

He waves me forward. "Come in, come in. We are enjoying some wine from the mortal lands while Colette finishes dinner."

I follow him through an arched doorway into a drawing room with tall curved ceilings and a cheery ambiance. With the extra ceiling height, I can stand to my full height, and even Orthello appears able to straighten his spine as long as he avoids the outer edges. The lanterns hanging from the ceiling are all whimsical blown glass and remind me of the carnival in Saule Da took me to as a child. The flicker from the gas lamps bounces off the shades and textures of the glass, creating a kaleidoscope of color.

Sam thrusts a goblet of wine into my hand. I am caught up in the way it was delivered. The goblet is not wood or metal as I'm used to, but blown glass. It's beautiful, with shades of orange, red, and yellow. It's a fall maple tree, and a warm fire all rolled into one smooth vessel. "This is lovely, " I say.

"Yes, my spectacular wife has been experimenting with using glass for cups of all shapes and sizes," he says, sticking his thumbs in his pockets and leaning back on his heels.

"It's good to see you, Miss Lavinia," a familiar voice says, and I turn to find Asher Covington standing in the corner next to Orthello.

I fight a groan. Kessia was right. I throw Sam a look, and he shrugs apologetically. He could've told me Asher would be here. But I suspect he knew I might not come if I had known.

I school my face into neutrality. "Well met, Asher. I was not aware you knew Sam and Colette."

"Oh," Sam says, "Asher's been to our home several times. He has a keen mind for science and has put forth more than one excellent suggestion to advance my research. Even with all of the hullabaloo with the tournament, he promised to come for dinner, and so here he is."

I force a smile. "How lovely." I am grateful for the wine, and I am even more pleased when I taste the familiar flavors from home. I shall need a few glasses to sustain me this evening.

"Ah, Asher, there is a book I have been meaning to show you," Sam says, abandoning me and crossing the room to where Asher is studying the book selection.

I turn my attention to Orthello and smile. "Is Lenora not with you?"

He nods, "She would not miss the chance to sample delicious wine. She is in the solarium."

I follow his gaze to an opening in the rear of the house, where an orange light glows, even though the sun has long set.

"Suppose they have proper seating for dinner?" he asks quietly, glancing at the drawing room furniture.

I chuckle. "I hope so, or we shall be sitting on the floor."

He considers. "That might be ideal. The table would be the perfect height for polite dinner conversation."

I lift my glass in agreement. "Then that shall be our plan." My view keeps being drawn to the orange glow. Surely there is a reason for such a bright light. "I must see what your wife has found interesting."

"You go. I will be standing here where I don't have to worry about hitting my head."

I leave him to it and move towards the solarium. As I approach, I resist the urge to shield my eyes, but blink rapidly, adapting to the unusual brightness. As my vision adjusts, I see a glass-enclosed garden with all manner of plants. Some I recognize as herbs used medicinally, but others must be unique to the Fae lands. Lenora stands in the corner, leaning over what appears to be a large daisy. As I move closer, she drops a small piece of something into the middle of the petals, which immediately snap shut and begin to undulate.

"What is that?" I ask, keeping a safe distance away from the mysterious flower.

"Death Daisy," Lenora says. "They love chicken."

I swallow hard. "Carnivorous?"

She nods. "Indeed."

I tentatively step closer, keeping my hands and glass of wine tucked in close. Lenora has no such reservations, and she breaks off another piece of chicken, repeating the process.

"Are they not remarkable? When I was a girl, these lined the side of our cottage."

I raise an eyebrow. "Isn't that dangerous?"

She chuckles. "Everything is dangerous in the Fae lands, especially if you are human."

Indeed. It is easy to forget, in the relative safety of the valley, that danger lurks just outside the wards.

"Dinner is served," Colette's voice calls out.

Lenora sighs, drops the last piece of chicken into a flower, and brushes her hands off on her skirt.

I follow Lenora through the drawing room to the other side of the house and into a dining area. Orthello greets us with a smile. He is standing beside a full-sized table with a height-appropriate chair. Sam sits at the head of the table in a chair with legs longer than usual and a ladder on the back, which I imagine he uses to reach the seat. He watches me survey the space and smiles. "My carpentry skills are improving, yes?"

"Yes," I run my hands over the carved back of the chairs. "This is exquisite work."

He motions to a chair next to Orthello, and I slide into the seat. More evidence of Colette's glass blowing covers the table, bowls filled with pasta, chicken, and sauces. Asher sits across from me, and Lenora sits across from Orthello.

"Everything looks delicious," Lenora says, leaning forward to peruse the offerings.

Colette beams from her place at the opposite end of the table.

"My wife is an excellent cook," Sam says, lifting a dish to fill his plate. His movement signals the rest of us to partake, and we do.

As we enjoy the meal, occasional conversation emerges and then slips into comfortable silence. It is a surprisingly wonderful evening, even with Asher in attendance. As we finish the meal, Sam says, "Shall we enjoy drinks among the books?"

"I'd love to speak with you and Colette about your collection of plants," Lenora says, wiping her mouth with a cloth napkin.

Colette climbs down from her chair and begins to clear

the dishes. "Unless you want to know about cooking herbs, Sam shall be the better informant."

Lenora slides her chair away from the table and says, "Then I must insist you give me the tour, Sam."

"By all means," he says, hopping down and leading her through the house. Their height difference is pronounced as they walk together.

"Since my wife has absconded with your husband, Colette, I shall help with the dishes," Orthello says, gathering silverware and stacking plates.

I hand him my place setting and sip my wine, unsure of what to do. Colette returns from the kitchen with a fresh bottle. "Let me top you off."

"Thank you," I say, watching her fill Asher's glass next.

"You two are acquainted, yes?" she asks.

"Indeed. We met at the tavern. He rescued Marinn and me from a beast in the woods," I say, working to keep the smirk off my face.

"Well, isn't that a story?" She says. "You're a hero, Asher."

He shakes his head, "No, I am not. She exaggerates."

"Oh?" She looks to me for clarification.

I widen my eyes innocently. "I would not exaggerate about such an important topic."

Colette smirks and then lets out a snort. "You two are peculiar, to be certain." She disappears into the kitchen, where I can hear Orthello clanging dishes together.

When something crashes to the ground and breaks, I wince. "That doesn't sound good."

"How is it that you find it so easy to converse with others?" Asher asks, rubbing a hand across the back of his neck.

"You seem perfectly capable," I say, tracing a finger along the smooth edge of my wine glass.

A flush creeps across his cheeks, "Adequate, at best. But more than that, I am often at a disadvantage."

"You ride dragons into danger. Perhaps you do not need to excel at shallow conversation to be amiable."

Asher grunts, and when I turn to look at him, he has this strange look on his face. I watch as he fidgets in his chair, mentally assembling a response. My lips part slightly. We hold the stare for a moment.

"You believe me to be amiable?" he asks, each word costing him something.

I search for the words to respond, but can find none. A simple nod of my head will have to do.

A slow smile spreads across his face. "Thank you, Miss Livinia, for your encouragement."

His smile completely changes his countenance. It is a smile that must be earned and is not easily given. It is a shame, because if he smiled more, he might be irresistible. But I am pleased to be on the receiving end of it, just the same.

Sam breaks the tension, "Livvy, you must come to see my new invention..." His voice trails off. He must have sensed that he walked in on a private moment. "Please excuse the interruption."

I push away from the table and stand, and Asher does the same immediately.

"Not at all," I say, "I would love to see your workshop." I turn to Asher, "Thank you for the conversation."

"The pleasure is mine."

Sam's eyebrows rise and he throws me a look. I ignore the question and say, "Lead the way."

I follow Sam towards the drawing room, giving Asher a backward glance. He is staring at me, hands balled at his side. He dips his chin, and I smile.

30

*B*eside Sam's cottage is a path leading into a heavily wooded area. I follow him tentatively. I do not wish to offend Colette by abandoning the party. But my curiosity drives me forward, lantern in hand. Soon, the path becomes littered with wood, metal, wagon wheels, and rusting metal objects I cannot identify. Sam seems unconcerned about the mess as he leads me to a small hut under a thicket of bushes.

As he reaches for the door handle, he seems to remember himself. The door and entire workshop are gnome-sized, with a moss-covered roof and small windows on two sides. Unless he had an invention to reduce my height, I won't be able to enter. "It appears I did not think this through," he says.

I smile. "It is all right. I can watch through the door if you'd like to show me what you are working on."

He blusters for a moment, clearly unsettled by his lack of foresight. I place a reassuring hand on his shoulder. "No worries, my friend. I am delighted to see your workshop."

"Yes, well, right then." He enters and flits around the shop, turning on the oil lamps.

As each light begins to blaze, it unveils more of what I picture as the inside of Sam's mind. There are crates and supplies stacked everywhere, floor to ceiling. In the middle of the room, he has carved out a table for working. I kneel to get a better view of the space.

On the table is what appears to be a cider press. But the basket for the apples is missing. In its place are two large pieces of wood with parchment peeking out from the edges. "What is that?" I ask.

Sam pushes his glasses up on his nose, "This is my creation." On top of the machine is a bar that, when spun, lifts the top piece of wood. I watch, spellbound, as he slides the parchment from between the blocks and shows me what he has made. On the paper is a line of symbols. I squint, and he steps closer to the door. It looks like a dragon, then another dragon, then a sun, a stick, and finally a dragon.

"What does it mean?" I ask.

He looks at the parchment and then to me, "Isn't it obvious?"

I smile and shake my head, "No, actually." When his face falls, I continue, "It could be me. I am terrible at puzzles and games." That's a lie. I am excellent at both. But clearly, he is pleased with his accomplishment, and I don't want to steal his joy.

"Ah, I understand." He lowers the parchment so he can point to the symbols. "Dragon, Dragon, Sun, Stick, Dragon." He looks up to me as if his explanation is sufficient.

I grimace and bite my lip.

He lets out an exasperated sigh, "Two dragons, next sunrise, jousting with lance, one dragon wins." He sweeps a hand out in front of him, as if all of this should be obvious.

"Oh, but what *is it*?" I ask. Perhaps it is art? Although it seems simple to be considered art.

He tosses the parchment on the table and retreats to the press. "It's a printing press." He begins to explain how it works. "I use blocks of wood to carve shapes. Next, I slide them into grooves on the bottom board. Then brush ink onto the raised shapes. When I press down, the images show up on the parchment. I can make many of the same print. It will be quite useful."

I rack my brain to think of ways to utilize this machine. "Of course," I say. The machine itself was impressive. How he might use it, I am not sure. But if anyone can figure it out, it's Sam.

He brushes his hands off on his pants. "We had best get back."

I wait for him to dim the lanterns and meet me outside. "Your mind is astounding," I say as we walk to the house.

"You have the mind of a scientist, Livvy. You're curious, and curiosity will lead you down all sorts of unexplored roads."

I smile. This is one of the best compliments I could receive. "Thank you."

"Although it's a burden along with a blessing. Colette appreciates my idiosyncrasies. But she is a rare gem."

I trip over a tree root and push my hand against the rough bark to keep from falling. He doesn't seem to notice my stumble, and I race to catch up to him. "You and Colette have a love story to envy."

He turns to smile at me, "I agree. But what about you? Is there anyone you admire?"

Asher. "Not at the moment," I say.

He continues to walk and says, "The village is teaming with young men. What about Asher, he seems a pleasant enough fellow."

"He is quite pleasant." I agree, thinking of his shy admissions earlier.

Sam pauses to inspect a tin bowl sitting on the ground next to a rock. "And he is a loyal companion. He recently came to the aid of his best friend and kept him from making a disastrous decision."

"Who was the man?" I ask, my voice pitched higher than usual.

"Thaddeus Cedar. Asher prevented him from sure heartbreak by a woman unbefitting of his serious attention."

"How would she have broken his heart?"

"Apparently, she did not share his strong feelings. It is assumed she pursued Thaddeus for his station, not for love."

"So he separated them?"

He nods. "Yes, to spare Thaddeus from heartbreak."

Surely he is speaking of Marinn. Sam knows Marinn is not a fortune hunter. But my mortification over the entire affair keeps my confession silent. We reach the side of the cottage and can hear laughter coming from inside. I grit my teeth against the anger that roars inside my head. How dare he? He does not know Marinn. He does not know her character or heart. All I want is to get as far away from Asher as possible. I can't bear to see his face.

Sam opens the door and turns to find me paused in the yard. "Are you quite well? Would you like to come inside?"

I blow a breath out of my nose, "No, thank you. It has been a lovely evening, but I fear I must head home."

His brow furrows with concern. "Are you ill?"

"No… yes," I stammer, "I have a bit of a headache coming on. Please give my regards to Colette for an excellent dinner." Before he can respond, I turn on my heel and stride down the path and away from Asher.

31

The following day, I'm filing the claws on a Red Kurenti when his low growl gives me pause. I check to ensure I haven't nicked the rough leather hide on his feet. Finding nothing, I look to see if he has noticed something amiss. I scan the treeline, my pulse speeding at the memory of the night with Marinn. The village established patrols to ensure the safety of the tournament guests and maintain a general sense of order. Still, I remain on guard.

A moment later, I see what the dragon had been growling about. Emerging from the path into the clearing is Asher. He is wearing his flight leathers and strides towards me, his long coat billowing behind him. What is he doing here? Another growl rumbles through the dragon.

Does his pride know no bounds? You cannot simply approach a dragon at random. I return my clippers and claw file to my belt and pat the top of the dragon's foot. I stand and say to Asher, "You are brave approaching a dragon to which you are unknown." My voice has a sharp, chill edge.

He pauses and glances nervously at the Red Kurenti. "I was hoping I might have a moment of your time."

"All right." I look down at my skirts, my hem soaked in mud. Not that anything can be done about it. My hand goes to smooth my hair, which I'm sure looks a fright. What am I doing? I do not care about his regard. He has done nothing but bring pain and disappointment. I move towards where he has paused and meet his gaze. "What can you have to say to me?"

His throat bobs, and he swallows as if gathering his courage. Laughable. Is this man who flies on fire-breathing dragons nervous? For what reason? I cross my arms and raise my eyebrows, waiting.

"Livinia, I have come here today because I can stand it no longer. Despite your lack of magic, mortal background, and rough associations, I am drawn to you. You fill my thoughts." He runs a hand through his hair.

What in the world is he talking about? He has done nothing but demonstrate strained tolerance where I am concerned. "Asher..."

He raises a hand to stop me. "Wait. I must say this." He takes a deep breath. "You are not what my family would choose for me. You have never traveled our lands beyond this village. Your family is of little standing in the mortal lands. Perhaps you are betrothed to another; perhaps you never plan to marry. I do not know. But if you are free and willing, I must say that despite all the shortcomings of your station, I desire to know you more with the goal of marriage."

He leans towards me, and I resist the urge to step backward. He clenches his jaw and then continues, "Please end my distress by saying you feel the same."

My palms sweat. My nose itches. The Red Kurenti chuffs impatiently, and I glance over my shoulder to ensure he isn't too agitated. Turning back to Asher, I watch as his eyes flit to the ground and then to mine. I study his face and consider what he has said. If you focus on the end of his sentiment, it sounds potentially romantic. But it came at the expense of a tirade of insults, adding to the insult of his interference with Marinn. On the whole, this is a terrible declaration of love.

I clear my throat. "I appreciate the struggle you have been through. I must say that your manner of declaration is quite surprising. You come here and insult me, my family, my dearest friend, and my station. Is that how you normally court women, Asher? If so, you are terrible at it."

His eyes flash for a second, and his spine stiffens. "Is that your answer? You think me a fool?"

I scoff. Is he offended? He is the one who issued the offense. "No. You are not a fool. But your pride will be the death of your endeavors, at least with me. And I have other reasons to reject you."

"What other reasons could you have?"

"Do you think I would ever take an interest in a man who has dashed the hopes of my best friend by taking away the one man she loves? She cried in my arms for days."

He shifts on his feet. "I regret that she was hurt. My efforts were in loyalty to Thaddeus, who has fended off many women in search of fortune and fame. I feared she could be counted among them."

"Why would you think that?"

"I watched her closely. She showed no more interest in Thaddeus than she displayed for a dozen other young men in the village."

His words snag on the truth of the observation. But he did not know her character. "She is friendly and engaging with everyone. The fact that she was shy around Thaddeus is precisely the indication that her feelings were sincere and deeply rooted. Now she has joined Julian in the wake of your prideful destruction."

Asher takes a step backward. "Julian?"

"How can you explain your treatment of him?"

Asher runs a hand across his chin, "As I said before, we do not get along. The kindest thing I can say is that he makes friends easily."

I bite my cheek and then say, "Yes, and you do not- for reasons that remain an eternal and incomprehensible mystery."

Asher sighs. "I do not like to speak ill of my colleagues. You're being uncharitable to put me in this position, but if you must know, Julian has repeatedly broken my trust. Saying this brings me no pleasure, but it seems the least I can do since you have delighted in painting me as a monster.

"Is that it? You have no defense?" I lift my chin and land the final blow. "Your treatment of not only my best friend but also Julian is indefensible. There can be no adequate explanation. You are the last man I would ever be interested in."

"You misunderstand my intention. Please give me a chance to explain."

"I have heard all I need to know." I turn on my heel to resume my work.

"So that is your opinion of me?" he asks.

I stop, but do not move to face him.

"I see," he continues. "If you find me this reprehensible, rest assured, I will not repeat the sentiments I have expressed this day."

I can feel Asher's eyes on me momentarily before he turns and leaves without another word. I hold my breath as his steps disappear. Pain grips my chest, and I press my palm to my breastbone and attempt to slow my pounding heart. How could he show up and ambush me with insults? And what, a proposal?

Irritation drives me forward to the waiting dragon. I lift

the nail I had been attending to and retrieve my file, shaping the claw into a smooth curve.

This entire conversation has been an exercise in futility. He vexes me so. I detest letting my anger rule good sense. It is done now. My mind narrows to the task at hand, pushing out the thoughts of Asher. The only residue from our conversation is the silent, conflicted tears I wipe away with my sleeve.

32

"I cannot believe you are abandoning me," Mr. Bennet says, licking his paw.

"I am not abandoning you. You are perfectly capable of caring for yourself. Sam will be over to let you out later this morning and ensure you are safely in tonight."

Mr. Bennet rolls over onto his back and wiggles against the carpet. "Let's not pretend he could ever replace you. But I suppose he will have to do."

I sling my satchel over my shoulder and cross the room to scratch Mr. Bennet behind the ear. "I shall miss you every moment."

He pushes his head into my hand and purrs. He really is the best companion I could have asked for. Who needs a man when I have him?

This trip has come at the perfect time to distract me from my conversation with Asher. I wish Marinn were here. Last night I had penned her a letter and dropped it at the tavern. My words had been as messy as my heart.

Each time I try to sort my feelings, I become lost in the tangle of emotions. Asher has turned me inside out. He has vexed me beyond measure. If he had merely declared his love without qualifiers, would I have accepted him? No matter. I shall likely never see him again outside of my responsibility to his dragon.

I pull the cabin door closed and turn to find the sky painted with hues of yellow, orange, and magenta, the sun still low behind the mountains. A thin layer of ice coats the porch, which I discover when my boot slips and I comically stumble before finding purchase.

Kessia, Orthello, and Captain are waiting with horses, all three struggling not to laugh at my folly. I clear my throat and school my face. "Well, met," I say to the group.

Kessia beams with excitement. "Well met." She is clothed in a sheepskin coat and black leather pants.

Orthello steps forward, reins in his hand, "This is Clover. I brought you a gentle horse for the ride. I was not sure how experienced you were at riding."

"Thank you. I have ridden, but it has been a while," I admit. Trepidation slows my steps towards the light brown mare. If I can groom dragons, I should not be afraid of a horse. But then again, I don't ride the dragons.

My mount seems peaceful enough. I can absolutely handle this. "Oh," I say, slipping my hand into the satchel for the extra apple I brought for her. "Here you go." I present the apple to Clover, and she sniffs the fruit, then pulls back her lips and chomps it down with one bite.

I pat the side of the flank, and then Orthello stands by as I step up into the stirrup and swing my leg over. I am grateful for my pants, unacceptable for a woman in Tevyne, but fine here. They certainly make riding easier. I shift in the saddle, getting used to the feel of being on horseback again.

We follow the path up the mountains, rising with the sun. The route is quite different on this edge of Eshan, with gentle slopes and easy riding. I long to speak with Kessia about Asher, but now is not the time. The peaceful silence of the morning is interrupted by Orthello clearing his throat and beginning to sing off-key and with no discernible melody.

"There once was a sailor brave and true.
　　Upon the seas he heard a tune
　　A maiden voice so fair and light
　　He said I'll marry you."

My horse shakes her head, as if trying to get Orthello's voice out of her ears. I lean forward and whisper, "Hang in there. It cannot go on forever."

I hear a snort and catch Kessia choking on a laugh. We both smile, and Orthello looks at us, mistakes our smiles for encouragement, and launches into the next verse.

"They married on a moonless night
　　He never saw her face alight
　　She dragged him to the sea below
　　A siren song was her delight."

My brows furrow. For being a romantic and aspiring wedding singer, that song seems a bit depressing. "Is that an ancient tale?" I ask.

Orthello puffs out his chest. "Indeed."

"To sing at weddings?" Kessia asks, catching my eye.

"Of course. It is a standard during ceremonies in Jura."

Captain nods in agreement. There are so many things in the Fae lands that remain a mystery to me. I have learned to accept the odd traditions as being somewhat unknowable.

We crest the hill and begin our descent. In front of me, the plains stretch out to the horizon. A village is visible in the distance. "Is that where we are headed?" I ask, pointing.

"No," Orthello says. "You don't want to go anywhere near there."

"Why?" Kessia asks, pushing a branch to the side as she passes under an Iron Wood tree.

"If you make it to the village, you'll face a coven of witches who would consider you a tasty morsel. But the other issue is what lies between the mountains and the witches."

I strain to identify any manner of creature on the plains below, but can see nothing. Perhaps tree spirits? They punish trespassing in their groves most brutally. Or root folk? Root folk ensnare passersby and slowly absorb them into the root system, trapping them forever.

"Forget-me-not mushroom sprites. They live under mushroom caps and feed off memories. They cause confusion, hallucinations, and complete amnesia. They are terribly wicked," Orthello says.

"I had a cousin who was simply out to pick some apples when she came across a forget-me-not," Captain says. "When she returned, she had been convinced she was a fairy princess, and let me tell you, a princess she was not. Even by my standards, she was most unfortunate-looking."

"So what became of her?" I ask. It did not sound so terrible to believe you were a princess. It could have been much worse.

"Ahh, I know what you are thinking." He wags a finger at me. "A fairy princess might sound like an innocent delusion, but it did not end well for her. She went straight to the local dressmaker and demanded a new gown, which she could not pay for. When the dressmaker, a cranky old hag, refused her, the situation escalated. My cousin pulled a blade, and the dressmaker responded by stabbing her in the neck with a needle. It was quite terrible."

"*Berries*," I say.

"Aye, her story has become lore by which we warn children."

I nod. "We have such stories in Straume as well."

We are quiet as we navigate a rocky outcropping. When the entire party is safely through the switchback, Kessia asks me, "Were you told many stories about the Fae?"

"Ma focused her tales on changelings and dragons, ever trying to dissuade my interest in the Fae lands."

Kessia rides beside me, smirking. "I imagine she was not pleased when you became a dragon groomer."

"Indeed. She would rather I be tucked away in a cottage near her, children on my hip and a husband in my bed."

"She's proud of your work in the tournament, isn't she?" Captain asks.

I press my lips together. Is she proud of me? "She does not show pride easily, and when she does, it is most certainly directed to my sisters."

Our group slips into silence, awkward at first, but then becomes comfortable as we approach the valley floor.

"There's a stream ahead where we can stop for the horses," Orthello says, pointing towards a copse of trees to the south. "The portal is just a bit further after that."

My stomach clenches, and Kessia meets my eyes. Neither of us has any idea what is involved with using a portal, or even what a portal looks like. We have only traveled by horse or by foot. According to Marinn's books, portals can be anything from a door to a tin cup. I hope the experience is not nauseating.

We continue to ride, and sure enough, there is a crystal blue stream running through a tangle of trees. The thick canopy shades our approach, and I am so thankful to slide my sore rump off the horse. My legs are stiff, and I take a few moments while my horse drinks to stretch my spine and legs.

What is Asher doing today? Is he still in the village? My

face heats. Has there been a worse proposal in the history of the world? I venture to say not.

"How does the portal work?" Kessia asks, bending down to fill her water skin from the stream.

"It is most convenient," says Orthello. "We will ride through a cavern and come out on the other side close to our destination."

"Really?" I ask.

Orthello nods. "We can take the horses and ride through. It will feel no different than our journey thus far."

Relief replaces the anxiety I had not fully acknowledged. I fill my water skin and hang it over my neck. My hair is less cooperative than usual, so I untie the leather strap and redo my braid. I wet my fingers and smooth the strands from my face.

"We'd better get on," Captain says, climbing onto his horse.

We all follow suit, and it is mere minutes before we are faced with a hill rising from the plateau at a sharp incline. A cave stands directly in front of us, pitch black and ominous. Even my horse must sense possible unknown danger as she slows to a halt and stomps her front hooves. Orthello notices our hesitancy.

"Easy, girl," Orthello says to my horse. "Once we enter the portal, mage lights will guide our path. Nothing to worry about."

He's right. As we ride into the cave, with Othello leading, lanterns flicker to life on the edge of our path. It is mere minutes before we see light on the far end of the cavern. Even with the mage lights, the walls of the cave seem to close in on me as I ride. My breath is coming in shallow gulps when we finally exit the tunnel. Breaking into the sunlight, I am greeted by a spectacular view.

33

Every nerve in my body is on edge as I take in the scene of unfettered magic. It is as different from Eshan as Eshan is from the human lands. A forest stretches out before us, with the sun peeking down through the canopy. The trees seem to touch the sky as their branches intertwine with gnarled branches and thick vines that hang across the path.

I pause next to Kessia as we wait for Captain to emerge from the tunnel. "Do they let you pick the tattoo design, or is there a special style they must use?" I ask.

"I am not sure. If I am given the option to choose, I think I would like a flame vine or perhaps a rose."

I nod. "Both would suit you well."

She turns to me. "You're getting one too. I insist."

"I haven't decided." Dragons seem unaffected by gold, so it would not interfere with my duties. After the mysterious growling in the woods, it couldn't hurt to add another layer of protection. But what sort of marking should I have done? If there is an option, I should have an idea before we arrive. Hopefully, inspiration will strike along the road.

"We are a mere half hour from Kaimas," Orthello says.

As we ride, the world seems to sharpen into focus. It's as if the more concentrated the magic is, the more it affects my senses. Fragrant star flower and stone sage grow along the path. Birds sing symphonies instead of mere songs. I cannot wait to see if the tales of water wielders and spell casters are true.

My cloak lies in front of me across the horse, the warmth of the midday sun causing a sheen to break across my brow. Beside me, Kessia grins as she drinks from her water skin. "Are you glad you joined me on this adventure?"

"Indeed. I am most pleased." I tip my chin to the sky, letting the sun soak into my skin.

We come to a clearing, and a city wall rises before us. It is massive stacked stone stretching as far as I can see in either direction. Down to the left is a gate made of vertically stacked tree trunks. The gate is large enough for any cart or caravan to pass through. Kessia and I share a grin, both of us giddy with anticipation. I am ready to sally forth, but Captain pulls his horse to a stop.

"There are some warnings I am compelled to relay before we enter the gates."

I turned my horse to face him, not wanting to miss any portion of his speech.

"We shall go straight to the tattooist without haste. Then we can visit the markets. Under no circumstances are you to leave our party and wander off." He pauses before continuing, "There is more than one creature behind those gates that would gladly take a human girl for nefarious purposes."

I nod. My heart races with fear or excitement, I cannot tell which.

"That's enough warning, these women are not foolish girls who will ride off with the first man to crook his finger at them," Orthello says.

"Fair enough," Captain replies, then turns his horse and heads for the gates.

I raise my eyebrows at Kessia, who rolls her eyes and moves to follow Captain.

As we approach the gates, the sound of a large chain begins to grind, and the doors slide open, revealing the city beyond. Directly inside the gate is a courtyard of stone, and beyond are buildings of all shapes and sizes bustling with all manner of people. Heavily armored dwarves man the gates, working a complex pulley system to close the doors as soon as we are through.

A pair of halfling women skip across the path in front of us, their shoeless hairy feet peeking out from simple linen dresses. Their joy is contagious, and I can't help but smile.

A beautiful black-haired elf woman hangs tapestries on a rope strung outside her shop. An orc drives a cart of bleating sheep. My senses are overwhelmed with the sights and smells flooding the city.

"Come along, Livvy," Orthello says.

I turn to see Kessia and Captain are already riding ahead, disappearing into the throngs of people. I give my horse a squeeze with my thighs, and she follows Orthello.

Soon, we are caught in the current of activity and swept towards the center of the city. We pass shops of every kind, apothecaries, dress shops, wand shops, tea houses, filling the block. After a bit, we turn down an alley and see Kessia and Captain tying their horses to a post in front of a darkened tavern that appears to be closed. They wait for us to catch up, and then I take a moment to survey the area.

The alley is empty, but for a hunched-over creature, face hidden by a cloak, sticking close to the wall across from us. It is the first creature I have seen here that causes the hair to rise on my arms. I take a step closer to Orthello, who is untying a saddle bag from his horse and throwing it over his shoulder.

"This way," Captain says. He leads us down a narrow space between the buildings to a side door of the tavern. Orthello's shoulders brush the sides of both buildings, and he grunts as he maneuvers past a board that has come loose.

Again, Captain pauses and turns to us, and I expect another warning. "When we go into the shop, please do not be alarmed by the appearance of the tattooist. She is," he clears his throat, "a witch."

Kessia sucks in a breath. Witches are a thing of nightmares for humans. They will hunt and kill humans for sport. A single coven can destroy an entire village. Some believe they hide in the human lands. Others believe they wait for humans to wander into the Fae lands and herd them like cattle for slaughter. Cunning, cruel, and callous, witches strike fear in my heart.

Do we absolutely need these tattoos? Is there no other option? I would never have agreed to come if I had known. Kessia shifts on her feet, and I can see she is facing the same struggle. "Is it safe?" I ask. I trust Captain and Orthello with my life. They would never steer me wrong.

Orthello chuckles. "Safe is as safe does."

That does not fill me with confidence.

"I am not sure this is a good idea," Kessia says, biting her thumbnail.

"Nothing to worry about," Captain says. "She is a half breed. Half human, to be exact. Her father was from your lands. He found a witch in the woods, near death. Despite the danger, he took her to his cabin and cared for her. Against all odds, they fell in love and had Ragana. Eventually, the witch was called back to her coven. Ragana grew up in the human lands, tucked away from society to protect her."

Orthello nods and strokes his beard, "Only came here

when her father died. Been tattooing for as long as I can remember. Long-lived, witches, even half-bloods"

With that, Captain pounds his fist on the door three times and steps back, straightening his tunic.

The door creaks open to reveal a sitting room most unexpected.

34

A woman with long white hair loosely braided down her back, white irises with just the barest hint of lavender, and porcelain skin stands before us. She looks nothing like what I imagined a witch to be. She appears no older than I am. She is dressed in a lilac gossamer gown tied with a gold sash. Her smile reveals the witch's heritage, her teeth terrifyingly lethal points. "Ah, well met. My name is Ragana. Please come inside." Her voice is like honey, casting a calm over me that is unnerving.

We step into her sitting room, a remarkable, cheery room with tiny rose wallpaper and bookshelves filled with tomes, jars, and trinkets.

"You are here for magical protection, I presume?" Ragana asks. Her fingernails are razor sharp and painted black.

Kessia and I nod.

"Very well, please have a seat." She points to a pale pink ruffled settee, and we obey. "You men can go into the kitchen. I have some freshly baked bread in there for you."

Orthello and Captain immediately abandon us. I scoff. My confidence in their protection is faltering if a loaf of bread can lure them away. What do we really know about this woman? She could have enchanted the bread or mixed in herbs that would harm them.

"Do you have a desired image to hold the tattoo? If not, I can propose a few options." She raises her eyebrows and waits.

I rub my sweaty palms on my pants. There is no doubt what I will choose for my image. But before I can speak, Kessia does. "A skull and crossbones, please." She smiles triumphantly at me. "Isn't that a fantastically eerie choice?"

"Indeed," I reply. Then I meet Ragana's eyes, "A dragon."

She gives us a brief nod and smiles. "As you wish."

For the next hour, Ragana uses her pointed fingernails to carve into our skin, adding a gold tint to the open wound and then healing it almost instantly with her magic. I watch, entranced, as she works. There is no pain besides a tingling sensation. When she finishes, I survey the shimmering outline of a dragon on my forearm.

Kessia holds up her arm, grinning at me. "Isn't it terrifying?"

I chuckle. We both thank Ragana and present our coins for payment.

She snatches them from our hands and slips them into her pocket.

Orthello and Captain reappear in the sitting room. Crumbs litter Orthello's beard as he shoves a piece of bread into his mouth.

"Did you eat all of her bread?" Kessia asks.

"Were we not supposed to?" Orthello asks, his mouth full.

Captain elbows him. "I told you we should have but one slice each."

Ragana waves them off. "It is easy enough to bake more. I am glad you enjoyed it."

As we exit the alley and make our way back to the horses,

I ponder the strange meeting. I have never met a witch before. Ragana is a peculiar mix of youthful beauty and grandmotherly affection. But when I glimpse her pointed teeth and nails I remember that she is a predator, or has the potential to be one. Still, I am so pleased to have met her. The added layer of protection from the tattoo is welcomed even as we traverse the city.

The next few hours are spent in a flurry of dashing into shops and bartering with street vendors at the market. Captain watches the horses while we fill our saddle bags with the spoils of our efforts. My favorite shop is the bakery we wander into after my stomach rumbles so loud, Kessia crooks an eyebrow at me.

The bakery is like nothing I have ever seen. A large display case is filled with chocolates of every type and size. There are small enchanted chocolate dragons that hop around and flap their wings. An army of chocolate soldiers with swords, crossbows, and maces stands guard. I wonder if they battle?

"Did you see these?" Kessia asks, drawing my attention to a barrel on the other side of the shop. "Gingerroot everdrops"

"What are those?" I've never heard of such a thing.

"I have no idea." She lifts the lid and plucks out a small semitransparent ball.

"You touch it, you buy it," says a squeaky voice. We turn to find a gnome woman sliding a tray of freshly baked cookies into the display case.

"Of course," Kessia agrees, "But what exactly is a Gingerroot everdrop?"

The gnome woman clucks her tongue. "Just as it sounds. A Gingerroot drop that never disappears." She seems to consider for a second and then says, "Actually, never is a very long time." She holds up a finger. "It will last for at least a year. And that's a good bargain."

Kessia and I grin. "Indeed," she says, taking her Gingerroot everdrop to the counter for purchase.

I could spend all day in this one shop, but the hour is getting late, and this is our last stop. After picking out some cookies, a chocolate bar for Marinn, and a chocolate dragon for myself, Kessia and I pay for our items and proceed outside. "Do you think the dragon will still be enchanted when we get home?" I ask.

Kessia shakes her head. "Probably not. But it should still taste delicious."

I hold up the box that contains my chocolate pet. I can hear him hopping around inside, his wings flapping.

We ride out of the city, quieter now that the dinner hour is near. As we approach the city gate, a roar fills the air. Our party glances nervously at each other. Orthello takes the lead, preparing to head off danger if needed. The roars are intermingled with shouting. Something is definitely amiss.

As we emerge from between the buildings, the situation becomes clear. A small Copper Veris dragon stands on its hind legs, a thick chain around its neck being held by three Fae men who are attempting to lead the dragon out of the gate. As we ride closer, I can see the dragon has an angry red patch underneath its scales on the side of its neck. No wonder it is furious. Do these men not know even the very basics of dragon care?

I grit my teeth. As we approach, I slide off my horse and wait for Kessia to dismount before handing her the reins. After a beat, I decide to sacrifice part of the chocolate bar as an offering. Copper Veris dragons have a taste for human food, and who doesn't love chocolate? Marinn will certainly understand.

I slowly approach the dragon. The dragon sniffs, and her eyes move to my hand holding the chocolate. Then she dips her head briefly in acknowledgment.

"Step away, miss," one of the handlers says, eyes shifting in my direction.

I keep my voice even and calm. "It is all right. I am a trained dragon groomer."

"She is quite dangerous. Please stay back."

I smile. This is not the first time men have underestimated me. It isn't worth trying to explain my expertise. An object lesson is often the best approach in these situations. I ignore the handlers and proceed, pausing to break the chocolate bar in half and slipping the partial bar into my pocket. I hold the treat in my hand, bow my head, and continue my mission. I must get a closer look at her scales. If there is an issue, that would explain her obstinate behavior.

When I am within the distance of the chain length, I stop. Then I extend my flattened hand. The dragon stops pulling on the chain and settles. I am sure she is considering me, but I dare not look up. She chuffs, and I see her feet turn towards me. I slow my breathing. Although I have been around dozens of dragons, a sliver of fear is always present upon a new interaction. A healthy respect for dragons is essential for any dragon groomer.

The ground rumbles as the dragon steps closer. The handlers and spectators have grown silent, probably anticipating my demise. Goodness, I hope they are wrong. I swallow the lump in my throat and lift my gaze to meet those of the dragon. She lowers her maw and sniffs the chocolate. I push my hand out further in encouragement. She snatches the chocolate from my hand, and I wait to see how she will respond.

She sits back on her haunches and stares at me.

"My name is Livvy. I'm a dragon groomer, and I'd like to check your scales. I believe you may have an injury that is likely causing you pain."

The dragon lowers her maw and proceeds to lie down. As she lowers her body, I stumble backwards to give her room. When she settled, I moved to her side, where the scales had drawn my attention. People around me begin to mumble. I am sure they expected to see me devoured.

"Miss, we must insist you move away from the dragon," a blond Fae man says. His voice carries a note of desperation. Is he concerned for my well-being or about my being proven right in front of a crowd? Likely the latter. These men are prideful to a fault. Either way, I shall not be moving away from the dragon until I am able to examine her.

Sure enough, as I examine the scales, there is a thorn lodged deep into her hide. The flesh around the thorn is inflamed, and if it is not removed, infection will follow. No wonder she was irritated. How had these men missed this? "Please stay still. I will return promptly."

A low growl rumbles from the dragon. As I cross to my horse to retrieve the small tool kit I always carry, the handler strides toward me. "Have you found something?"

I only pause for a moment before continuing to my horse, where I unlatch my saddle bag and rummage for my kit. My hands shake. How dare they chain this beautiful creature, not even attempting to communicate with compassion and ignoring her obvious injury?

"Did you not hear my question? I must demand an answer. This is my dragon."

Who is this impertinent person demanding things from me? With my kit in my hand, I turn around to investigate. His arms are crossed before him, and he scowls at me.

"You must?" I spit, "That is fascinating. I must help an

obviously injured dragon that you insist on disrespecting." I shoulder him out of the way and return to the dragon. He matches me stride for stride.

"I do not disrespect my dragon. You can have no true understanding of the bond between a dragon and rider. If there is an injury, I did not intentionally ignore her plight." He grabs my elbow and pulls me to a stop. "So please, explain what injury you speak of."

I brush my hair from my face and explain my findings. He shifts on his feet, casting a furtive glance toward the dragon, still resting comfortably. "What can I do to assist?"

I blink rapidly, processing his change in demeanor. "Um, perhaps you can help me keep her calm. I need to remove the splinter, and you will need to retrieve a poultice for her irritated skin. The apothecary should have what you need."

He dips his head. "Thank you. I do care for my dragon a great deal. We have been through many trials together."

His words are water to the fire burning behind my eyes. "It is easy to miss. I am the dragon groomer for the Drakonas tournament, so I am adept at quickly assessing possible injury."

He stands behind me as I begin to work the splinter out of the dragon using my recently acquired tweezers.

"You have met the riders and dragons?" he asks.

I nod. "All of them."

"I hope that some of them have made a better impression on you than I did, with my shameful oversight," he says.

"Some are certainly more agreeable than others." I inspect the sliver from different angles to decide upon the best approach.

"Ah, you are speaking of Asher Covington without speaking of him, aren't you?"

Heat rises in my cheeks at his name. "Do you know him?" I ask. Perhaps this man can give me some insight into Asher's character. The dragon groans as I press deeper into her hide. This sliver is stubborn.

"We went to school together, though it was long ago. I can't imagine he's changed much."

"He's just as disagreeable now as I'm sure he ever was." The sliver might come out in one piece if I am careful. If it breaks, there is a chance that part of it might remain embedded and could cause an infection.

"He has his own opinion and his own way of doing things, but his honor was always steadfast. I would take honor over agreeableness, any day."

I start to work my way around the sliver with the tweezers. If I can loosen the area, it will come out easier. I am also keenly aware of the unique opportunity I have with this man to gather insight into Asher and possibly Julian. "Did you know Julian Kilric? He is also in the tournament and grew up with Asher."

"I did."

I lick my lips. I wish I had brought my canteen with me. "Were you his friend?"

There is a pause before he responds. "I wouldn't call myself such. He kept others at a distance as a rule, but left school suddenly after some accusations were made."

I turn to look at him. "Accusations?"

He holds his hands up in defense. "More rumors than accusations. I cannot be sure. With enchantment magic, it is hard to prove fault." He leans in to inspect my progress. "Will you be able to help her?"

Julian has enchantment magic? I tuck that information away and turn my attention back to the dragon. "Of course."

After a few minutes, I am finally able to extract the sliver in one piece. It is at least three inches long. How did she manage to get this so deeply embedded? I hold the sliver up for her rider. He sucks in a breath. "That is awful. How can I thank you?"

I stand up and slip the tools and sliver into my bag—a slow rumble of applause ripples across the courtyard. I ignore the crowd and pat the dragon on the side to let her know we are finished. "The best thing you can do is care for your dragon. Go to the apothecary and purchase the appropriate medicine right away."

He smiles, "Of course. If you see Asher, please tell him his old mate Ovin says hello."

"Of course," I say. I hope never to see Asher Covington again. His smile comes with unnecessarily complicated feelings. Then my nose tickles and I sneeze twice.

I return to the group and climb onto my horse.

"That was impressive," Orthello says.

"Yes, I thought we were about to see you burned to death," Captain says, patting his forehead with a handkerchief.

I arrange myself in the saddle and reach down for my canteen, drinking deeply.

"I had no doubt you would be fine," Kessia says, beaming.

"Thank you." My throat is scratchy, and I take another drink of water. "I think I have had enough of the city for now." As much as I have enjoyed the experience, I yearn for my cottage and my bed.

Captain strokes his beard, "Yes, I'd like to be home in time to enjoy a mug of ale with my wife."

Orthello nods and clucks twice, causing his horse to turn and head towards the gates. We follow him with Captain in the rear of our party. We ride back to the portal and arrive just as the sun is setting. The passage through the tunnel is less disconcerting than earlier. I ruminate on the revelations from the dragon rider. At least I can be sure Julian was not using his magic on me. He doesn't need it. He is charming enough on his own. How awful to be accused of misdeeds just because of your magic. At least he confirmed my opinion of Asher being disagreeable. Overall, the trip was quite enlightening.

My heart swells with a sense of accomplishment. I have officially traveled beyond the valley, used a magical portal, and received my first tattoo.

ong after dark, I collapse into my bed, my backside and legs aching from the long ride. I fitfully sleep and then wake up sometime during the night, covered in sweat. Throwing off the covers, I push myself to sit, and my skin instantly pebbles from the chill. A coughing fit erupts from my heavy lungs. Mr. Bennet lifts his head in concern. "Are you quite all right?"

I shake my head. That is all I can muster as a response before I roll to the other side of the mattress, where the blankets are not soaked, and curl up into a fetal position. I wish Ma were here. She was always attentive when we were sick, ready with a cool cloth or remedy.

My teeth begin to chatter. Soon, I feel the warmth of Mr. Bennet curling up against the small of my back. It soothes me, and I drift into a fevered sleep.

My dreams are filled with monsters hidden in the woods, growling and following me. I run and run, but they keep catching me.

When next I wake, I stay wrapped in a blanket, slip on my boots, and venture out to the outhouse. While the door is open, Mr. Bennet slips out and races into the woods. "Traitor," I mumble.

He has still not returned, as I force myself to build a fire. My nose is dripping, and coughing fits wrack my body. The fire takes every bit of my energy, so I drop into a chair by the hearth and pull the blanket tight around my shoulders. I wish Julian were here. I could use some cheering. Even as I think it, Asher's face flashes in my mind. At some point, I doze off again and awaken to a knock on my door.

My voice is raspy when I call out, "Come in."

Kessia's smooth black hair appears at the door. "Oh, Livvy. You look awful."

I smile weakly. "Thank you."

She has a satchel with her and sets it on the table. She lifts the flap and fishes inside to retrieve bottles of tonics and tins of creams.

"How did you know I was ill?" I ask.

She unscrews the top from a tin, and the faint smell of eucalyptus fills my nostrils, starting to work its way through the stuffiness. She hands me the cream, and I scoop out a fingerful and rub it under my nose. A second dose gets shoved down my tunic and over my lungs. Once I take a decent breath, she says, "Aside from watching you sneeze the entire journey home last night, Mr. Bennet came scratching on my door and would not desist until I answered his call. He told me you were ill, so I stopped at the apothecary first thing."

My eyes swim with tears, and I quickly wipe them away. I detest emotionalism when I'm sick.

"Oh, sweet friend, don't cry. It leaves your face splotchy." She smiles and hands me a handkerchief from her pocket. "Is there anything wrong other than your fever-induced sorrow?"

I slump into the chair. "I am unsure, though I'm under a

lot of stress. There's still so much to be done for the tournament. Marinn returns soon, and I can't begin to imagine if her trip went the way she hoped it would. And now I cannot even stand without the world spinning."

Kessia crosses to the water jug and sets the pot to boil. "A cup of tea, a few days' rest, and you'll be ready for battle."

I manage a chuckle. "For someone who appears as if you could take down a Mammoth Lokys all on your own, you can be quite sweet." She is a contrast to Marinn, who looks sweet, but can be fierce if challenged.

Kessia stokes the fire. "Don't you dare tell anyone. It would completely ruin my reputation." When the kettle starts to boil, she pours two cups and adds pouches of medicinal tea.

When she delivers the tea, she sits across from me and holds my gaze until I shift in my seat. "Why are you staring at me? Is my appearance that dreadful?"

She rubs her finger along the edge of the cup. "No. I do have a question for you."

My back aches. All of my muscles ache, and this chair is not helping. "You are welcome to ask as long as I can retreat to my bed."

I hobble across the cottage carrying my tea and sigh when my bones sink into the soft mattress. I may never get out of this bed again. I focus on Kessia, who seems to be waiting. "Alright, ask your question. But be warned, I may or may not answer."

Kessia leans back in her chair and crosses her legs. "Are we going to talk about Asher Covington?"

I purse my lips and then school my face into a blank slate. "Who is Asher Covington?"

She groans. "Honestly, Livvy. If you would admit your feelings, you may find they are reciprocated."

"Perhaps there is another I prefer," I say, thinking of

Julian. Then I shake my head. "My heart is a convoluted mess unworthy of examination." I slink down into my pillow. "Besides, I am going to be much too busy with the tournament."

I can tell she does not believe me, but she lets the conversation drift to other subjects until I fall asleep.

For the next two days, I sleep, wake, eat the soup Jasmine delivers, take the tinctures Kessia brings, and pray for this to pass. Mr. Bennet stays close to my side the entire time—finally, my fever breaks and the fog lifts. I ease myself out of bed and take inventory of the cottage. Has it really only been two days?

The cottage is tidy, thanks to Kessia. I put the kettle on to boil and investigate the jars of medicine lined up on the table. Next to the jars is a letter addressed to me, written in unfamiliar handwriting. Kessia must have dropped it off this morning. I run my finger beneath the wax seal and unfold the letter. I look at the bottom of the paper to identify the sender. Then I suck in a breath and begin to read.

36

Miss Lavinia,

Be assured, I am not writing to persuade you to reconsider my offer of marriage. You made your feelings quite clear. I do wish to address the offenses laid against me.

First, I indeed persuaded Thaddeus to leave the village. I will not deny my actions. I watched your friend closely, and she showed him no more affection than myriad other men in the village. His feelings were quite entrenched, and I determined it to be better to take our leave than wait to find out that his feelings were not recip-rocated. I know my actions may seem cruel to you. I may have been mistaken, but I believed I was acting in the service of a friend.

Second, as to Julian. He was the son of a General in my father's military. When the General was killed in battle, my father took Julian in as his mother had died in childbirth. Julian was given every advantage: education, connections, and finances. He followed his father's footsteps into the military. When Julian was caught in a compromising position with a high-ranking woman and forced out of service, my father covered up his indiscretion and allowed him to return to the keep with his dragon.

When my father died, Julian was left a stipend, which he

demanded immediately and proceeded to gamble away. When he returned needing money, I sponsored his entry in several jousting tournaments. Despite my family's generosity, last year he attempted to persuade my sister to elope. When he discovered he would never have access to her fortune, he disappeared. She was heartbroken. I had not seen him until now. Given all that has transpired, I believe my contempt is well-earned and reasonable.

I apologize if I offended your sense of propriety.

Asher

37

The letter folded in my pocket is as heavy as a boulder. I am not sure why I brought it with me. I had read it so many times last night that I could almost recite it from memory. But no matter how many times I studied the words, my confusion persisted. Was I mistaken about Asher? Or was he merely trying to cover his mistreatment of Julian and manipulation of Thaddeus?

Ranger nickers as we traverse the snow-covered ground leading to a keep beside a small lake to groom an Orange Zarijos who recently returned from a trip to Ezera, where she had a run-in with an ancient sea creature and was wounded. While she was tended to immediately after the altercation, I must check and clean her wounds. The lake is stunning, crystal clear to the bottom, where it seems trees were frozen in time, forever reaching up for air.

The keep is built into the side of a mountain, featuring a four-story turret on top, and is connected to an outcropping of rocks. The dragon appears to be inside the turret at the moment.

As I approach the wide plank wooden door at the bottom,

a stout goblin bursts forth, and flames chase him into the morning.

"I'm just doing my job," he shouts up the stairs to where the dragon resides.

He pulls his hound-tooth cap from his head and smacks it against the side of his pant leg. Smoke billows out from the flames he extinguished with his efforts. I'm frozen in place as he takes a moment to inspect himself and realizes the entire back of his clothing is charred. "I just bought this outfit. I cannot believe she ruined another one." He continues to grumble.

I step forward and clear my throat. "Well met. Are you all right?"

He waves me off. "Oh yes, yes. She is a bit temperamental this morning."

I smile. "Dragons can be like that."

He pulls on the hem of his tunic to smooth the damaged fabric. "Are you here for grooming?"

I nod.

He scoffs. "Best of luck."

"Are you a new caretaker?" I ask.

He slips the cap onto his head. "No, I was sent to deliver the necklace her rider commissioned for her. When I tried to hook around her neck, I must have pinched a scale. She was not pleased."

"I imagine not." I tie Ranger to a tree and begin loading my satchel with extra tools. I want to make only one trip up the stairs.

"I'm going to have to raise my rates if I keep losing clothing to dragon fire."

I chuckle. "An occupational hazard, to be sure."

He bids me farewell. I move to the bottom of the turret, staring up at what I know is a long white spiral staircase inside. Dragging my ladder and satchel, I begin to climb.

Dust hangs in the air, driven from where it had rested by the dragon, stomping around the keep.

On my way over, I had stopped at Captain's house. He has a greenhouse and grows fruit year-round. He has set a few aside for me because orange dragons share his fondness for tropical fruit.

When I reach the top of the stairs, I lean my ladder against the wall. I slip an orange from my bag- best to start the appointment off well.

The dragon is facing away from me, but lifts her snout and sniffs, then slowly turns around. Her eyes narrow in on the orange in my outstretched hand.

"Well met," I say, "I've brought you an orange, and I'm here to ensure that you are feeling well, would that be all right?"

She steps forward to the middle of the room. Dragons would rarely lower themselves to cross a room for a mortal. I bow my head and walk to meet her. Holding the orange in my flat outstretched hand, I wait for her to take it. She flicks out her tongue and scoops up the orange into her mouth.

I can hear the orange pop as she bites down on it and then pauses, letting the juices flood her mouth. Her tail swishes, and she chuffs.

She is wearing the necklace. A ruby the size of my fist hangs on her breastplate. The ornate setting is exquisite, but I don't think I shall mention it, given her recent interactions with the jeweler.

The dragon rests on her haunches, a signal for me to begin.

While I inspect her injuries and clean her scales, my mind wanders to the trip with Kessia. There is so much of the world I have not seen. Eshan has my heart, but I find the idea of longer journeys to Jura or some of the other kingdoms quite exciting.

An image drifts through my mind unbidden. Asher and I are on the back of his dragon, his arms wrapped around my waist. The wind is in my hair, and the horizon stretches out before us. The vision is visceral. I groan. This is ridiculous. I am not a silly schoolgirl.

I chuckle and roll my shoulders. The dragon chuffs, and I lean back to meet her eyes. "You are lucky you do not have to worry about male machinations."

She pulls her lips back and bobs her head.

I climb down the ladder and stand before her, taking in the full height of this magnificent creature.

I used to know exactly what I wanted - a dragon. If I could bond with a dragon, my life would be complete. But just as my world opened when I crossed those mountains, I fear the trip to Kaimas has fundamentally changed me. It has awoken a wanderlust.

At least Marinn comes home tomorrow.

$\mathcal{M}$arinn is waiting on the porch when I arrive. She smiles when she sees me, keeping her back straight and chin up. I admire her resilience. Although I understand why Asher convinced him to leave, I still believe Thaddeus was foolish to go along. Hopefully, he will quit being an unmitigated arse and beg her forgiveness. If not, it is undoubtedly his loss.

I don't say any of this. Instead, I stride up the stairs and fold her into a hug. "Well met. I'm so glad you're home."

"Me too", she mumbles, her face buried in my shoulder. When she pulls away, she straightens her cloak and must see the concern on my face. "I'm over him, Livvy," she says, taking my hands. "I'm hopeful we can be civil if we meet in public."

I swallow my smile. She is trying to be brave, but I know better. It is inconceivable that she has fallen entirely out of love with Thaddeus. But if the match is not to be, she is right to hope they might both move on. I won't tease her for it.

Instead, I open my cloak to show her the skin of ale clipped to my belt. "I brought refreshments."

"As did I," she says, retrieving a bag from her pocket, "Biscuits."

"We are well stocked. Let's go."

Arm in arm, we weave our way through the village and throngs of spectators. There are carts and makeshift stands set up selling everything from exotic ale to little jars of every type of potion ingredient imaginable. We take our time, investigating each of the stalls. I buy a caramel apple, and Marinn chooses bright pink spun sugar that resembles a cloud on a stick. I've never seen anything like it.

I smile at a goblin wearing team hats stacked on top of each other, twenty feet high. His hands are full of pennants and banners for each of the teams. I see Asher, Thaddeus, and Julian represented. It is surreal that these men who have plagued my thoughts are actually famous enough to have hats and banners in their honor. I don't point it out to Marinn, lest I sour the mood. Instead, I lure her over to a cart teeming with blown glass.

As we draw closer, I spot Colette perched on a ladder, hanging colorful gourd-shaped lanterns from low branches on a tree above her station. She nimbly moves between answering questions from admiring patrons and carefully arranging her glass pieces to their best advantage. We admire her creations for a few minutes, but Colette is so busy, I don't want to interrupt her. When I can catch her eye, I give her a bright smile and a wave. She is beaming with pleasure, and we leave her to it.

If many more people descend into the valley, we may burst at the seams. I will have to conduct my first official exams in the morning, but today is just for Marinn. As we walk, she tells me stories about her mischievous little cousins. I tell her about the latest village gossip.

"What of Asher? Have you seen him?" she asks.

My shoulders sag. "Only in service of his dragon." I don't

know why I withhold additional information. My conflicted heart isn't sure how to explain all that has transpired with Asher and Julian. No matter. With the tournament beginning in earnest, I will have little time to ruminate on either man. I hope I can keep my thoughts in order. With dragons, distractions can be deadly.

"And have you heard from Julian?" she asks.

"I had a letter. He said he will be back for the tournament."

Marinn seems to sense my reluctance to discuss either Asher or Juilian and moves on to other tales of her travels as we wind our way up to a rocky outcropping only known by the locals. It is the perfect location to take in the valley view.

The sun has melted the snow on the rocks and warmed them, making them comfortable for sitting. We can see down into the village, packed with spectators. Wherever there are clearings in the valley, crowds gather. A symphony of chatter echoes off the canyon walls and then turns to a roar when the first competitors appear at the starting points for their final practice runs.

Marinn lays out a napkin and produces biscuits and jam. I slip the wineskin off my belt and unscrew the top, handing it to her. She drinks deeply and wipes her mouth with the back of her hand.

"How ladylike," I say, chuckling.

She laughs. "Yes, I am quite the lady. That is why the line of suitors stretches to the edge of the village."

I bump her shoulder with mine. "You do not need a line of suitors."

Her smile falters for a moment. "Perhaps I shall get my own caracal and forget about love."

"Love is vastly overrated," I say, taking a pull from the wine skin.

"Isn't it wonderful how all of the trees are so full and bright now that magic is back?" Marinn asks, gazing at the valley. The entire world looks as if the sun had been hiding behind a cloud and finally emerged, casting everything in a bright glow.

"Yes, but nothing compares to the never-ending hearth fires. I could get used to those." We had been warned that at midnight every hearth in the valley would be lit with magical everflame. The fires will keep homes magically warm as long as the ward is lifted. Waking up to a cozy cottage is a luxury I am not eager to give up.

Unfortunately, we were also warned that extra precautions would need to be taken to protect us from the effects of spells and enchantments. Luckily, I have my tattoo and my gold necklace.

"That reminds me, " Marinn says, digging into her pocket and retrieving a red velvet pouch. "Father had these made. I have one, too." She holds it out to me.

I open the drawstring and sniff. Lavender, lemon verbena, and sage fill my senses. This would lend an additional layer of protection against Sprites and Tree Gnomes. "Thank you."

"Father has made me promise to stay out of the woods. He's worried that whatever we heard growling might still be around and even emboldened with the wards down."

I nod. It is a legitimate concern.

"What are your duties during the tournament?" Marinn asks.

I suck in a breath. "Each day, I will examine the dragons set to compete and ensure they are healthy. If any of the dragons receives an injury, I will assist in caring for them. Of course, I am not a Mender, but I can change bandages."

Marinn stares at her hands.

"What is the matter?" I ask.

Without lifting her eyes, she says, "You will be quite busy. I shall be lonely."

I slip my arm around her shoulders and pull her into my side. "I would never leave you lonely. My duties will be done by noon, and we can watch the matches together, rooting for our favorite dragons."

She peeks up from under her lashes. "You mean favorite riders?"

I shrug and smile, "Either way." My stomach flutters as I think about seeing Julian again. Perhaps we will have time to talk soon.

"And what shall we do about Thaddeus and Asher?"

I straighten my shoulders. "Ignore them. They are of little consequence, so it shall be easily done."

She nods. "Right."

We sit in silence, watching the practice runs and not daring to speak the truth about our hearts or the men who have stolen them.

39

The next morning, I don my official tournament cloak and head out. There are no lengthy speeches or formal ceremonies to mark the competition's beginning. With thousands of people all jostling for a place to view the matches, it would be like corralling cats to attempt such an event. I leave early for my first tournament client and take every back trail I know of to avoid the village. Even so, I weave through crowds of people carving their own paths through the woods.

The first client is a Gray Sirvis dragon. They are one of the most unpredictable dragon breeds and can be quite dangerous. They have an insatiable need to hunt. It takes a strong rider to bond with a Gray Sirvis. During our preliminary exam, I spent an hour with the dragon before I even touched him. When I reach his cave, his rider, Suetta, is pacing. "Well met," I say.

She stops abruptly, "Finally. I have been waiting for an hour."

I pause. This is not the welcome I expected. Did I have the time wrong? No, I had triple checked the schedule. "Were you expecting me earlier?" I dig into my satchel for the paper. "Because the schedule-"

"I care not about the schedule," she interrupts, "My dragon is refusing to move." She points to the cave in frustration.

I secure my cart and mule and take a deep breath. Why would a dragon decide not to move? If it is an issue between the dragon and the rider, there is not much I can do. But I will need to check him over. If there is something physical, I'll find it.

Inside the cave, the dragon lies with his head on his crossed front legs. As I enter, only his eyes rise to greet me.

"Well met," I say, bowing out of habit.

The dragon grunts and closes his eyes. "See, something is terribly wrong with him. He went hunting at dawn, and when he came back, he was like this," Suetta says from behind me.

I frown. "Why did you not call for a Mender?"

She runs a hand through her hair. "If I call for a Mender, he will be disqualified. I was hoping you could help."

I shake my head. She cares more about the competition than about the health of her dragon. "Please give me a few minutes to evaluate his condition."

She grunts and steps back against the cave wall. I lick my lips and step forward. "It seems you are not feeling well. Can I help?"

The dragon chuffs and tips his head to his back flank. I move to the area and begin searching for the cause of his distress. There is nothing obviously wrong with his foot, claws, or leg. I run my hands along his scales just behind his leg and feel something lodged below. Carefully lifting the scale to see what it could be, I find the telltale spikes of Bittersweet Nightshade, a poisonous plant native to the valley. He must have run into a bush while hunting.

Bittersweet Nightshade can be lethal to humans. No wonder he is so miserable. Luckily, if I can remove the spikes, he should recover in time for her match. I retrieve my leather gloves from my bag along with my long tweezers. I painstakingly remove each spike. In the middle of my work, I must pause to ask for a lantern. Instead of a lantern, the rider approaches and holds her hand out; light shoots from her fingertips, illuminating the space and allowing me to finish. "Thank you," I say as I drop the last spike into a pouch. "He should be feeling better shortly. Dragons metabolize poison quickly, and with such a small amount, it should be out of his system in an hour."

Suetta puts her hands on her hips and tips her head up, sighing. "Thank you."

When she meets my gaze, her eyes are shining, the relief clear on her face. I slip my gloves and tools back into my satchel along with the pouch of poison spikes. They can be helpful if combined with the right ingredients. I am sure the apothecary will appreciate the donation. I pat the dragon on the flank. "It's my pleasure."

As I move on to the next dragon, a sense of pride travels with me. It's reassuring to know I can assist with minor medical emergencies. In moments like this, I am thankful Ma was a Healer. She did not have official training, but knew enough of the herbs that grew in our area to help with many ailments in the village. Her homespun medicine was the best that most of the miners and their families could afford. She taught me from an early age how to treat wounds, illness, and even how to deliver a baby. Pairing those skills with my training in dragon grooming has proved beneficial.

The tournament passes in a blur of excited crowds, dragons, and little sleep. Even on the days between rounds, I still must attend to my regular clients. I have not seen Julian yet, although I search for him everywhere I go. Marinn and I have formed a habit of meeting up to watch the matches from our secret spot.

Marinn and I have watched almost every match. Some are close, with points being given to each rider during the three runs. Other times, the victor is declared early. Three days ago, Leonardo and Metsaloo, the Copper Vesti who loves art, made a strong showing, knocking the other rider off on the first pass, which is an automatic victory.

Then one of the blue-eyed twins with the Red Kurenti lost his match in the third pass after his shield was struck hard enough to break his opponent's lance. The Red Kurenti dragon was so angry that he sent a fireball across the tree-tops. It could have been a disaster, but a water-wielder stood above the tree line in a satin pale blue cloak. She moved her hands in wide circles as if shaping the water from nothing and then sent it streaming down to where the trees burned. Her actions were met with applause and admiration from the villagers, who were not accustomed to such displays of magic.

After today, the field will be narrowed down to four teams, including Julian, Thaddeus, Leonardo, and either Asher or Fedryc. I ruminate on Julian as I walk across the valley to Honora. I still haven't spoken to him since he returned. During my inspections of his dragon, he has been busy talking to others or absent. Most recently, he had gone into the village for some reason. Irritation and disappointment had danced within me. His letter had been affectionate, promising even. And yet I have not spoken to him since he returned to the village. Is he avoiding me? Have his affections changed? Besides all that, it seems irresponsible to disappear before such an important event.

When I arrive at the outcropping, Asher is deep in conversation with one of his men, for which I am grateful. I assess Honora and find her in excellent condition. She has a scrape on her rear leg from a previous match, but it is healing nicely. Asher comes to lean against the wall of the cavern, watching me. I clear my throat. "She is ready for today."

Asher uncrosses his legs and steps forward, then pauses. "Yes, thank you."

I press my lips together. "You are welcome." He looks handsome in his riding leathers. I resist the urge to run my fingers along the crest embossed on his chest plate. We stand and stare at each other for longer than is comfortable. I bite my lip.

He absently pulls on the cuff of his sleeve and says, "I heard you were ill. Are you feeling better?" The side of his mouth lifts, threatening a smile.

"Yes, much better," I say. Why is he asking me about my health? Do I look ill? I smooth my hair. Perhaps I should have been more judicious with my washing. I tip my chin down toward my shoulder and sniff to make sure I don't smell.

"Good. And your morning, has it been pleasant?" Our eyes meet, and he holds my gaze for a moment before averting his eyes.

"Quite pleasant," I say. I quickly survey my surroundings. Honora chuffs and lifts her head from where she has stretched out on the ground.

I shift on my feet. Asher balls his hands into fists and then stretches his fingers out, as if trying to release the tension between us. I search for something to say. When the silence becomes so uncomfortable that I can no longer stand it, I say, "Good luck and have care," and then quickly leave.

My chest heaves as if I've been holding my breath for the entire encounter. It takes a moment for me to realize what has me so flustered. It is fear. I am afraid for Asher. His earlier matches have been easily won. Today, he faces a Black Jouda dragon and rider from Ezera, who have easily beaten their opponents thus far and are sure to be tough competition.

Two hours later, Marinn and I sit on what has become our favorite outcropping of rocks, with a clear view of the winter sky.

I wipe my sweaty hands on my cloak and lick my lips. My heart is in my throat as Asher mounts his dragon and takes up his lance. Marinn grabs my arm and squeezes. "Oh, I cannot bear to watch." She attempts to hide behind my back

I pat her shoulder. "Come now. The dragons need our encouragement."

Marinn groans and straightens. "Oh, very well. My nerves may not survive it." She leans forward to wrap her skirts around her feet and unfold the blanket she brought to protect herself from the chill.

I try to think of something reassuring to say, but come up empty. Marinn will need to manage her emotions. I am consumed by my own nerves, which threaten to overwhelm me.

The ground rumbles as the massive dragons step towards the ledge, their scales shimmering against the pale blue sky.

The horn echoes across the valley, signaling the start of the match. A cheer erupts as the dragons leap into the air, their wings unfurling, casting shadows, racing towards the center of the sky. Jousting sticks tipped in gold extended ahead of the riders. My vision flits between the two dragons, closing in fast. I hold my breath as they collide, Asher's lance hitting Fedryc in the chest, pushing him flat on his dragon's hide. The cheers follow the dragons as they circle back to go again. I watch Fedryc as he struggles to right himself and reposition his lance.

Once they reset on the edge of the cliff, they are ready for the next round. If Asher lands another blow, the match will be his. Fedryc must at least get a strike or be eliminated.

"I expected this to be a close competition," Marinn says.

"Isn't Asher supposed to be the best rider on the field?"

Marinn nods. "Indeed. But Fedryc has had such a strong showing, the odds are split even."

We sit in anticipation of the next round. My mouth is dry. I wish this wasn't so stressful to watch. I used to hate the idea of the tournament because of the dragons, and now I see that the riders are more in danger than anything. And that terrifies me.

I hold my breath as they launch for the third time. My focus bores into Asher, willing him to be safe and victorious. Marinn grasps my hand and squeezes so hard my bones grind together, and I squeeze right back. I swear I can see Asher's eyes narrow as he waits until the last moment and then turns his body to the left. The other rider has no time to react before Asher swings his lance from the side, knocking the rider off the dragon, making it a clean win. Marinn and I erupt into applause, joining the cheers across the valley. Relief courses through me.

fter each round of matches is a day of rest, so it is two days later when I enter the cave of Julian's dragon. Julian is standing against the wall. When he sees me, he smiles slyly. "There you are. I was hoping I would see you."

I lift my chin. "Really? You haven't bothered to seek me out before today."

He runs a hand through his hair. "I've been busy. I was called away on urgent business. I looked for you in the village yesterday."

His smile, once charming, now seems false. I had been in the village most of the day and had not seen him once.

I furrow my brow. "No matter. I'm here to care for your dragon."

He steps forward. "Surely you have a few moments to spare. Did you receive my letter?"

"I did." I say, "And had assumed you wanted to spend time with me."

He smiles sheepishly. "I wanted to. But I have had to meet

with the families who are funding my entry into the tournament. It was a dreary affair." He looks up at me from under his lashes, "The only thing that kept me going was thoughts of you."

A sense of wanting tries to snake its way around my body, and I recognize it for what it is- magic. How dare he? I school my face into neutrality and hope my words cut enough to sting. "Are you attempting to charm me on purpose, or does it happen unbidden?"

His smile falters. "I am not doing anything other than sharing my feelings with you. Why are you cross with me?"

I am thankful for the herbs in my pocket and the gold tattoo, both of which serve as protection against the kind of magic used by Julian. Squaring my shoulders, I say, "I do not have time to play games with you, Julian. I have a job to do. Now, please leave me to it."

He lifts his hands in defense, "No need to be hostile. I thought we were friends."

I ignore his last comment, turning to face his dragon.

She chuffs and turns her head away from me. I reach up and pat her on the side of her snout. "How are you, Zelena? Ready for your match?"

Julian huffs and walks out of the cave, leaving me to my work. Good. I quickly conduct my exam. When I exit the cave, Julian is nowhere to be found.

I am bitterly disappointed in Julian. As I pack away my tools, I hear footsteps behind me. I turn, and it's Julian.

He clears his throat. "I owe you an apology. I have behaved badly. I do not blame you for hating me. Can you give me a chance to make it right?"

I squint at him. "How would you do that?"

His shoulders sag in relief. "Tonight. We can find someplace quiet and talk."

I sniff. I am unsure how to respond. I do not desire to

give him another opportunity to disappoint me. I force a smile and say, "We will see."

Across the valley, I am surprised to find that Asher is not at his cave. According to Osso, the little boy from the village who has taken to bringing the dragons water, Asher is having his midday meal with Sam at his house. My heart warms at the attention Asher pays to Sam. "He left a while ago, so should return any time," he says.

I tussle Osso's hair, and he scampers off to his next assignment. I'm not sure if the tightness in my chest is from the anxiety of possibly seeing him or the likelihood that I would not see him.

As I've met with Honora, I've decided she is my favorite dragon. Fierce and sweet, she is patient while I work and moves her body in anticipation of my needs. I slow my work, and begrudgingly admit it's because I hope to see Asher when he returns. When I can come up with no other tasks to be done, I rub my hand against the side of her maw and whisper, "Good luck today. I am not supposed to have favorites, but I hope you win."

After a quick bite at the tavern, Marinn and I meet in the village square. She grabs my hand and squeezes. My jaw clenches, and I force my shoulders to relax, but that does nothing to stop the worry that clings to my ribs and wraps around my heart. Asher and Julian are up next.

I used to wonder what would make someone want to participate in this sport. For Asher, at least, I have the answer. He is defending his title at the behest of his family. What motivates Julian, besides a need to prove himself? In any case, I have no desire to see either man hurt. I close my own eyes briefly and send up a prayer of protection. It does little to dissuade the pit in my stomach. But there's nothing else to be done except wait and watch. So that's what I do.

Usually, Marinn and I sit on the rocky outcropping she

had shown me the day before the tournament began. It has an excellent view, but is also observable by much of the valley. I desire more anonymity today. Luckily, Marinn did not press me on the issue and agreed we could seek out a clearing in the woods. Once we arrive at the clearing, I realize the change of position means we cannot see the dragons from their starting points. However, we will have a fantastic view of the battle from below. Marinn unfurls a blanket and lays it across a bed of pine needles. We lie down and stare at the sky, waiting for the announcement to signal the beginning of the match. When the sound of the horn rings across the valley, I suck in a breath and hold it.

I hear the flap of the wings before I see the dragons hurrying towards each other on a collision course. The gold-tipped lances catch the sun as they fly. The dragons approach each other without slowing. I scramble to my feet, keeping my focus on the dragons. Julian crashes his lance into Asher's chest, breaking the lance in half. Gasps echo across the valley, and my hand covers my mouth.

Marinn is beside me, clapping. "That was an exciting start to the match, don't you think?" She grabs my arm, shaking me.

I study Asher, who is palming the middle of his chest. Is he hurt? He will likely have a nasty bruise. At least he wasn't knocked from his dragon. That is little consolation, as a hit to the chest can be just as fatal. I can hardly breathe. The riders disappear as they return to their ledge for another go, and I'm assuming a new lance for Julian.

"That was a terrible hit," Marinn says.

I swallow the lump in my throat and nod. I cannot find my voice.

Marinn seems to notice my distress and grasps my hands. "Oh, but Livvy, he will be all right. It was a hard hit, but not a damaging one, it seems."

I look to my friend whose eyes are shining with excitement. "I know it must have been hard to break his lance."

She nods, and her face falls into a serious expression. "We shall have to see what happens in the next round. I am sure Asher will be victorious." She pauses and raises an eyebrow. "That is who we are rooting for, right?"

Ignoring her, I look up at the sky, now clear and blue, with no sign of a dragon.

Once again, the horn blows and the match begins. This time, I imagine Asher, his face twisted up in concentration, ready to fight. There is a great deal at stake for him with his family and his title.

I slow my breathing and force myself to stay calm as the beating of wings rumbles across the sky. The gold and green scales of the dragons reflect the sun in a blinding brilliance. Asher flies hard and fast, his lance out in front. They might collide mid-air. At the last minute, Asher leans forward and thrusts his lance out to strike Julian in the shoulder hard enough to push him backwards onto his dragon. Only the footholds keep Julian from falling from his dragon.

The crowd gasps and cheers. This is truly an epic battle of two great riders. "It's tied. It's tied. I can't stand the excitement. I want it to be over, but I can't look away." Marin's voice is pitched higher than usual as she joins in the cacophony of noise.

Meanwhile, my mouth is a bucket of sawdust. The best I can do is lift my lips and stare at the sky as the dragons circle back to their ledge for one more pass.

"Liv, just think, if Asher wins, you might be on stage with him when he is presented with the trophy." She points at the emblem on my cloak and waggles her eyebrows. She continues to prattle on, but my mind drifts, and I'm hit with a pang that constricts my heart. My da should be here with me. He would have loved this. I don't know if he would rather root for the noble with a mantle of weighted expectations or the man who is out to make a name for himself.

I chew on my lip and wait for the horn to blare for the third time. A chant begins from somewhere in the village and is quickly picked up by the crowds dotting the valley. "Asher, Asher, Asher." As the chanting gains strength, they begin to clap along. Marrin joins in, but I can't bring myself to. If I open my mouth, I may vomit.

The horn sounds. The pace of the chant increases as the dragons leave their perch and fly towards each other. By the time the dragons meet, the valley is filled with thunderous shouting, clapping, and screaming. Then Julian hits Asher in the shoulder with his replacement lance hard enough to cause Asher to fall backwards and tumble off his dragon.

It takes a moment to comprehend what exactly is happening as Asher's lance drops from his hand and he follows, everything happening in slow motion. Asher doesn't flail or flounder. He falls as if he's falling into a feather bed. Bile rises in my throat as the ground rushes up to meet him. The entire crowd gasps and then falls silent as we all watch to see if Honora will be able to catch him. This cannot be happening. Honora growls and lets out an unearthly scream. She dives out of sight, presumably to circle back and capture Asher before he hits the ground.

A horrifying thought crosses my mind. Am I watching Asher die? If Honora cannot get to him in time, what hope does he have? I can see where they're going to land if he does fall. He will need medical attention if he survives.

My heart is in my throat. Marinn is frozen in horror. Without a word, I sweep my satchel from the ground, and I start to run. Branches whip my face as I sprint through the trees. I keep looking for any sign of the dragon and the rider. My feet barely hit the ground as I trip over branches, catching my sleeves on vines. My breath comes in heated pants, and the only thing I think about is getting to Asher.

Honora roars over my head, flying in the same direction. Her gold scales glint through the trees as she dives closer to the ground. She's skirting the tops of the trees, and if she doesn't catch him quickly, she risks injury. I can't stop. Then comes a monstrous noise, and it has to be Honora, hitting the trees.

I choke out a sob. Was she able to get Asher, and now they are tumbling together to their deaths? Or will she sacrifice herself for him? All of the options are horrifying.

41

The undergrowth is thick, and the foliage rips at my cloak. Yet, I continue to run. This infuriating man has inconveniently carved himself into my heart. Not that I love him or anything as foolish as that, but he has earned my begrudging respect. And Honora does not deserve to be hurt.

Every breath is a struggle. Panic drives me forward. I knew this tournament was a terrible idea. It is ludicrous to think it is a good idea to joust on the back of a dragon between mountains with no safety net of any kind. Anger blazes behind my eyes, and I'm glad for it because fury is better than any other emotion I might feel at this moment. I must keep my wits about me because Asher and Honora will need my help. In the back of my mind, I remember that the magic band is lifted, so Menders are in the village.

I force myself to inhale through my nose and out through my mouth. Mentally, I run through everything I know about emergency dragon care. I also learned from an early age how to treat human wounds, illness, and even how to deliver a baby. I always carry my satchel containing basic medical supplies. Hopefully, I can be of help to both Asher and Honora.

Finally, I break through a dense tree line, and Asher is lying on the ground unconscious. I scan the area for Honora and hear the low rumble of her growls coming from up in the trees. She is entangled in the canopy, with a branch embedded in one of her wings. I suck a breath at the sight. I have no idea how the trees are holding her. If she falls, she will land on Asher. I don't know what to do for her right now, so I turn my attention to Asher, racing to him and falling on my knees at his side.

"Asher, can you open your eyes?" I slip the helmet off his head and brush the hair from his face. Before I begin to examine him, I look up and say, "Honora, don't worry. We will take care of Asher and you. All will be well. Please stay still so you don't damage your wing further.

Honora grunts in an acknowledgment and stills. I carefully unbuckle his chest plate and remove it. Then I put my ear to Asher's chest, holding my breath so I can listen for any sounds of a heartbeat. The thump of his heart is loud and strong. His chest rises and falls with his breath. He moans and tries to reach out to me. "No, stay still. Don't move."

I pull cloth from my satchel and press it against his head. When the bleeding has slowed, I begin to run my hands carefully over his arms and legs to ensure that nothing is broken. When I get to the junction of his left arm and hand, I can feel that indeed there is a break in his wrist. I carefully straighten it and reach into my satchel for a roll of bandages. I scan the forest floor and reach out to retrieve a stick suitable for stabilizing the break. I snap it in half over my knee and attach it to the underside of his wrist, and wrap the bandage around, securing it in place. Just as I tuck the end of the bandage into my wrapping, my work is interrupted by a sound that sends a chill through my bones.

The familiarly haunting low growl that has stalked me twice before is now here, behind me. I freeze. My heart is pounding in my ears. A stick breaks as the animal steps forward. Honora thrashes in the trees. I look up to her and silently will her to stay still. Maybe if I stay still, the animal will leave. It must be wary of the dragon above me.

This is a disaster. I am alone- without any real defense. While there is a slim chance I could run and hope to escape, Asher would surely die. I slip my hand into my satchel and withdraw my blade. My hands sweat, and I wipe them off on my skirts and grip the blade till my knuckles are white. Then I take a deep breath and force myself to stand and turn- ready to face the growling menace. "You will not hurt him," I whisper as I stand.

Before me stands the most enormous Dykuma wolf I have ever seen; the coloring on his tail marks him as a male. He is about thirty feet away, staring at me with black eyes. His silver fur is raised. He takes a step towards me, growling, and the hair on my arms raises. Where are the Menders who should be assisting Asher? They saw him fall just as I did. My mind races as I hold the wolf's gaze. What am I to do? Ma will never let me live this down if this wolf kills me.

"Leave us alone," I say, my voice shaking. I am keenly aware of Asher, defenseless behind me. I try to find the courage to keep facing this predator down. Instead of courage, I hear every voice that ever told me I could not work with dragons because I was human. I would fail because I was a girl from the mortal lands. Most of those voices had the distinct sound of my mother, but not all. I learned early not to share my dream with too many people. Even the well-intentioned villagers I told as an excited little girl would pat me on the head and tell me it wouldn't be possible.

I refuse to prove them right, so I stand taller and spread

my arms out to my sides, not out of courage or valiant duty, but out of obstinacy. The wolf paws at the ground and continues to stare. He seems to hesitate. Good. I begin to wave my arms around and scream. I jump and flail. If I make myself a threat, he may move on to easier prey. He tips his head and looks at me inquisitively. Breathless, I finally stop jumping and stand.

Instead of scaring him away, he steps forward. Why won't he leave me alone? I blink back tears. Crying will not help anything. The last thing I need is blurred vision.

Was this how Asher felt before Honora rescued him? Terrified and utterly alone? Now would be an excellent time for a dragon to come to my aid. The blade hangs heavy in my hand. I must do something. I could climb a tree, but that would leave Asher exposed. Before I can decide, the wolf comes for me.

42

The wolf's maw is wide open, teeth flashing. I scramble backwards, lifting my hands to defend myself. I will not stand here like an offering. The weight of the knife in my hand reminds me I am not helpless. I will not go down without a fight. I lower my arms with my blade outstretched. I widen my stance and take a deep breath.

The wolf is coming straight for me, his pupils blown wide and filled with death. His paws scrape the snow and forest floor. I grip the knife and ball my other fist. He leaps into the air. And as he does, the world narrows. There is no sound. There is only this wolf, me, and my knife. He is planning to attack me from above. He is planning to attack me with his teeth and claws. He will kill me and drag me into the woods.

Some primal survival instinct takes over. I let out a guttural roar and thrust the blade up as the wolf comes towards me. It flashes in the sun before slicing through the wolf's neck and into his head. His growl turns into a high-pitched yelp. The oppressive weight of him falling on top of me as I crash to the ground.

I lay there for a minute, eyes closed, trying to breathe.

The wolf is warm and heavy. I hold my breath to see if he is breathing. His body is still. I think he is dead.

I scramble to push the wolf off of me. My hands are covered in blood, pine needles sticking to them as I crab walk away from the wolf, as if he can come back to life. Once I am out of reach, I let out a sob and frantically wipe my hands on my skirts. The handle of my knife protrudes from the wolf's neck, the blade buried to the hilt.

I rise to my knees. My hands shake as I straighten my skirts. My heart is racing. I can hardly believe what has happened. Asher begins to moan, and I crawl over to him, brushing the hair from his face. "Asher, don't move. You fell." I scan his face for signs of comprehension. I begin to panic anew as he lies there without responding. Tears fall onto his face as I hover.

Finally, his eyes flutter open, and he stares at me. "Am I on the ground?"

I chuckle. "Yes." I wipe my nose with the back of my sleeve. Blood still stains my fingernails. I'm unsure if it is from Asher or the wolf. "I'm here. I am not going anywhere," I say.

He moves his head from side to side as if clearing the fog from his mind and then focuses on my face. "Don't cry, Livvy. You are too pretty to cry." He reaches his hand up to touch my cheek.

I choke out a laugh. "I believe you may have hit your head."

He scans my torso, "What about you? Are you injured?"

I shake my head. "I am fine." The last word gets caught in my throat like a dry piece of soda bread.

"Is Honora injured?" he rasps.

I look up to where Honora is trapped. "She is hurt, but alive. She tried to rescue you and was caught in the canopy."

Asher's eyes widen in panic, and he tries to sit up,

moaning when he moves his wrist. "I need to get to my dragon."

I place my hand on his chest. "You need to stay still. There could be injuries I missed, especially to your spine and neck. You are in no condition to help her right now."

He stares at me and then up at the trees, his eyes trying to focus on his dragon.

"Do not worry. I will help her," I say, brushing a strand of hair from his face.

I climb to my feet and begin to pace, avoiding looking at the dead wolf. What do I know about Gold Vesti dragons? They can heal themselves, but not from being impaled. If she shifts while impaled, the wound might be catastrophic. How can we get her down without causing more damage? If she shifts into her human form, we can help her climb down.

Asher swallows and says, "She needs to be resting on the ground to heal herself with her dragon fire. If she shifts, she should be able to climb down."

"That is good news because I don't know how to get her down otherwise." We both look up to see golden scales shimmering like autumn leaves against the sky.

"Right," he says, sounding exhausted and closing his eyes again.

"Asher, you must stay awake." I don't know if he has a severe head injury or perhaps his lungs are in peril. "Asher, what hurts? Can you tell me?"

Just then, Kessia and Captain break through the trees. Kessia quickly takes in the scene.

"I was at Captain's house, and Marinn came running and told us. It seems the tournament officials believe Honora was able to catch Asher before he reached the ground. I believe Marinn was going to find a Mender. What can we do?"

I look up to them, tears pricking my eyes. "I'm not sure. I

need to determine if Asher is hurt anywhere else besides his wrist, and we need to figure out how to get Honora down."

Kessia pushes up her sleeves and notices the wolf. "What is this?"

"Later," I say, my voice sharpened by all that had happened.

Kessia nods. "I can help. We had some general medical training in school. Let me examine him, and you can help Honora."

I swallow and back away to give her room to work. "Okay. I already wrapped and braced his wrist, but I'm not sure about the rest of him." My voice breaks, and I'm almost embarrassed. I'm supposed to be a great dragon groomer, and here I am, breaking down at the first sign of real trouble.

Captain puts a hand on my arm. "You've done well. Now pull yourself together and do what you do best for that dragon."

He looks up, and my gaze follows. He's right. I can do this. I climb to my feet. I scan the trees and evaluate which one will be the best one to climb without jostling the dragon. I decide on a tall oak tree that's just out of the reach of the injured wing, with three branches extending out toward the dragon. I walk to the base of the tree and then call up to Honora. "Honora, Asher is going to be all right. I know that you are hurt, and I will do everything I can to help you. I'm going to climb up so I can look at your wing. Please don't burn me alive."

Captain chuckles and Honora chuffs in response.

I empty my satchel of anything Kessia might need and slip the strap over my neck and across my body. Then I begin to climb. My hands skim over the rough bark. More of the sky opens up around the dragon as I get it closer to the top of the canopy. I try not to look down. I wrap my arms around the tree and swallow the panic closing in on me.

Kessia's voice rises in concern. "Livvy, are you okay?"

"No, I am not." It has been an awful day. First, Asher's devastating loss and injury, then the unprecedented and terrifying wolf attack. I focus on the branches as I climb. The bark is woven with rivers and texture, serving as roads for the purple ants as they go about their business. Green spotted beetles stare at me as I pass, probably wondering what I am doing here. I don't blame them.

Finally, I am level with Honora's wing, stretched taut over the branch. She whimpers, and my heart aches.

43

I brush my hand against Honora's flank. "Hello there, I want to help you."

She lifts her head and turns so I can see her eye, which is full of pain and what I can assume is worry for Asher. But she's barely able to move anything else because of the way she's pinned in the trees and her impaled wing. I look down at Asher, lying on the ground with Kessia and Captain hovering over him.

I climb two branches higher so I can better view the branch protruding from Honora's wing. Several tools in my satchel might help remove the branch. "I am going to free you from the branch so you can more easily get down. But it's going to hurt because I'm going to have to cut the branch. It is likely to shift as I cut it." I bite my lip.

I consider my options. Typically, it is better to cut below the entry point and remove it only when you can control the bleeding. However, I don't know if that applies to dragons. They have membranous wings, so perhaps it would be better to cut the branch above and lift the wing off? I survey the jagged entry into the hide of the wing. Nothing significant seems to have been hit. My voice shakes as I explain my hypothetical plans to Honora.

Once I am wedged between the branches, I carefully saw through the bottom of the impaling branch and then lean back in case the change in position causes Honora to shift. When I'm sure she isn't moving, I return to the task of removing the barky spine from her wing.

I need to pull it out straight to avoid causing further damage. I won't be able to remove it with one hand, that's certain. I'll need to climb one more branch to get the best leverage.

Above me is a sturdy limb, and I can use it to accomplish my goal. Reaching into my bag, I retrieve the rope and lean over to tie it around the branch, just above the cut and below a knot in the wood, to prevent it from slipping. After ensuring the knot is secure, I climb to reach the sturdy bough, slip the rope over the bark, and let it drop to the ground. I adjust the position of the rope until it is likely to pull the oversized thorn cleanly from the wing. "Captain, I need assistance. Please grab that rope, and when I say, pull as hard as you can straight down."

"All right. Give me the signal."

I check the knot and the position of the rope on the branch. "Alright. On the count of three." I pat Honora on the side and count down. Kessia joins Captain, and at the bottom of the countdown, they tug hard on the rope, moving their hands up as the anchor point begins to move.

I wince at the tearing sound of the wood against flesh. The dragon grunts but manages to hold still during the process. "That's it. Keep going. It's halfway out," I call down to Kessia and Captain.

Captain strains to pull the rope, his face flushing red and eyes bulging. But after so many years on a ship, he knows his way around a rigging, and it shows in how he wraps his hands around the rope and uses his entire body to pull. With a grunt, Kessia releases the rope and retreats, apparently deciding she is only getting in the way. Snow crunches under her feet as she crosses to Asher and kneels beside him.

The branch releases its hold on Honora and flies through the tree, bringing leaves along as it drops to the ground with a thud.

Honora grunts when her wing is liberated. I scoot back to the trunk. My sleeve snags on a bit of lifted bark, and I yank it free, ripping the edge. Shoot. As I inspect the damage, a bright light flashes. My hand involuntarily rises to shield my view. Captain, apparently startled, lets out a string of curses he must have learned on the sea.

When I dare look, Honora is no longer in the tree. She has transformed into a woman and is standing before Asher. Her gold skin shimmers under the loose shift hanging to the ground. I shimmy down the tree and join them. Honora is breathtakingly beautiful. Only a small mark on her shoulder indicates she was injured. Her hair is a wave of gold, twisted into braids that fall down her back. Her eyes are closed, and she whispers something. A golden light emanates from where her hand touches Asher. The glow spreads across his chest and to the rest of his body. Asher visibly relaxes as the dragon works. I have never seen a more beautiful sight. Few are privileged enough to witness this transformation, as it can be a time of vulnerability for dragons. The fact that Honora is willing to risk shifting in our presence is a testament to her love of Asher and, I hope, her trust in me.

Kessia hands me a water skin, and I gratefully take a drink. Sweat drips down my back. My hands sting from the scrapes and slivers I will need to dig out later.

As Asher unwraps his wrist and moves to sit, voices approach, calling for Asher and Honora. Relief floods me as a group of officials in tournament cloaks arrives, including

Marinn's father. He immediately crosses to me, folds me into a hug, and says, "Marinn has returned to the village, she aggravated her ankle with all the running. I imagine you had everything to do with the outcome of this potential calamity?" He lifts his chin to where Honora and Asher rest.

"It was a group effort," I say, leaning against his chest. Tears stream down my cheeks as I embrace his comfort. After a few moments, I slip from his grasp and kneel beside Asher, who is sitting against the base of a tree. "Are you feeling better?" I ask.

He smiles shyly. "I am. Thank you for everything." He tips his head back to rest against the tree.

"You're most welcome. It was quite a hit you took." I look around. "Where is Honora?"

"She returned to the cave in her human form to rest. She used immense energy today."

"Yes. You should rest as well."

"I am joining her shortly. I wanted to ensure you were well."

I fold my hands in my lap and search for something to say. I bite my lip. "I admit, I am quite shaken." I survey the aftermath. "It could have been much worse."

He grunts. "I suppose you're right." Then he meets my gaze. "But are you hurt? It must have been an awful trial to assist Honora."

My cheeks heat, and I dip my head to hide my flush. He is being quite considerate. It seems so unlike him. Perhaps he hit his head after all. I flash him a brief smile followed by a slight nod.

"What happened to this wolf?" Captain asks in his gruff voice.

"What wolf?" Asher's voice echoes. He leans forward to see what Captain is talking about.

I sigh, standing and wrapping my arms around my body,

and daring to step closer to the wolf. How do I share a story I can hardly believe myself? If not for the carcass taking center stage, I could have imagined the entire scenario. Alas, the proof is at the feet of Captain, who is inspecting the animal and waiting for an explanation. Taking a deep breath, I tell them the story. As I'm speaking, I realize I am minimizing the danger and horror of the situation. It is a habit deeply ingrained from growing up under my mother's critical eye.

Even so, the group's reactions are appropriately filled with shock and dismay. Asher scrambles to his feet as if the threat is still imminent. Captain continues to look between the wolf and me. Kessia covers her mouth with her hand. When I'm finished, everyone stares at me. I blink rapidly, waiting for someone to speak.

"Oh, Livvy," Kessia says, coming over to my side and slipping an arm around my shoulder.

I lean into her, the exhaustion of the experience beginning to take hold. I am flooded with a tide of accolades and support. The only person not eagerly adding a comment is Asher. He stands apart from the group, eyes flashing with emotion. The muscle in his jaw twitches as he stares at me. I meet his gaze and shrug. He takes a step towards me but stops himself.

I wipe away the solitary tear threatening to break down the dam on my emotions. If only he would come to me, it would comfort me so. I quickly realize I am losing my struggle to maintain my stoic demeanor. My teeth begin to chatter, and I start to shake. Along with the barely concealed emotion, my limbs grow incredibly heavy, as if they have been transformed into sandbags.

Kessia squeezes my shoulders. "Come, Livvy, let's get you home."

With one last look at the wolf and then at Asher, I allow Kessia to lead me away.

44

The next day, I am up with the sun. Mr. Bennet is sitting nearby, curled in a chair and staring at me with unblinking eyes. My mind fills with snarls and teeth. My hands are clean, but I can still smell the blood. I shake my head, trying to clear the overwhelming sensations.

"Are the rumors true? The entire village is talking about it," says Mr. Bennet.

"Yes, I am sure they are. Asher was expected to win."

"Not about Asher, about you. About your heroic rescue of Asher and epic battle with the Dykuma wolf. You know one bite is fatal, yes?"

I pause. "I did not know that." My *Field Guide to Dragons* only mentions the wolf as a food source for dragons, but gives little additional information. Dykuma wolves are rare in this part of the continent. Still, I should have known more about them.

My hands tingle and tremble. No. I cannot go down the dark road of what could have been. I have a job to do. My only plan for today is to check in on Asher and Honora.

"Well, try not to die today. I have grown fond of you over the years," Mr. Bennet says.

I can't help but smile. "I shall do my best."

On the way through the village, I stop by Marinn's house. She must be nettled after yesterday, feeling both worried and disappointed that she missed the excitement. She answers the door and immediately drags me into an embrace so tight I cannot breathe. Apparently, her ankle injury wasn't serious. "Oh, Livvy. I heard all about what happened. You could have died."

I peel her off of me. "But I didn't die. And I'm fine."

She purses her lips. "Are you certain?"

I smile. "Yes." I spin as if on display. "See? No harm done."

"I'm so glad." After a beat, she continues, "Oh my, I bet you have not heard the latest news."

"What news?" My blood runs cold. Is Asher all right? I thought so yesterday, but so much can change overnight.

She leans in conspiratorially, even though we are alone on her porch. "It is Julian. They suspect he was cheating. He's facing disqualification from the tournament."

I am rarely surprised, but this is astonishing news. This cannot be true. "Tell me everything."

"I don't know all of the details. Father said he was being investigated. Please don't say anything. It is a secret for now."

I run my fingers through the ends of my braid. "And Asher… is he all right?"

Marinn grins. "More than all right! He will be ruled the victor if the accusations are proven true."

My fury over Julian's treachery could only be eclipsed by the wave of relief that rushes over me. "I am so glad to hear that. I'm on my way to see him now."

"Really?" she asks, her tone loaded with a thousand innuendos.

I playfully smack her arm. "I am doing my job."

"All I am going to say is that I have never seen you run so fast as when you thought he might be hurt."

"Yes, well, I have no comment about that."

Marinn chuckles and then seems to remember herself. "Please don't say anything about Julian."

"I will not say anything."

"Thank you. Now get going. Asher is waiting." She smiles as if she knows something I do not. While Marinn is a song made flesh when she is glad, I know that I'll never outrun her teasing.

Thirty minutes later, I approach Honora's cave. Asher steps out, and I stop at a distance to watch him unencumbered. He is quite handsome today. His neatly pressed coat cuts across his broad shoulders perfectly. I roll my shoulders.

As I approach, Asher flashes me a smile. "Well met. It is good to see you."

I return his smile. "Well met." My chest swells under his approving gaze.

A willowy woman with salt and pepper hair piled in an elaborate style steps into view, and a long, green silk scarf flutters behind her in the breeze coming off the mountain. She lets the hint of a smile momentarily flash across her face, looking between Asher and me. "Asher, who is this?"

This woman is the embodiment of Fae royalty- a beautiful, icy presence. This woman is too old to be his sister. Maybe his mother or another relative?

I smile and straighten my shoulders, "Well met. I'm Livinia, but my friends call me Livvy."

"I see. I am Duchess Covington, Asher's aunt." She lifts her chin and turns to Asher. "How are you and Livinia acquainted?"

"I am a dragon groomer and working for the tournament," I say, eager to prove myself and then immediately irritated that I feel the need to.

She ignores me, addressing her question to Asher. "They hire humans for that?" She picks a piece of invisible lint from her cloak. "A Mender would be more appropriate."

I stand there as Asher shifts on his feet. Why is he not saying anything? I press my tongue to the back of my clenched teeth. Heat rises in my cheeks, and I want to fling myself off the cliff's edge.

"Livinia was instrumental in our rescue yesterday."

"I see. And you are well acquainted?" Her words are heavy with insinuation.

"Yes, we are acquainted. There have been several occasions where our paths have crossed," he says.

She looks down her nose at me. "I can assume you have not introduced Miss Livinia to your parents?"

Asher looks confused. "No, of course not."

I cluck my tongue. Asher quickly clarifies, "My parents and my sister are on a ship to Jura to work out trade agreements with the King. They will not be here. But when they do return, I would be happy to introduce you to them."

"I see no reason for an introduction if she is simply a human employed in service." The Duchess's words drip with vinegar.

Silence hangs in the air. Finally, Asher speaks. "Livvy has taken excellent care of the dragons."

My heart warms at his comment- not only at the compliment, but at the use of my name.

His aunt grunts. "They should be more selective about the location of the tournament. Traditionally, it is not to be witnessed by humans, let alone have them so intimately involved. This should be brought to the attention of the tournament Guild."

Asher clears his throat. "Perhaps we should give Livvy a chance to look over my dragon. She is on a tight schedule."

I flash him a grateful smile.

"Excuse me," I say, and suck in a breath as I turn my attention towards the cavern. The last time I saw Honora, she was in her human form. As I approach, her gold scales catch the light, and I am once again impressed by her size.

"Well met, Honora. I am glad to see you doing well."

The dragon chuffs and meets my gaze. I cross to the wing that had been impaled the previous day. Upon inspection, it seems to be completely healed. How extraordinary to have that kind of power.

"How is she?" Asher asks.

I straighten and turn to where he is watching me work. "Perfect." I survey him for a moment. "And you?"

He spreads his arms out to make the point. "Fit as a fiddle."

I nod and smile. "Good to hear."

"It seems there is some controversy surrounding my match."

"Yes, I heard something about that."

He runs his thumb across his chin. "It seems that when Julian broke his lance, he proceeded to use an enchanted replacement that had not been inspected prior to the competition. It was imbued with additional strength. When he was confronted, he denied any wrongdoing and then fled."

"How dishonorable. You were certainly right about him."

"Yes, I just wish I had been honest with the tournament officials about his deceitful nature." He steps closer to me and touches my arm briefly.

I don't dare move. I can barely breathe with him standing so close. His eyes are the most beautiful shade of gray. I have the sudden urge to touch the tips of his pointed ears. Are they as sensitive as I have read? Butterflies flutter in my belly. What is wrong with me? I am a fool.

"Are you all right?" Asher asks, drawing my attention back to his face. His brows are furrowed.

I lick my lips. "Of course. I am fine." I scuff my foot on the ground, unsure of what to say.

"Do you have any other appointments today?"

"No. I was given the day off by the tournament committee. However, I wanted to ensure you were well."

"Thank you. I am quite well, and glad of your company. Can I walk you home?"

Walk me home? Although the day is getting late, the thought of walking through the woods alone makes my pulse race. I know the wolf is dead, but I cannot escape the thought that another might be out there, waiting. If I say yes, does that give him the wrong idea? Despite my reservations, I find myself saying, "That would be nice."

As we walk, Asher tells me about a time he visited Straume. He had been a boy and enthralled by the size of human families. Fae have a much lower fertility rate, and having two children is considered a favorable family size. I share stories from our home, including the first time I saw a dragon pass over my childhood cottage. Time passes quickly, and soon we find ourselves walking by the tavern. "Oh, please let me stop and see if there is any mail from home."

Jasmine has a letter waiting and pulls a face when she sees Asher standing behind me. I give her a smile that says I will fill her in later and take the letter.

As we continue to walk to the cottage, I inspect the envelope. It is from Ma. Hopefully, it contains some good news.

"If you would like to open the letter, there is still enough light to do so," Asher says.

I am anxious for news from home, so I unfold the parchment and read as we walk the path to my cottage. I stop when I get to the second paragraph. My ma's words stop me in my tracks, and my hand flies to my mouth.

"Is something wrong?" Asher asks.

I fear that if I try to talk, I may burst into tears. I attempt to suck in a breath and find that I am choking on my tears. I manage to stammer out, "It's my da. He is dying." I look to Asher, whose face is filled with concern. I continue, "The healer has been to the house. "

"This is grave, indeed. Can I be of assistance?"

I shake my head. Everything inside me desires to beg him to send a Mender to my home. I cannot bring myself to ask such a thing. My heart is shattering. "There is nothing more that can be done. I must go home as soon as I can." I sniff and sink into the chair.

Asher shuffles his feet and moves about the room, as if considering his next steps. "I shall take my leave."

I barely hear him as I reread the letter.

My Dearest Livvy,

I pray this letter finds you well. Your sisters send their best wishes. You are missed every day. I look forward to the day you come home.

I must share with you news of a distressing nature. Your da is not well. We have had a healer come from the neighboring village. He has said there is nothing more to do for your da but make him comfortable. We are grieved at this news, as you can imagine.

Oh, daughter, we know not how long Da has on this side of the veil. Da has impressed upon me to make sure you promise not to come home before the tournament is over. After the tournament is finished, make haste, for we know not the number of our days.

All My Love,

Ma

45

I pace inside the cottage, chewing my thumbnail. I cannot simply remain here while Da slips into the darkness. I need to see him. But if I leave the tournament early, I will forfeit half my pay. Emotion roars inside of me. For the first time, this hamlet is more a prison than a refuge. Surely something can be done.

For possibly the first time in my life, I am at a complete loss as to what I should do. I feel as if I am a knee-high child again, wanting to hide my face in Ma's skirts, or later, in my da's pant leg—the memories from home flood back.

Growing up, I asked Da a million questions about dragons, most of which he couldn't answer. "I'll be your dragon," he would say. Then he would heft me onto his shoulders and run through the yard. I would stretch my arms wide and tilt my head back, laughing. Those were the good days, when his lungs were clear and strong.

When I was ten years old, Da came home with a cloth-wrapped package. He handed it to me, and over my shoulder, I heard Ma cluck her tongue. "What is it?" I asked. I never received gifts unless it was solstice or my birthday, and even then, it was usually small candy treats or perhaps a new dress.

He smiled. "Open it and find out, Livvy Lou." He tousled my hair, and I raced to the wide-planked oak table next to the hearth to unwrap the package.

I gingerly touched the soft leather cover and opened to the first page, barely able to breathe. It was a *Field Guide to Dragons*. On the inside of the cover was a space for me to write my name, which I eagerly did. I spent hours poring over the tome. With every turn of the parchment, my love of dragons grew. It wasn't until years later that I understood the financial sacrifice contained in those pages. It is still my most treasured possession.

With three children under six, Ma had no time for my obsession. "You would do better tending to your chores and keeping your skirts clean," she would say, kneading a loaf of bread or hanging laundry on the line. "The Fae are not to be trifled with." Like all humans, I had heard the stories about the Fae stealing children and leaving changelings, ensorcelling pretty young women and enslaving humans for menial labor. But the powerful, thunderous beat of wings was a song to my young heart, calling me to the sky.

As the summers passed, I kept my dream tucked in the corner of my heart, lest my ma find it, study it, and again explain in great detail why it would never happen. She prided herself on being practical, which shared a border with negativity, and I did not have time for either.

Over the years, the dream had not faded, but grown, layer by layer, and was now an intricate oil painting in my mind. I had no chance to act on those dreams, however, until I was in my twenty-first summer and encountered a trader my father knew. Craige traveled to Saule, trading magic-dampening gold mined from hills near our village. Every time he returned, it was with little silver bowls, jars of enchanted ointment, and other trinkets to sell to mortals eager for a bit of magic. While gold dampened magic, silver enhanced magic. Objects made of silver were thought to bring luck to humans and Fae alike.

The grass was still wet with dew that morning as Craige set up a rough-hewn table atop two logs to display his wares. His long overcoat was probably light brown at one time, but was now stained with shades of ale and who knew what else. A scar ran down the side of his face from brow to chin. I was busy unpacking my wooden cart full of jams I sold in the summer months at the village market. He asked about my father, and we shared the latest local news about the mines and his travels.

"The things I've seen would curl your hair," Craige said, pulling a rag from his pocket to polish a small brass object.

"Like what?" I asked. Most people never traveled outside the immediate area, but the idea of leaving the barriers of our village was intriguing.

He dropped the rag on his table and held a rectangular talisman in his palm. "This is a Charm of the Wild Hunt. It will bring good fortune and protect the wearer from trouble."

I lean in to get a closer look. Vines snaked along the edges, and a stag was carved in the center. A loop along the top begged for a chain to hold the talisman close to the wearer's heart. He looked at me expectantly, waiting for a reaction.

I nodded appreciatively. "It's lovely," I said, and pointed to my cart. "I'd have to sell a lot of jam to purchase something so magical."

He smiled. "Ah, that you would." He turned to rummage through a satchel tied to his mule.

I began to arrange my jam jars, making sure the twine

bows faced forward, my eyes occasionally flitting back to him.

Finally, he let out a satisfied grunt and turned to me, holding something behind his back. "I have a sixth sense about things. All that time I spent in Saule has rubbed off some magic on me. Some call me Fae-blessed." He shot me a toothy grin. Well, not precisely toothy, because he was missing half of them. But friendly, to be sure. I raised an eyebrow. If that was him, Fae blessed, I would hate to see the alternative.

He squinted, as if studying my face, then said in a solemn tone, "I sense a longing in you." As he continued, his manner grew more animated, adding sweeping one-handed gestures. "You have the heart of an adventurer. You shall leave these lands and go west." He paused dramatically. "And I have your destination."

My throat closed up. How could he know I longed for winding mountain roads and exciting adventure? I had seen him speaking with Da many times, but we had never had a real conversation before. Perhaps Da shared with him my desire to see the world. I glanced around the thatched roofs of our village, decorated with the wildflowers that had been there each summer for as long as I could remember. Familiar voices called out greetings and traded gossip. I'd lived in Tevyne my whole life. How could I leave? Where could I go? But even as these thoughts raced through my mind, my carefully hidden dream began to rumble in that secret corner of my heart, demanding to be set free. I shook my head. "I don't know of what you speak."

He gave me a sly smile. "I think you do." His callused hand finally revealed what he'd been hiding- a piece of parchment rolled and tied with twine. He held it out to me.

My hand trembled as I reached out and took the scroll. "What is this?"

He lowered his voice to a whisper. "It's a map."

I waited for him to continue, resisting the urge to rip off the twine and see for myself.

"This map will take you to Eshan, where mortals and Fae of all kinds live together."

I had never heard of such a thing. Saule was off-limits. Bedtime stories warned us of the danger waiting there. Was he suggesting I go to Saule? My heart pounded. I ran my thumb along the edge of the paper.

Perhaps I misunderstood. Maybe the village he referred to was in the mortal lands. I had heard rumors, but Fae usually tried to blend in or evade detection by building their homes in the forest. Superstitious villagers did not react well to magical creatures in their midst.

There had been peace between our lands for generations. It was a peace held together by the mountains that separated us. Anyone who consorted with the Fae was courting trouble, at least according to the stories. I wasn't sure how true any of it was, but villagers were wary, and Ma would take to her bed if she thought Fae were in our land. "Fae are living in the mortal lands?"

He tipped his head side to side. "Yes, but you wouldn't know them for what they are." He scanned the crowd gathering to trade wares. "Most just want to live a quiet life."

I slipped off the twine and let it float to the ground, then unfurled the map.

The grizzled man straightened and continued. "The village I speak of lies west, in the mountains. Technically, it's in Saule."

I stared at the map, trying to orient myself to the landscape. It was roughly divided into Saule and the mortal lands. The Skadaris mountain range divided the two, stretching the continent's length. The mountains provided a natural barrier, helping to maintain peace between the lands for the last six hundred years.

I squinted and searched for the name of our village, Tevyne. When I found it, I used my finger to track it over to the mountains. The trader leaned in and pointed to a small spot on the edge of the mountain range closest to the mortal lands. "Here is where you need to go."

I leaned in to read the name. "Eshan?" Why had I never heard of this village before?

I looked up to meet his gaze. He nodded and smiled. "That is where your future lies."

Now, after so many years, it turns out he was right about Eshan. But I cannot imagine a future that does not include Da. I kick off my boots, crawl into my bed, and cry. At some point, I must doze off because a hand on my shoulder rouses me. It's Marinn.

"Oh, Livvy, I'm so sorry about your da."

My eyes work to focus on her through the swelling and redness resulting from my crying fit.

"What are you doing here?"

She perches on the edge of my bed. "Asher stopped by and told me about your da. He thought you could use a friend."

I sit up and lean against the wall.

Mr. Bennet pounces on the bed. "You really must tell me what all this is about. First, you are almost eaten by a feral wolf, now I find out Asher was here without a chaperone."

I chuckle. "He walked me home, nothing more."

Mr. Bennet curls up on my legs. "Then why is your face so puffy and red? If he hurt you, I shall scratch his eyes out."

I reach out and scratch him behind the ears. "No, he is a perfect gentleman. It is my da." I sigh.

Mr. Bennet looks at Marinn and then at me. "What has happened?"

Marinn speaks up. "Livvy has received grim news from home. Her father is quite ill and may not have long." Marinn takes my hand. "I do not want to give you false hope, but I do feel it is right to tell you that when Asher came to the house, he asked for any information I may have about your family's location."

It takes a moment for the words to sink in. "Why?" My heart swells with possibility. Could he be taking a Mender to Da? Is that too much to hope for? Of course it is. Still, it is peculiar for him to inquire about my family.

"I am not certain. I told him what you have shared with me. When we parted, he was quite determined to take action, although I do not know what he means to do."

I wave her off. "He's likely returning to his family to prepare for the next match."

"I do not think that is his plan. You realize he has access to Menders? Perhaps he means to help."

Mr. Bennet pauses his grooming to say, "Unless you have some surity, that is a cruel false hope."

Marinn's face falls. "I did not mean to cause pain. It's just that his questions were quite specific and detailed. He asked as someone wanting to travel to the destination."

For the first time since I opened the letter from Ma, I have a sliver of hope. Would Asher help?

Marinn looks up from under her lashes, tracing her finger along her skirts. "You did save his life. It wouldn't be unreasonable to repay your kindness with such a gesture."

"Honora saved his life. I was merely there to assist. I could not accept such a gift from Asher." I could not bear to tell her about my rejection of him. But after such a speech, how could I endure such a kindness?

Marinn shakes her head. "If you had not been there, that wolf surely would have gobbled him up."

I swallow. That is true. Asher had been in no shape to defend himself.

"Did your ma request you return at once?"

"No. Da made me promise not to come home until after the tournament. I shall honor his wishes, although it may break my heart beyond repair."

Marinn pulls me into a hug. "We must trust in a favorable outcome." She releases me and places her hands on my cheeks. "You have a job to do. Come. Wipe your face, and let's venture to the tavern. Jasmine is making roasted chicken."

46

The next day, the village is in an uproar. It was confirmed that Julian's second lance was magically enhanced, disqualifying him from the tournament. He has disappeared in disgrace, and Asher has been declared the winner of the match.

Overnight, Asher left the valley with his dragon, forfeiting his position in the tournament. Speculation over where Asher has gone is plentiful, but without certainty. My ears perk up every time his name is mentioned. I cannot fathom a reason good enough to abandon the tournament now that he has the opportunity to move forward, but apparently, that is precisely what he has done. What will his family say?

I briefly consider all those betting brackets that could never have predicted this outcome. Who shall win the betting pool after all that has transpired? I hope it is someone in need of the coin and surprised by their good turn.

As for me, I am grateful for the distraction from the heavy burden of my worry. There are only a few more days left of the tournament, and then I can go home. It does me no good to fret about something I cannot control. Perhaps if I keep telling myself that, it will become true.

Since Asher has forfeited and Julian is disqualified, the tournament is now between Thaddeus and Leonardo. It has been fascinating to watch riders as they prepare for competition. One can tell much about a man's character when he is under the pressure of the tournament. When I arrive to see Metsaloo, I find Leonardo seated in front of a canvas, painting the valley in splendid colors. He has paint streaked across his sleeve, and his breastplate lies on the ground next to his easel.

"Ah, good morning, dear Livvy," he says with a broad smile as I tie up Ranger and cross to where he sits.

"Well met. You have captured our valley with such beauty," I say.

As I lean in to admire the painting, Metsaloo sweeps overhead and circles back to land. Leonardo scrambles to keep the painting and easel from being toppled over by the wind. "Metsaloo!" he exclaims.

I smile. I could spend all day in the company of this delightful duo. Alas, there is much to do. So, when Metsaloo has settled, I complete my exam and give him a clear bill of health.

"Best of luck today," I say, packing my tools.

"Metsaloo and I would like you to have this," he says. I turn and he is holding the painting.

"Really? How wonderful." I gratefully take the painting and lay it carefully atop my cart. Metsaloo covets paintings, and this would surely be a credit to his hoard. How lovely that they have blessed me with it instead. "I am truly honored. I will hang it in my cottage with pride." The gift warms my heart, and I give them a bow before departing.

After visiting Leonardo, I turn my attention to Thaddeus. He may have some information about Asher's sudden departure. My visit to his dragon shall serve a dual purpose. The cold air fills my lungs as I hike up the mountain, Ranger by my side and pulling my cart. I scan the forest for any sign of predators. I'm grateful for the reassuring sounds of birds and squirrels. If they are free from threat, then so am I.

By the time I approach the break in the trees, my emotions are once again in turmoil. My hands tingle, and it's as if I am being tightly laced into a corset. I pause and close my eyes, waiting for the panic to pass. *I am safe. I am safe. I am safe.* When my chest relaxes, I shake out my hands and continue.

Thaddeus stands on the natural rock shelf at the cave's opening. He stares out at the horizon, looking uncharacteristically serious. Is he nervous about the match? I would certainly be nervous. "Well met, Thaddeus."

He turns, and a smile breaks across his face. "Well met, Livvy. How are you today?"

My smile falters. That is an excellent question. However, sorting out my current state is a task for a different day, so I settle for, "Ready to embrace the day."

"Excellent. Shall we go see Starlight?"

I tie up Ranger and follow Thaddeus into the cave. His beautiful blue dragon is sitting before what looks like a roasted boar. Cobalt Toris dragons use lightning magic to cook their food, although I have never seen it in person.

Thaddeus clucks his tongue. "Starlight, you need to eat. We must fly soon, and you need time to digest your food. Plus, Livvy is here for your pre-flight check. We mustn't make her wait."

I have no desire to get between Starlight and her food. "We can delay the perusal until she is finished," I offer.

"Yes, that would be best. Would you like some tea?"

"That would be lovely." Did he bring tea from his home? I have never had Fae-brewed tea. As children, we were warned against eating or drinking anything offered by the Fae. However, Thaddeus has given me no reason to doubt his integrity and sincerity. I allow him to lead me out to the fire, where chairs are placed in a circle around the warmth. After motioning for me to sit, he pours me a mug of hot water and unclasps a beautiful carved wooden box, offering me a choice of tea from within.

He grimaces. "The selection is limited. However, we have Starflower and Maza Bloom."

I peer into the box. I have never had either, although I know they are sought after by dragons and Fae alike. I choose a bag and lift it to my nose. It smells like mint and blueberries. The second option is reminiscent of lemon and rose hips. I select the blueberry tea and drop it in the mug to steep. "Thank you for the hospitality."

He wipes his hands on his trousers and prepares his mug. After he is seated, he clears his throat. "Are you enjoying the tournament?"

I sip the flavorful liquid. "I am. Although I was quite surprised to hear that Asher had left the tournament prematurely." I let the statement hang in the air, hoping for insight.

He shifts in his chair and scratches his neck absentmindedly. "Yes, it is curious."

He knows more than he is sharing. "Do you know why he left?"

He sniffs and finally meets my gaze. "I do."

I clench my jaw. Why is he being so cagey? How scandalous can it be? "Are you permitted to satisfy my curiosity?" I keep my face blank and wait.

The silence hangs in the air, stretching uncomfortably between us. I will wait as long as it takes to hear his confession.

My patience pays off as he finally begins to speak. "I am not sure it is my place to share this information, but I understand your need for explanation." He sips his tea. "Asher left to return to his home."

"But why?"

"What I know is this: he left last evening to return home. His mission was to retrieve his Mender and go to the mortal lands. He mentioned a village by the name of Tevyne."

My jaw falls open. Could this be true? Does he intend to bring a Mender to Da? "What would motivate him to do such a thing?"

"Our conversation was brief and focused almost entirely on his praise of you, actually, and your actions yesterday. He was keen to repay your kindness."

I cannot speak. Dare I hope that Da might be healed? Asher was under no obligation to me. Even if he believes he is in my debt, sacrificing his probable victory is too much. How can I ever return his kindness? My mind swirls with this revelation. My heart is just as conflicted.

"How is Marinn?" he asks, looking sheepish.

I clear my throat. I am thankful for the subject change. "She is quite well."

His throat bobs. "Will she be at the match today?"

I smile. He is in love with her more than ever. "She is planning to attend. Perhaps we shall see you in the village later?"

He looks at the ground. "Surely she has no desire to see me."

I lean forward. "I believe she would very much like to see you again."

He tries to keep a smile from lighting up his face, but fails. He runs a hand over his mouth and chin. He leans back and crosses an ankle over his knee. "Yes, I believe I will be available."

"Wonderful," I say, sipping my tea and reveling in the joy soon to come to my dearest friend.

When we have finished our tea, I complete my exam of Starlight, who is in perfect condition for flying today. "Best of luck," I say to Thaddeus as I prepare to depart.

"Thank you. Please give Marinn my best."

"I will."

My step is lighter as I retreat down the mountain. Once I return my cart and Ranger to the cottage, I plan to meet Marinn at her house and depart for our viewing location. Should I tell her about Thaddeus? I believe she still cares for him. The last thing I want for her is to be hurt again. If Thaddeus wants her heart, he will have to pursue her with determination. I shall have no part in breaking her heart should Thaddeus falter.

47

*M*arinn and I huddle together on our usual outcropping, now crowded with spectators.

"Our secret viewing location is not so secret anymore," Marinn says begrudgingly.

"Indeed. I suppose it is to be expected given the progression of the tournament," I say.

Marinn nods in agreement. "I pray this match is less eventful than Asher's."

I chew my thumbnail. I cannot bear to watch another rider fall from his dragon. When did I start caring about the riders? I need this tournament to finish quickly and without incident.

My mind returns to the possibility of the Mender. How could Asher do such a thing? My previous contempt for him has left me undeserving of such a gesture. My cheeks heat thinking about it. I long to tell Marinn, but I would also be forced to share how I learned the information, and I promised Thaddeus I would keep his confidence. Instead, I reach for the wineskin and tip it to my lips.

I find Marinn staring at me. "Livvy, are you thinking about your da?"

I nod. She puts her arm around me, and I lean into her comfort. Even with the warmth of my dearest friend, uncertainty persists.

Finally, the horn blasts, signaling the beginning of the match. I sit up in anticipation of the contest. As soon as the dragons leave their perch, the entire valley is on their feet, cheering. The roar is loud enough to cause my teeth to chatter. Thaddeus is just as Marinn had first described him so many weeks ago. His long red hair tied atop his head and streaming out behind him as he races towards the other team, lifting his lance and leaning forward. The other rider raises his shield and deflects the direct blow of the lance. The gold tip hits the rider in the shoulder and shatters, causing the volume of the crowd to increase. Both Marinn and I jump and cheer—two points for Thaddeus.

The riders circle and begin again. This time, Thaddeus sits up straight and throws his head back, letting the wind brush against his whole face. What is he doing? It's too early to declare victory, and he has no reason to give up. "What is he doing?" I ask.

Marinn shakes her head, her hands folded under her chin. The cheering is cut with murmurs as his peculiar behavior gives pause. I cannot look away from Thaddeus as he reaches the middle of the field. At the last minute, his casual stance disappears, and he swings his lance from the side, knocking the other rider from his dragon. As the rider falls, I gasp. This cannot be happening again. Marinn screams and wraps her arms around my neck, squeezing. I cannot react to the victory until I know the fate of the other rider. When his dragon scoops up the rider, who waves to the crowd to indicate he isn't injured, I can finally exhale and join Marinn in her exuberance. Thaddeus takes a victory lap around the valley. As the crowd disperses, Marinn and I make our way to the pub.

As we walk arm in arm, I can't help but hope that we run into Thaddeus, especially after his inquiry this morning. "Have you seen Thaddeus?" I ask Marinn, testing her level of interest.

She lifts her chin. "I have not. But no matter, I am over him, Livvy. I am just glad enough time has passed that we can be civil to each other in public. Of course, I am pleased he has won the tournament. I wish him no ill."

I swallow a smile. She is a terrible liar. "And if he still loves you?" I ask.

"If he still loves me, he shall have to prove himself. Otherwise, I shall look elsewhere."

"Of course," I say. Then I lean over to inspect the back of her dress.

"What are you doing?"

"I wanted to see if your backside is on fire."

She frantically looks over her shoulder, brushing her hands across her bottom.

I laugh. "I don't mean literally. Didn't your father ever say that if you were a liar, your pants would catch on fire?"

She looks confused, then clucks her tongue. "Mortals are so strange."

We walk in comfortable silence for a bit. I long to tell her about Asher, but now that much of the day has passed without broaching the subject, I am unsure how to introduce the information.

"Miss Marinn, Miss Marinn," a little voice calls out from behind us. We both turn to see Osso, his bright red hair weaving through the crowd before tripping over his own feet and crashing into Marinn.

"Oh, Osso," I say, peeling him off her skirts.

He is no worse for wear as he smiles brightly at us. He

produces a bouquet of blue Starflowers tied with a white ribbon and presents it to Marinn. She crouches before him. "Are these for me?"

He nods and smiles.

Marinn looks up to me as if I know who sent them. I shrug.

"Osso, did you pick these?"

He shakes his head. I chuckle. Little Osso could never be accused of being too chatty.

"Please, tell me who sent them?" Marinn asks.

"Thaddeus sent them. He says he misses you."

Marinn blinks rapidly and looks up to me. Her throat bobs. "Thank you. I will be sure to tell him you did your job admirably."

Osso beams. He turns to go, but then quickly leans in, kissing her on the cheek before running away.

Marinn laughs as she rises and brings the flowers to her nose to smell.

"Apparently, Thaddeus has not forgotten about you." I cannot help but grin as Marinn pretends to be under-whelmed by the gesture.

"They don't even smell." She says, her eyes sparkling.

Marinn and I notice the change in the street at the same time. The crowd has stopped moving and is murmuring all around us. Are we being singled out for some reason? We begin to scan the crowd and then turn to see if whatever has changed is behind us.

When we turn, Thaddeus, still in his tournament uniform, is kneeling on the ground, a ring in his hand. The entire crowd quiets, watching the drama unfold. Is his hand trembling? He glances nervously around at the crowd. He clears his voice and begins to speak. Then he pauses before he begins again.

"Marinn, I have been to see your father, and I cannot wait

another moment. I made a most egregious mistake when I left without declaring my feelings for you. I ask you to forgive me for my behavior, and if you'll have me, please do me the honor of becoming my wife."

Marinn's hand covers her mouth. Her eyes fill with tears. She nods. "Yes. Yes. A thousand times, yes."

She laughs as he slips the ring on her finger and stands to pull her into an embrace. The crowd claps and cheers. More than one person wipes their eyes. I cannot imagine a more perfect proposal for Marinn. It is a storybook romance, to be sure. Before I can move to congratulate the couple, they are swallowed by people lavishing them with well-wishes.

From the edge of the crowd, I watch for a moment. They do make a fine pair. There will be plenty of time for Marinn and me to relive this glorious moment. For now, I have the urge to escape to my cottage. As much as my heart swells with joy for her, I cannot help but grieve the ongoing disaster that is my situation with Asher.

48

Later that night, I sit by the fire, my arms wrapped around my knees, feet on the chair. My hair hangs down in a loose braid over my shoulder. Candle-light flicks along the walls, only an hour or so left on the wick. The night has slipped into that time when only the most nocturnal creatures move about, yet I cannot sleep.

Marinn's joy is a balm to my soul, even while my pain and worry over things at home cut into my heart. I have been rendered useless, without solid knowledge about what is happening or any power to intervene. Asher's face flashes in my mind, and I bury my head in my knees to block out the memory of his fleeting touch. The sound of horses' hooves pulls my attention to the window. They are likely passing by on their way home. The sound stops outside the cottage. Perhaps they have paused to adjust the horses? A hard knock on the door causes me to flinch. Who would be here at this hour?

I reach out for my candle.

Mr. Bennet lifts his head, where he lies at the foot of my

bed. "Send them away. It is rude to appear at such an hour without invitation."

I tell him to keep quiet and pad over to the door, lifting the handle. The moon illuminates the woman standing on my porch.

It is Asher's aunt, her hair uncharacteristically mussed, her jaw set. Over her shoulder, I see the platinum trim of her carriage gleaming in the moonlight. Her team of large horses stands sentinel.

"Duchess Covington, how nice to see you." I move to the side as she sweeps forward to push past me into the room, surveying the accommodations.

"You have a very small cottage." She tugs her gloves off and drops them onto the table.

I hold my arms to my side, fighting to keep my composure. Was something wrong with Asher? Was she here about the tournament? Scrambling for something to say, I glance at the kettle. "Would you like some tea?"

Her gaze snaps to mine. "Absolutely not."

I swallow hard. So, not a friendly visit, then. Curled up on the end of my bed, Mr. Bennet growls. I shoot him a look, then cross my arms and wait for her to continue.

"You must know why I have come," she says.

I lick my lips. "I have no idea." I search her face for some clue, biting back my growing fear. The question swelling my gut works its way out, and I must ask. "Has something happened to Asher?"

She scoffs and lifts her chin. "Indeed. A most disturbing report has reached my ears. A report you and that Marinn have surely cooked up."

"What kind of report?"

She hardens her gaze. "That my nephew has made you an offer of marriage."

"Asher?" Of course, she's speaking of Asher. I worry my lip.

She nods curtly.

"I have never heard of such a report." How can she know he had proposed? I certainly have no desire to discuss this with her. I'm not sure of where things stand between Asher and me.

The candlelight flickers on her face menacingly as she narrows her eyes. "Let me be clear. My nephew has responsibilities to this family and his station. His future cannot include any relationship with a human." She spits the last word, as if it is hard even to say the word.

My face heats, and I drop my arms to my sides, balling my fists. "If that is the case, it makes no sense that you would travel through the night to discuss an impossibility."

"Have you no shame? Asking Asher to give up so much to extend the short life of a mortal by what, ten years?"

"Pardon?"

"Asher left the tournament to retrieve our Mender and travel to the mortal lands, for you."

"I never asked him to do such a thing." I blink back tears. It is true, then. Da is going to be well. It cost Asher the tournament, his family's approval, everything. How could I ever repay him? I sniff. This woman does not deserve a window into my heart.

"And yet he did," she says, flashing her teeth at me.

Tension hangs in the air. After a moment, she shifts her feet and squares her shoulders. "Are you engaged to my nephew or not?"

Despite my best efforts, I feel my shoulders slump. "I am not."

Something like relief flashes across her face. "And will you promise not to enter into any kind of arrangement with him?"

My mouth goes dry. Who does this woman think she is, barging into my home and bullying me into making a promise such as this? "I will never make such a promise to you." Even if I didn't know if I would ever see Asher again, I would not give her the satisfaction of capitulating to her demands. A low growl from Mr. Bennet seems to signal that it is time for this intruder to go. I lift the candlestick and shift my body towards the door. "You have insulted me in every way possible. Please leave." I yank the door open and shiver as a gust of cold wind extinguishes the candle I'm holding.

"I have never been thus treated in all my life," she mumbles and strides onto the porch, her back rigid. Her driver scrambles to open the carriage door, and the horses stomp in anticipation of their departure.

I watch Asher's aunt climb into the carriage. She turns around to give me one more scathing look before the driver closes the door. Once the carriage is out of sight, I let out a deep sigh. Mr. Bennet rubs against my leg. Once inside the cottage, my body shudders with all that has happened. I'm angry, mortified, and somewhere mixed in is the slightest flicker of hope.

---

49

*T*he next morning, I rise before the sun after a fitful sleep and am greeted by Mr. Bennet hissing in front of the door. "Open, please," he says, lifting his paws.

My head is heavy with lack of sleep and tension over the unexpected visit from Asher's aunt. I rub my eyes. "I'm sorry. You could have woken me if you needed to be let out."

I pull on my boots and coat.

"I tried. Unless you want me to use my freshly sharpened claws, I am at the mercy of your sleep schedule. Now, please release me."

I lift the handle, and as soon as the early morning light slips through the opening, Mr. Bennet pushes past me and leaps off the porch. I follow him out to attend to my own needs. When I am finished, I stand outside letting the morning chill push the sleep from my mind. My breath billows in front of me as I release a sigh.

What is to come of this day? My heart is full of hope this morning. Marinn is engaged to her great love. There is a chance a Mender is at Da's bedside even now. And if I am honest, my heart leaps at the idea that Asher's actions are possibly driven by anything other than obligation. What else could have driven his aunt's midnight visit?

I drop down on the steps of the porch and lean against the post. I rest my eyes and drink in the sounds of the birds. I must doze off because when I wake, it is to someone touching my shoulder. I startle and open my eyes to a silhouette blocking the sunlight.

I stand, pulling my coat closed. "Asher," I say. He is dressed in a long cloak, riding boots, and a white tunic. His hair hangs loose to his shoulders.

"My aunt…" he says, sheepishly.

"Yes, she was here." I smile.

"What can I say to apologize for her behavior?" He rubs a hand along the back of his neck.

"After what you have done for Da, it is I who should be apologizing."

His face holds so much restrained emotion. "You must know. Surely, you must know it was all for you. You have always been forthright with me. The conversation you had with my aunt last night has taught me to hope, as I have not allowed myself before."

My heart swells. If he continues to speak to me this way, it may burst out of my chest. Yet, I am willing to risk death to hear him share his affections for me.

He continues, "If your feelings are still what they were before the tournament, tell me immediately. One word from you and I will be gone."

He steps forward, so close that I can count his eyelashes. "If, however, your feelings have changed, I would have to tell you that you have enchanted me body and soul." He reaches up and tucks a strand of hair behind my ear. "And I love you."

I cannot breathe. Is he going to kiss me? I know nothing of my future except that I love this man. Should I kiss him? It would be so easy. I lick my lips.

He glances around my homestead. "I know you have built a life here, and I have no desire to take you away from your friends, unless you want to go. Whatever the terms, I never wish to leave your side from this day forward."

I could never have imagined such a speech directed at me. Every part of me tingles as I resist the urge to throw my arms around him and kiss him until the end of time. His lips part, and he tips his head towards mine. I stand on my toes to meet his soft, full lips halfway. The kiss sends a shiver through me, and I slide my hands up his chest and around his neck. He finally breaks the kiss and pulls me to his chest. "I should tell you. I have already spoken to your father, and he has given his consent to marry if you wish."

I step back and study his face. "Is this a proposal, Mr. Covington?"

"Only if you would like it to be." He smiles and kisses me again.

50

*L*ater that day, Asher brings me to a clearing where Honora is waiting. It is a Fae tradition to reintroduce me to the dragon as Asher's fiancée.

Even saying that word in my head is strange. I look down to where our hands are intertwined. I cannot imagine how Marinn will react when I tell her. For now, I am enjoying the private time with Asher after so much uncertainty.

"Well met, Honora," I say, stopping a safe distance away. Asher continues forward until our connection grows taut. He turns back to me.

I shrug. "There is never a reason to be careless around dragons."

He smiles. "You are going to have to be a little careless if you are to fly with me."

My brain cannot comprehend what he is saying. "I don't understand."

"It has been your dream to fly with a dragon, yes?"

"Since I was a child," I answer. I look to Honora with fresh eyes. Will she let me fly with her? Since I was six years old, this has been my dream. What a surprise that Asher of all people is the one to fulfill my greatest wishes.

"Flying can be quite jarring. This will be a short flight around the valley. Eventually, we will be able to fly to your home for a visit."

I did not think I could love him more than I already do. I was wrong. "I cannot believe this is happening."

He smiles down at me. "It is my pleasure, you headstrong, obstinate girl." He taps my nose with his finger and then brushes a kiss across my lips. "It is time to go."

I take a deep breath. This moment is one I have dreamed about for so many years. My heart thumps as I follow Asher up to mount the dragon. He demonstrates the best way to climb the front leg and swing my foot over to mount the dragon. As I climb onto the back of Honora, the rumble of ancient power echoes through me. I tuck my skirts under my legs to keep them from billowing. Then I tuck my hair into my cloak. Asher climbs on behind me, his chest pressed against my back. It is strange how natural this feels.

Honora rises to her feet. The movement is jarring. Asher wraps his arms around my middle, and I cling to the dragon's scales. With a few beats of the massive wings, we lift into the air. My stomach drops as we ascend. The muscles of the dragon shift below me as she takes us higher. The wind whips at my face, and I cannot stop smiling. The valley stretches out below.

Asher's hot breath brushes against my ear. "Is this all you thought it would be?"

I nod. The buildings of the village peek up at me. I see the tavern, Sam's house, and the Inn. The blue and yellow of Marinn's house stand in stark contrast, even from the sky. Is Marinn outside watching? Even the trees, towering high above the ground, seem minuscule.

Honora glides as she gracefully swoops down towards the

village. I let go of her scales and throw my arms to the side. I tip my head back and laugh. I can feel Asher chuckling behind me. This is what it must feel like to be a bird. How extraordinary. I could spend the rest of my life in the air.

After circling the valley again, Honora begins her descent, aiming for the clearing from which we started. "Tighten your legs and hang on," Asher says.

I am thankful for the instruction as Honora drops to the ground, abruptly coming to a stop. My senses, which had been filled with screaming wind, are now assaulted by silence. "Is it too soon to fly again?" I ask, leaning into Asher as Honora settles.

He chuckles. "I'm having food brought to the cottage. If we do not return soon, Mr. Bennet will consume our specially prepared meal."

We climb down from the dragon, and I thank Asher for the flight. "I shall never forget this. You have allowed my dream to come true. Thank you."

His face grows serious, and he shakes his head. "I appreciate your gratitude, but this is not enough. It is unfathomable that you cannot bond your own dragon. I plan to do everything in my power to correct that injustice." He reaches out and takes my hand. "You are the bravest person I know, and I will need you by my side if we are to take on this fight."

My heart beats so fast at his touch. Is he serious? "Won't that be dangerous?"

He doesn't flinch or look away. "There will be much opposition, but I also know of a growing number of fae who desire more equality between the fae and humans." He smiles. "Besides, Honora and I believe you have earned the right to bond a dragon. I will not rest until that opportunity is afforded you."

Honora nods and chuffs. My mind is surprisingly conflicted. Yes, I want to be able to bond with a dragon if I am deemed worthy by one of the beautiful creatures. But what will the cost be for Asher and the rest of Saule? Will there be war? Will Asher's family stand in opposition?

He seems to notice my concern and says, "Livvy, this is not only about you. The injustice of the decree has plagued my thoughts since before we met. You just solidified my conviction."

I nod, unable to respond without another silly show of emotion. What a journey this has been. And apparently, it is just beginning. I straighten my skirts and hair. Asher takes my hand and leads me back to the cottage.

That night, I am sitting on a chair listening to the rhythmic motion of the axe outside, grateful to be near the cozy fire with my book. Asher volunteers to cut wood, and I gratefully allow him the task.

The scuff of his boots on the porch, alerts me to his return and I mark the page with a scrap of paper before closing the tome. "How are you doing this evening, my dear?" I ask as Asher enters the cabin with an armload of wood.

"Very well, only I wish you wouldn't call me 'my dear.' It's what my mother called my father when she was cross with him."

"What should I call you then?"

"Well, let me think. 'Asher,' for everyday. 'My love,' for Sundays. And 'dragon rider extraordinaire,' but only on very special occasions."

He sets the logs down next to the hearth.

"And what shall I call you when we inevitably argue? Mr. Covington?"

"No. No. You may only call me Mr. Covington when you are completely, perfectly, and incandescently happy."

I untuck my leg and lay my book down on the chair. Rising, I cross the room. "And how are you tonight, Mr. Covington?"

He smiles.

I sweep a loose piece of hair out of his face, loving the feel of his name on my lips. "Mr Covington."

His eyes cloud over with longing. My heart flutters. How could I have ever thought he was unworthy of consideration?

I rise on my tiptoes and place my lips a breath away from his. "Mr. Covington." We stay like that for a moment, our eyes locked.

Then a smile lifts the corners of his mouth before he closes his eyes and kisses me.

Five months later, the Maza Blooms lining the edge of the forest hold the promise that summer is on the way. Bright green leaves shimmer in the midday sun, and the smell of new growth fills the air. Marinn and I stand with our betrothed in Eshan's village square, she in blue and I in green. Both Asher and Thaddeus are dressed in black formal coats, hair slicked back and tied at the nape. We are surrounded by family and friends who have come to celebrate with us.

Beside me, Marinn and Thaddeus fight back fits of giggles. Given the time and effort she has invested in this day, I am surprised she is not insisting on the most formal of decorum. But I must admit, her joy is contagious. Asher shares a shy smile with me as we wait for the Royal Cleric, an exceptionally old man with a crooked nose and purple robe, to begin.

My sisters couldn't make the trip because a stomach virus was running through their children. Ma and Da sit in the front row of the large and varied crowd, beaming. Asher and

Thaddeus flew to Tevyne and brought them back on their dragons. I can't imagine Ma making that journey, but by all accounts, she bore it well. This might be the first time Ma has actually been proud of me. It is likely due to her belief that I am now to settle down as a proper wife. I could shock her with the long conversations Asher and I have about changing Saule to be more inclusive and equitable. I do not believe "settling down" will ever be high on my agenda.

Da sits next to her in a new suit. For the first time in a long time, his cheeks are pink with color. He has gained weight and is healthier than I have ever seen him. My heart swells again for the man who made this possible, my Asher. Scattered throughout the rest of the audience are my dearest friends, dressed in their finest and sharing the joy of the day.

Asher's family is seated beside mine. His father was displeased when Asher announced our engagement. Luckily, his mother and sister have welcomed me most sincerely into the family. I am thankful his aunt did not choose to attend. Her absence is a perfect wedding gift. I cannot keep myself from smiling as I reflect on the past year and what's to come.

Marinn will leave to join Thaddeus at his family's estate, with a promise to visit often. Her father seems to be holding his emotions in check, but just barely. Asher, who never liked court, will be moving in with me for now. It is quite a departure from the usual luxury he is accustomed to, but he insists he is up to the challenge and ready for a change.

I clear my thoughts as the Cleric begins to speak. Marinn has ensured the ceremony is a blend of the traditions from all our communities, which is a perfect reflection of Eshan. My eyes shine with tears as we promise to love each other for all time. In keeping with High Fae tradition, Asher slips a simple silver band on my right hand.

To honor the human side of our new union, Da steps

forward and binds our hands together with a woven cord. His voice catches as he says, "May this binding unite your hearts, minds, and hands through any storm that may come. May you find joy in each day. May you forgive quickly, be slow to anger, and always remember that nothing can separate the ties that bind."

Emotion causes flushed patches to appear on Asher's face. My tears turn into laughter as I watch him fail to maintain his stoic facade. When the vows have been exchanged and the newly married couples presented, Orthello steps forward and clears his throat.

Having Orthello sing was not on Marinn's list of ideal wedding activities. She only relented when I pointed out that she was given full rein to plan the rest of the ceremony and the subsequent celebration.

I smile at my towering friend. He strokes his beard and begins to sing a song from my village in a voice that is surprisingly improved, almost on key, even. Apparently, his lessons are paying off. His deep voice reverberates through the valley.

"There is a love that some will know,
    Sacred and unending.
    If you should find this kind of love,
    It would surely be a blessing.
    The seasons change, the moon shall wane,
    This much is true:
    A thing most rare, this kind of love,
    Is the love I see in you."

As the ceremony comes to a close, I am ready for some ale and dancing. My face flushes as I realize I am also looking forward to my first night as Asher's wife. As we walk hand in hand to the tavern, where tables have been set up outside and covered with flowers, my thoughts move to the future. After the guests have gone and life has settled, the real work begins.

DRAKONAS TOURNAMENT

The Drakonas Tournament began after the Great War to encourage cooperation between the Kingdoms. Every three years, the tournament is held in a different location within the Realm. The tournament council determines the location and selects the riders to be included. The Realms' top 32 dragon riders and their mounts are invited to participate.

Riders are permitted to practice at the tournament location during the four weeks preceding the tournament's start. This is done to reduce injuries and deaths due to unfamiliarity with the terrain.

Once the tournament officially begins, a round robin single-elimination tournament takes place.

- Round 1 - 16 Matches
- Round 2 - 8 Matches
- Round 3 - 4 Matches
- Round 4 - 2 Matches
- Round 5 - Championship Match

Between each round shall be a day of rest for dragons and riders.

No more than four matches shall be held in a single day.

Each match shall have three runs. The competing pairs start at separate points on the field, and the distance is decided by the committee based on the location.

Each rider shall wear a chest plate and helmet. They shall carry a shield and lance. The committee shall inspect all equipment before it is used. No magical enhancements are allowed.

Scoring shall be as follows:

- 3 points awarded for breaking lance on the shield
- 2 points awarded for breaking lance on the body or arm
- 1 point for a touch on the shield, but no break (which happens somewhat regularly)
- Knocking the rider from his dragon is an automatic victory.

LEDA
EZERA
LAUKS
SAULE

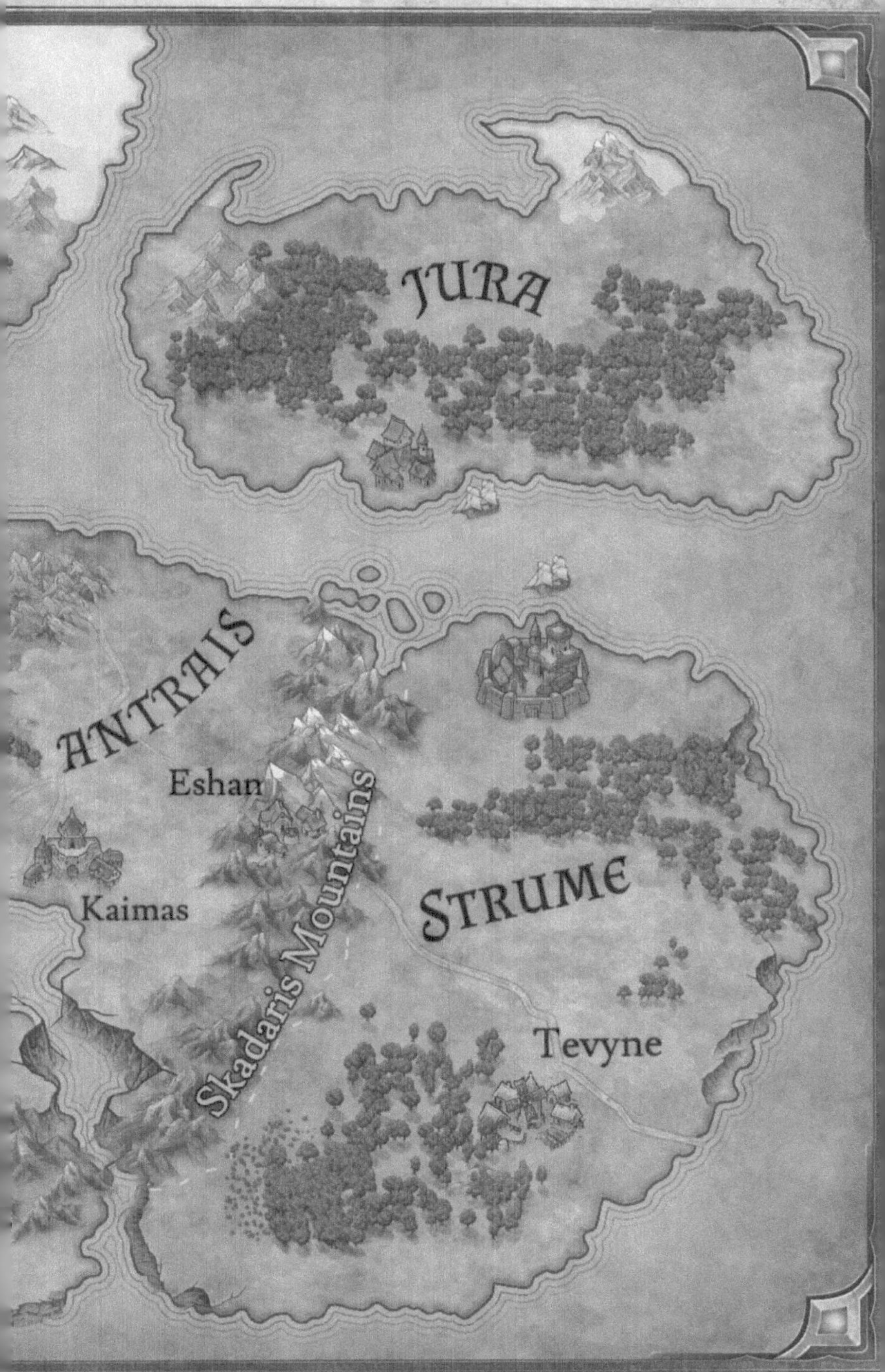

JURA
ANTRAIS
Eshan
Kaimas
Skadaris Mountains
STRUME
Tevyne

ACKNOWLEDGMENTS

Thank you to everyone who supported this project! My family has allowed me to work the crazy hours of an author and tolerated my strange questions about imaginary scenarios.

As my first Kickstarter project, I was blessed to have the support of 177 backers, including these fine folks:

Ainsley Kubicki
Allison Day
David Day
Jeffrey Ebbeler
Debbie Baker
Alexis Wright
Lindsay Marcum
'Will It Work' Dansicker
Abbie Caruso
Aingeal Wroth
Alex Blackstone
Alex Harlequin
Alexandra
Allison E Culley
Amanda Corbin
Amanda Tallon
Amber Cutrer
Amsel
Anais
Andrea Martin Kidder
Anna Vranopoulou
Anne-Mette Brandt
Antoinetta Aquila
April Ayton
Ashley
Ashley Gelease Millis
Ashley Orndorff
Ashley Reynolds
Ashley Woodbury
AuroraTheDragon174
Becky Flores
Belinda Mullinix
Beth Morgan
Bethany Gutner Diakis
Brittini Ramsay
Brittney Anderson
Candis Pike
Catherine Loving
Cara Beining
Carol Van Natta
Cerise
Cherelle H
Christina Schlickenmeyer
Christine Detrick
Christy S
Chumyshka
Corrie Pelc
Cortney Babcock
Cristina
Cynthia Anne Hurt
Dana Whitley
Denise Williams
Dominic Hilsbos
E. Leet
Eddie Runde
Eileen-Marie Charette
Elizabeth N. Carrillo
Ellen Sandberg
Emily Soto
Emma Esposito
Eris
Esther
Florentina
Franchesca Caram
Gabrielle Brisebois
Gena Rinckey
Giselle T.
Greg Donnell
H. Kjeldgaard
Haleigh Kirch
Hannah Jurina
Hannah McKay
Harmony Cartwright
Heather Aeschliman
Heather Zebley
Heidi Goddard
Jamie Rodriguez
Jena Byas
Jenna Daugherty
Jennifer Osterman
Jessie Marston
Jose Mahabirsingh
Julia Libby Julianna
Julie McAtee Kaarin
Borel Kai'lee Kaitlyn Rogers
Kaityn Stone
Karina Krogh
Karoline Baldwin
Kat Kuckens
Katanya Champion
Kate Durost
Katherine E. Melvin
Kathleen Burkepile
Katrina
KB
Kerriann Whitworth
Kevin Day
Kimberly Gonzalez
Kristin Pratt
Kristin Taggart
Kristina Raine
Lana
Larissa Green
Lauren Govert
Lauren Jesmer
Lauren Lennon
Lauren Peterson
Lauren Roller
Lin
Lisa Herrick
Lori Hout
Lorien Cord
Luke Golding
Maria Bossard
Marisa Valle
Marin Ito
Marte Drumheller
Megan Reichert
Melanie Stark
Melissa Desland
Melissa T
Michelle LaCrosse
Morgan G.
Nicholas Lawrence
Nicole Butler
Paul Drennan
Peggy Kimbell
Polinchka
Rachel Keiko Stark
Rebecca
Rebecca O'Neill
Rory
S. Black
Sadie Fivas
Samantha H
Samantha Keil
Samantha N Newerry
Sara Harricharan
Sarah Beth Barksdale
Sarah Tuttle
Shavon Bledsoe
Sierra Hillwig
Sigrún
Shi Hsiang Lin
Sophie Wyatt
Stacey Andrews
Stacy Mickelboro
Stephanie Diaz
Stephanie Lozinski
Sunny Ryan
Sunya
Suz Rodgers
Tina Stull
Tipanan Nomkuntod
Torre Gibson
Tracy Hennigan
Tracy Lee
Whitney Phillips
Whitney Rudeseal Peet
Ysabel Jardine
Zilla

ABOUT THE AUTHOR

Wendy Day is a prolific author who weaves her words into compelling cozy tales. Her books are your ticket to a world where the extraordinary is every day, where heroes are as funny as they are brave, and where every adventure is seasoned with a dash of pixie dust and a whole lot of laughter.

When Wendy Day isn't busy bringing her imaginative worlds to life on paper, she's a devoted mom and loving wife, spreading her joy and creativity to her family, including her two dogs and one entitled cat. Her life is an ever-evolving story, with each chapter bringing new adventures, challenges, and opportunities for growth.

https://www.wendydayauthor.com
https://x.com/WendyDayAuthor

instagram.com/wendydayauthor
tiktok.com/wendydayauthor

STANDING WATER

She survived the collapse of America,

now she just wants to live.

Nineteen-year-old Jamie dreams of adventure far from the small town where her family took refuge during the virus and subsequent war of 2027. Ten years later, the country is beginning to rebuild, and she even has a map hanging on her bedroom wall with push-pin plans.

But when her dad is suddenly dragged out of their farmhouse by government officials, Jamie's world is rocked again. Her mom is in denial, and her little brother looks to her for answers.

Can she rescue her father and protect the town she is so eager to escape? Or will this adventure cost her everything?

AND THEN IT WAS SEPTEMBER

A missing necklace, a backpack full of photos, and two women trying to outrun their family's disappointment and leave their mark on the world. Delightfully heartwarming, And Then It Was September explores the impact our lives have and the legacy we leave when we're gone.

MEXICO, MARGARITAS, AND MURDER

After her grumpy husband dies, Sally throws out his thread-worn plaid recliner, cashes the life insurance check, and lets her spunky best friend, Pearl, drag her to Mexico for an all-inclusive vacation using their Senior Citizen's discount.

They kayak, sing karaoke, and spy on the next-door nudist resort. Sally's not sure if it's the sun or tequila, but she is truly having fun for the first time in her life.

That is until a fellow guest turns up dead.

While Sally fearfully packs her bags for home, Pearl insists they stay and get to the bottom of what's happened.

Together, they become crime-fighting seniors who refuse to let the bad guys win.

CHRISTMAS, CABERNET, AND CHAOS

After her holiday plans fall apart, Sally drags her grumpy best friend, Pearl, to McKenzie Bridge- a small town famous for Christmas magic.

When a local woman claims someone is trying to kill her, and the Police Chief won't listen, the spunky senior sleuths jump into action.

Can Sally and Pearl save Christmas?

Best friends Sally and Pearl can't take the dreary January weather a second longer, but Pearl has a plan. She convinces Sally that a last-minute Caribbean cruise is just what they need to shake off the winter blues.

Charting a course for sunny skies, they board the Moonlit Dream. Between the mixology contest, sexy man competition, and making friends with the group of real estate agents they are assigned to dine with, the cruise is a blast.

That is until one of their dinner companions takes a nasty spill and dies. It's ruled an accident, but Sally and Pearl don't buy it, and they set out to solve the case. There's no shortage of suspects since almost everyone he knew had a reason to want him dead.

Brimming over with heart and humor, Sally and Pearl's third adventure will delight fans of the series and keep them guessing.

www.ingramcontent.com/pod-product-compliance
Lightning Source LLC
Chambersburg PA
CBHW061654190726
48289CB00006B/1869